Jesus F(orever) N(ow) Christ

Pádraig Standún

Gotham Books

30 N Gould St.
Ste. 20820, Sheridan, WY 82801
https://gothambooksinc.com/

Phone: 1 (307) 464-7800

© 2025 *Pádraig Standún*. All rights reserved.

No part of this book may be reproduced, stored in a retrieval system, or transmitted by any means without the written permission of the author.

Published by Gotham Books (February 8, 2025)

ISBN: 979-8-3485-1750-2 (P)
ISBN: 979-8-3485-1751-9 (E)

Because of the dynamic nature of the Internet, any web addresses or links contained in this book may have changed since publication and may no longer be valid.

The views expressed in this work are solely those of the author and do not necessarily reflect the views of the publisher, and the publisher hereby disclaims any responsibility for them.

CONTENTS

CHAPTER ONE 1
CHAPTER TWO 9
CHAPTER THREE 21
CHAPTER FOUR 27
CHAPTER FIVE 33
CHAPTER SIX 39
CHAPTER SEVEN 45
CHAPTER EIGHT 49
CHAPTER NINE 73
CHAPTER TEN 73
CHAPTER ELEVEN 97
CHAPTER TWELVE 103
CHAPTER THIRTEEN 109
CHAPTER FOURTEEN 129
CHAPTER FIFTEEN 141
CHAPTER SIXTEEN 149
CHAPTER SEVENTEEN 155
CHAPTER EIGHTEEN 171
CHAPTER NINETEEN 179
CHAPTER TWENTY 185
CHAPTER TWENTY-ONE 191
CHAPTER TWENTY-TWO 201
CHAPTER TWENTY-THREE 209
CHAPTER TWENTY-FOUR 217
CHAPTER TWENTY-FIVE 233

CHAPTER TWENTY-SIX 237
CHAPTER TWENTY-SEVEN 245
CHAPTER TWENTY-EIGHT 249
CHAPTER TWENTY-NINE 273
CHAPTER THIRTY 277
CHAPTER THIRTY-ONE 281
CHAPTER THIRTY-TWO 285

CHAPTER ONE

Margie, the shopkeeper was the first person to refer to the newly arrived film producer as "the Devileen" or little devil. It was on Pension Day, Wednesday, the day on which some senior citizens gathered to collect their old age pensions and maybe buy a newspaper or a few groceries on their way home from morning Mass in the local church. Margie referred to them as "the holy Joes" when they were not listening. She was happy to take their money and exchange a few greetings and comments about the weather or whatever was happening in the world at the time. She was aware that many of them might not see another human for the rest of the week.

Some weeks, Margie saw more of the drivers of delivery vans and lorries than she did of local people as they went about their work on land and sea. Lorries came through the mountains from Mayo with bread, eggs, meat, and soft drinks. Margie would have expected more of that traffic from Galway City than from neighbouring Mayo, but the country cousins seemed to be a more entrepreneurial breed. As they brought sausages from The Neale and Newport, eggs from Balla, loaves of bread as well as fish from Ballinrobe, and sweet-cakes from Foxford. Margie used to joke with the locals "If you are what you eat, then you are all from Mayo."

"I wonder who that is?" Tom Dharach asked about the small man with the big moustache and the wad of black hair stuck to his head with some kind of hair gel. There was a nervous look about him as he glanced at newspaper headlines. He had the look of someone who might run off with one of the newspapers without paying for it.

"I wonder would Margie be able to keep up with him if he made a bee-line for the dood?" Tom asked himself with a smirk on his face. "Our Margie would put on quite a sprint for the sake of a euro."

"He has a Spanish look about him," said Mary from the Mountain. "I saw a lot that looked like him when I was on my honeymoon in Marbella."

"Don't tell me that you were looking at other men when you were on your honeymoon." Margie said.

"There was none of them as nice-looking as my own man, God rest him."

"I wonder what would have brought the likes of that fellow to this part of the world?" Tom Dharach said as he sized up the stranger who had opened one of the tabloid newspapers as if he had an interest in some of the photographs. "He looks to me like some kind of a spy, or maybe a detective."

"You won't make much profit from that fellow," Mary from the Mountain said to Margie. "He reminds me of someone you would see in the Mobile Library, reading every page but not prepared to pay to bring a book home with him."

"He might have something to do with the film," Margie said. "They are supposed to start work any day now."

"We will not have room to walk on the roads," Tom Dharach said, "with strangers wandering about all over the place."

"The filming will not be starting for some time yet," Margie said as she gave the impression that she knew all about it.

"You seem to have the inside track on all of this," Mary from the Mountain said. "Isn't it a wonder that there is not more about it on the radio or television?"

Margie shrugged her shoulders "I would not know anything about it except that a man came on the phone the other day to make sure that there would be plenty to keep a film crew in food and drinks for a few weeks."

Tom Dharach gave a little laugh as he touched his peaked cap in honour something spiritual. "I hear that it is a play about Our Lord Jesus Christ. Sure won't he be able to make water into wine if they are running out of drink?"

Mary from the Mountain looked across at the strange man who now seemed to be absorbed in one of the newspapers he had not bought. "If this play is supposed to be about religion, that fellow over there is cut out for the part of Judas. I don't believe I have ever seen a man so much like a ragamuffin in my life."

"Isn't it wonderful that a play about God and religion is going to be filmed here." Tom Dharach remarked.

As she headed for the shop dood, Mary from the Mountain observe "Maybe they heard that the biggest hangmen and crucifiers in the world has come to inhabit this bloody place.!"

"They will bring money into the area, that is for sure," Tom said. "And every cent of it is needed. I wonder will they have parts for the ordinary people like ourselves as part of the crowd on the hill of Calvary? The people of Kerry made their fortunes when 'Ryan's Daughter' was being filmed down there."

"A lot of them were not impressed with the film when they saw the carry-on between Ryan's Daughter and that English soldier fellow in the wood," Margie said.

"What do they get up to?" Tom asked.

"Are you telling me you never saw the film?" she asked

"I didn't, or many other films either, apart from 'The Three Stooges' or 'Laurel and Hardy' when I was a boy. I saw some cowboy films too. I liked the action. The TV put an end to films in the local hall."

"Sure the television was much better," Margie said. "You would see all kind of stuff on it from all over the world."

"My mother never let the television into the house in her lifetime, and I had no interest in it when she died. Apart from the hurling and football matches. I used to come in here to watch them in the pud and have a few drinks at the same time," Tom said.

"Everyone has their own way," Margie said, as she seemed anxious for Tom to pay his grocery bill so that she would get a chance to speak to the dark stranger. She remembered the old adage that the customer is always right, so she dealt with Tom as patiently as she could.

Tom's mind was elsewhere. "What was it that happened in the wood?"

"What wood are you talking about?"

"The wood in that film you were talking about, the 'Ryan's Daughter?'"

"I will put it like this," Margie said. "It was not searching for mushrooms herself and the soldier were in the wood. I won't say any more seeing that you are on the way home from morning Mass."

"There would be nothing sinful in the kind of a holy film that is going to be made around here soon" Tom said. "But you would not know what they would come up with in this day and age."

Margie gave the impression that she was busy behind the counter as she kept one eye on the dark stranger. It looked like he had been waiting until all of the customers were served as he seemed to be reading the newspapers from cover to cover. He brought one of the tabloids to the counter when he saw that Tom's business was finished. He filled a cup of coffee from the machine before he approached Margie in order to pay for his small purchase.

"Isn't the weather great," she greeted him as he accepted his money. "Lovely weather for someone on a winter break like yourself. Are you hoping to stay for a while, or are you just passing through? There is just one road in to the place and one road out at the other side."

"I had not noticed that there was only one road through the place. Is that the road known as 'The Wild Atlantic Way.'"

"We are close to the end of that road alright. All good things come to an end as they say," Margie joked as best as she could. She seemed almost desperate to find out more about the stranger. "You don't seem to be planning to stay very long."

"A while." He was keeping his plans close to himself which was something Margie seemed to see as a challenge. "Have you something to do with that film that they are all talking about?" she asked.

"I have connections with that project alright."

"An actor?"

"Unfortunately, no."

"A cameraman?"

He stretched out his right hand to accept his change, which she held on to until he would answer her question. "Producer," he answered.

"That makes you the top dog?" Margie hesitated for a second. "Not that I am calling you a dog. I mean you are the person in charge of it all." She shook his hand as she gave him his change. "Margie is my name.. This is my shop, post office, and public house. No doubt we will be seeing a lot of you in the coming days and weeks. By the way when is the real work starting?"

"It has started already. We are studying the scripts."

"I am talking about the actual filming."

"That will take a while, a couple of months maybe as the actors get ready for their parts."

Margie showed surprise. "I would have thought that only a big film like 'The Titanic' would take that long."

"Our methods are different than those of a lot of other film-makers. I personally interview each actor. I set them the task of imagining their own part to see their character from every angle, go down really deep into their psyche before the cameras start to roll."

"That sounds very interesting," Margie said. "You are very clever."

"You are very clever yourself," he answered. "You know how to ask the right questions I would think you are able to get blood out of a turnip."

Margie smiled. "You are no turnip, but you know how to only say what you need to say. What did you say your name was again?"

"I didn't say"

"And you are not going to tell me now, either? You are a right little devil."

He held out his right hand "Nicólás Dowling is my name."

"You are well named for this Gaelic speaking area," Margie replied. "Nic a' diabhailín," she said, "Nick, the little devil."

"You are the smart one," Dowling said. "Not everyone could come back so quickly with an answer like that at the tip if their tongue."

"Have you done any acting yourself?" Dowling asked.

"Isn't that what I do every day of my life? You need to be quite an actress to run an establishment like this."

"I am serious," he answered. "There will be bit-parts available at the fringes of the story."

"Bit-parts. Hangers-on. Not for me, thank you. I have more than enough to do around here."

"The bigger parts are already filled, unfortunately. There would be no point in coming out here if we did not have professional actors. There are however some small but strong parts still available such as the Samaritan woman at Jacob's well. A good woman to ask a question or two of Jesus himself. I think you could fill that part. A strong woman. A couple of hours work. Someone else could hold the fort here for that long, I am sure."

"I am not a religious person," Margie answered, "and I am certainly no virgin or no Nun."

"Neither was the Samaritan woman. You could give it a try."

Margie shrugged "You could show me a script."

"We don't use scripts. That is not how we work. We learn on the hoof."

"I thought you told me you were professional actors and actresses?"

"We have our own way of working. I put the responsibility on the actors. They have to think for themselves, to imagine their parts as comprehensively as they can before we ever put together a final script."

"Interesting," Margie said, although it seemed that she was losing interest. "Please excuse me as I have a couple of customers to deal with in the Post Office."

"I'm sorry," Dowling said, backing away. "I wonder is there any way I could get to talk to you after you finish your day's work?"

Margie gave him a card "My number is on that, but I don't know if I have enough courage to take even a very small part in your film."

"We will see," he answered. "You can make a decision about that later. In the meantime, I hope to speak to you later in the evening."

Margie's next customer asked her if the man with the sticky hair on his head was going to buy the business from her.

"A pity he is not," she answered. "I would be in the Seychelles before the end of the week."

CHAPTER TWO

Nicólás Dowling went to speak with the local Roman Catholic priest that afternoon. He was of the opinion that it would help him to keep the local population on his side if he had the support of the local clergyman. It was not that he had any respect for clergy or religion. There was every chance that the film he was hoping to make would please either priest or people of the area, but that would not matter when he and his crew would have long left the area before the film was on screen. In the meantime, it would probably help their stay in the area if local people were not hostile to their work. Faith or clergy were not exactly popular because of many scandals that had attested the church not just in Ireland but all over the world. Child sexual abuse in parishes, schools, and communities was coming to light in recent decades, and the general consensus had it that it was because of compulsory celibacy among the clergy.

By getting the priest onside, Dowling hoped that their interpretation of the story of the Passion of Jesus Christ would not lead them to be denounced from the altar or driven out of the parish, at least until the film was in the can. Fr. Eamonn Ó Sé was a big strong man with shoulders almost as wide as the doorframe. His head was bowed slightly so that he would fit through the door of the old bungalow. He quoted an old saying to his visitor to explain why he had learned to bow his head every time he passed through the doorway. Locals have a saying in Irish – "A goose is smaller than you, but it always lowers its head."

Nicólás Dowling did not quite grasp the proverb so he asked "What exactly did it mean?"

"I am the tallest priest in the diocese, but they sent me to the oldest house with the lowest door. There must have been something to do with humility or taking me down to size in question."

"It is a very pretty little house," Dowling said, "especially from the outside."

The priest answered "There was a time the priest had the biggest and the fanciest house in most parishes, but the opposite is true now. But so what? Our boss man, by which I mean Jesus Christ said he had 'no place to lay his head.' We are coming down to earth at last."

The film maker stretched out his right hand "I am Nicólás Dowling."

"Éamonn Ó Sé." Hands were shaken, but the priest had a mistaken idea of whom his visitor was. "I don't keep any money in the house. For safety reason, but if you would like something to eat I can make you a sandwich or get you something from the local shop.."

Nicólás Dowling laughed. "I am not looking for alms, or whatever you call it nowadays. I can still afford to put a bite in my mouth."

"I am very sorry, Nicólás," the priest said with a touch of shame in his voice. "There is hardly a day that some stranger does not come to the door looking for something to eat, or the price of a drink."

Dowling laughs "I understand. That bloke that you follow, Jesus, I mean, set you up for lots of trouble with passers-by. He was far too nice for his own good, and maybe for your good too."

"It is hard to work out sometimes," the priest answered, "who needs help and who doesn't."

His visitor changed the subject "I am here about the film."

The priest waved him towards the sofa. "Take the weight off your feet. Could you tell me why you chose this place for your film?"

"We needed a remote place. If that is not an insult to your parish. We needed somewhere with space and time without the whole world looking over our shoulders, and the media especially."

"You must have something to hide," the priest said with a wink.

"It is hard to hide what the old film makers called 'The Greatest Story Ever Told'. In some ways or still is one of the best stories, but it might need to be told in a different way."

"It's your baby," Nicólás said. "I will not be telling you what to do, and even if I did I would not expect you follow my advice, but if there is any way the parish can help, feel free to ask. We have a good Community Council which I am sure will make the local hall and other facilities available. There will be nobody standing in your way and I am sure the community can only benefit from your efforts. It will be an honour actually for the whole parish to be chosen ahead of the rest of the country."

"Maybe everyone in the area will not agree with how the story turns out," Nicólás Dowling suggested.

"The two thousand years old story is hardly likely to change," Fr. Ó Sé laughed. "Jesus is bound to bounce back as he always did. You can't keep a good man down."

"Our version of the story is still a work in progress."

The priest was beginning to have second thoughts "You can't keep a good man down," I have just said. "Could it be that you are thinking of a woman Jesus? I suppose anything goes nowadays in your line of work."

"I don't think we will be going that far," Dowling said.

"Do you mean you are thinking about it?"

"I am now, since you suggested it,"

"I am not sure if that is not a bridge too far even in this day and age," was the priest's reply. "Are you telling me that the story or the script or whatever you call it has not been written yet?"

Nicólás Dowling explained how he and his crew worked and he eased the priest's worries somewhat by telling him the name of the actor scheduled to play the part of Jesus.

"I hope that you don't have as much savagery in the story as Mel Gibson had in his version", Fr. Ó Sé said. "I know that some of the scenes in that treatment certainly frightened children."

"What answer would you have to explain the title of the film," Dowling asked the priest.

"Sure, how would I know what you and your colleagues are calling it?"

The film producer spelt it out "Jesus F N Christ."

" Why that? Of all possible titles?"

"I am not a religious man but there isn't a day that goes by day I don't hear someone using the words "Jesus Fucking Christ" if they hurt their finger or kick against a stone on the road. There are lots of varieties of the same phrase, of course "Fucking Jesus Christ," not to speak of "Fucken Jaysus," or "I'll beat the bejasus out of you."

Fr. Ó Sé shrugged. "It is not as if it is meant an insult to someone they consider as their lord and master, to use the old phrase."

"Does it not upset you?"

"Not when I hear it so often, I suppose. It does cause me to repeat the words Jesus used at his crucifixion 'Father, forgive them, because they do not understand what they do.'"

"But they don't care. They have no respect anyone or anything."

"There are bigger problems in the world, bigger fish to fry," the priest said.

"When I was learning about religion," Dowling answered, "there was what was known as 'taking the name of the lord in vain.' What happened to that?"

"It was thrown out with the bathwater," came the casual answer. "The way I look at it is that I can't see that Jesus himself would have a problem with a bit of bawdy talk or what you refer to as 'taking the lord's name in vain'. It happens and for the most part it is not meant as an insult."

"That, for me," Dowling said, "is part of the malaise of the church in this day and age. Anything goes. There is no right and wrong. Ye have lost the plot and don't seem interested in finding it again."

"I think the church is beginning to learn from its many mistakes," the priest answered, "learning how to live in the real world, learning how to take the rough with the smooth. Learning not to make as many mountains out of molehill as we did in the past".

"You can use all the clichés in the world, but it is not getting you anywhere," the film producer said.

"I am a follower of Pope Francis myself. He will not be around for long because of his age and health, but he sees the ways in which the church is shaking off a lot of its hang-ups. I think that is what he means when he said in effect that clergy need to get down and dirty if they are to reach people. The way he put it was that the shepherds should smell of the sheep in biblical terms. I don't think he would be worried with how many 'fucks' you put between 'Jesus' and 'Christ.'" "So what?"

"We are trying to soften our title a little bit," Dowling said, "by adding our meaning to the F and N in the middle of the title."

Ó Sé smiled. "Do I detect someone not willing to take the hard road. Chickening out on spelling out what you mean exactly? Don't give it, if you are not able to take it"

"Give what?" Dowling asked.

"Give us shit. Give shit to the church. We have come through so much that we are actually able to put up with the shite.."

"I am not strong enough to be a Salman Rushdie," Dowling answered. "I hate your fucking church and what it stands for, but I recognize that millions, billions love it and give their lives for it. I just do want to insult those people by having 'FN' in the middle of the name of Jesus."

"So what have you suggested?"

"Forever new, maybe. What would you suggest yourself?"

"What about Forever Now, because we claim Jesus is there forever. Yesterday, today, and tomorrow."

"But is he there? Is he real? Is he a figment of the imagination?"

"He is real for me," the priest answered. "I have bet my life on him. I am an old-fashioned believer.. I accept the full package, Jesus of the gospels, Jesus, the son of God."

"You don't come across to me as being old-fashioned. You are not just black and white. Where do you stand on subjects like homosexuality, LGBT rights and all that kind of stuff?"

"I stand where I think Jesus stands, on the side of love and understanding." After a pause he added "And compassion. Just as the mothers and fathers whose children are gay or whatever have taught us in recent years."

"But the church does not support you on that?"

"Which church? The church of the people, or the church of the Vatican? When they will come around at their own slow pace. They have no choice really."

"As we are at the end-game already?" The priest said.

Dowling made exclamation marks with bent fingers on both hands. "So you don't support the 'actual church?'"

"The actual church, the real church is the communion of faith."

"So 'fuck the Vatican?' is what you are saying?"

The priest laughed. "It is thyself who sayeth it. The Vatican is slow and ponderous, but it eventually catches up with the people of God."

"You are saying your superiors have not got a clue?"

"They have lots of clues. Like myself they have given their lives for all of this. They are, I'm sure, following their consciences, but as I have said already, the people of God are away out in front of them."

"That is an amazing statement," Nicólás Dowling said.

"What is amazing about it? It was always such in the church. Peter and Paul had their differences from the very start. One of the great early Councils of the church hinged on one 'iota,' one letter 'i' in deciding Jesus was, is 'equally God and equally human.' Wars were fought, schisms formed on such issues, so why should we be surprised to find the churches of today stagger through the fog as best they can?"

"Sound like a lot of cock-ups to me," Dowling said.

Fr. Ó Sé gave a low laugh. "That is probably the greatest proof of all of the existence of God. The survival of the cock-ups as you call them, for two thousand years."

"You sound like you question it all every single day?" Dowling said. "And still believe?"

"There is not a day that I look into the chalice in the middle of mass that I do not have questions. And answers as well. It is a question of faith and I still stick with what I have. Maybe it is just the easy way out."

"You put your money on that horse every day. What if it turns out to be a donkey, or a mule or jennet?"

"All the better." the priest smiled. "Of course, it is on a donkey like the one that Jesus turned to carry him triumphantly to Jerusalem that I place my shekel. The laugh may be on the other side of my face when and if I reach the other side, but so what?"

"So you are not even sure about the other side?"

"I don't know in so far as there is nobody there to prove it that came back from the dead. Except Jesus of course according to my faith. I have also seen the powerful faith of the hundreds of people whose funerals I have celebrated. The strength of that faith is evident in the powerful desire so many people have to see their loved ones again in some form or other. That faith is just palpable at so many funerals."

"You could just say the prayers and take their contributions. Does not many a priest or minister do that?"

"What makes you think that?" the priest asked.

"Is it not a reasonable assumption?"

"Isn't it you that is cynical," Fr. Ó Sé said.

Dowling answered "I am just asking the questions, and answers seem not just scarce but doubtful as well."

"Did you have faith yourself once?"

"I still have an open mind," the Producer said. "I think. some answers may come from the story of Jesus and what I see and hear of people's faith. We will see as time goes on."

Fr. Éamonn Ó Sé sounded as if he was talking to himself for a moment. "I suppose everyone is searching in their own way. The answers seem to come to some people easier than others."

"It must be difficult to remain in that organisation," Nicólas Dowling said. "Given all the scandals that have occurred down through the years."

"Things are more difficult now than at any time in my lifetime," the priest answered, "but the community understand in ways that the media does not, that the vast majority of clergy have not abused children. I'm talking here of nearly ninety-five percent who have not abused anyone. Most people in the parishes accept that."

"You must admit that your crowd are a busted flush, a dead duck, a lost cause. A hangover in more ways than one, hanging on to the coattails of a society that has lost interest in most of that stuff.."

The priest joked "You sound like you are about to quote the old riddle."

"What riddle?" Dowling asked, before the other man could finish his sentence.

"Under the water, over the water, never touches the water: What's that?"

"It is too much of a riddle for me. Is it something religious?"

"It's an egg in a duck's arse. That is what it is."

"What has that to do with anything?"

"If a dead duck like me has an egg still in its arse, there is a future. When the egg cracks open."

"You seem to be losing the plot."

"Again?" The priest asked. "What I am trying to say is that it is your hole that has the problem. I am fairly ok with all this stuff we have been discussing. It is you that's full of sensitivity, that is looking for answers that are not there at the moment."

"So where are you going to find the answers?"

"They will be there when we reach really rock-bottom."

"You are very sure of yourself?" Dowling answered.

Fr. Ó Sé sounded as if he was trying to make a case in a court of law. "I give you two thousand years of experience."

"And I give you one unsinkable ship called The Titanic, which tan into an ice-berg. You and your crowd are heading for rock-bottom."

"And so, we have been for two thousand years."

"Up shit creek without a paddle," the film producer said.

"Do you remember the story about Jesus when he was really down on his luck, his followers drifting away when he was not giving them home-made wine, not to speak of loaves and fishes?"

"You are probably going to tell me what he said," Dowling said as if his patience was being tried.

"Will you also go away?" he asked his dwindling band of followers. It was Simon Peter who spoke up. "To whom shall we go. You are the one who has the words of eternal life."

"Go on. Keep trying to convince yourself," Dowling said. "You and by that, I mean your organisation are a lost cause, battered and broken beyond recovery. I do not rejoice in that, but if you are to have a future you have a long way to go to come back."

"We are battered and bruised, but we are still here," the priest answered, "and we are so important that a secular organisation is about to make a film about us."

"The last kick of the dying horse. Or should I say ass?"

"I live in hope, I suppose," Fr. Ó Sé said. "True enough the great days in which Nuns, Priests and Christian Brothers educated much of Ireland and quite a bit of the world as well are gone."

Ireland has moved on. The world has moved on. Others and in many cases, better educators have taken their place. That is progress a new church is emerging, smaller but in many ways fuller of faith as those involved will not feel that they have been forced into it against their wishes. The best thing that happened the church in ages was the freedom brought by the Covid epidemic. People who somewhere in their psyches' felt an obligation to comply with church attendance under the threat of mortal sin felt free to stay away. That does not mean that they cared no more about their religion but there was no psychological gun pointing at their heads.

His visitor shrugged. "I understand where you are coming from. You have no choice except to defend your own institution."

"I don't have to defend the indefensible," the priest answered, but there seem to be two opposing interests in this country, those who think the Roman Catholic church is finished and the couple of million people who still attend Sunday Mass. Media and arts people do not seem to be aware of this because they do not notice what happens other than in their own lives in the same way as believers ignore what happens outside their sphere of influence.

"Do that many people still attend Mass on a regular basis?"

Fr. Ó Sé said "I regularly come home from Sunday Masses attended by fairly large numbers of people. I switch on the radio while having my self-cooked Sunday dinner and listen to programmes in which the high and mighty pronounce the death and burial of religion in Ireland. I ask myself 'Did I not see three or four hundred people at each Mass I had today?' Why are they being dismissed as 'stupids' by people who have written a book or published a podcast?"

Dowling smiled. "You will surely kick our arses down the road so if we do not come up with a good Irish Catholic film."

"All we will expect is a bit of balance, not the dismissal of half the community as being ignorant mugs."

"We will do our best," Dowling said lightly.

The priest continued as if talking to himself: "What is the truth?" as Pontius Pilate asked "Give us the unvarnished truth as you see it. We cannot ask for anything more."

"Even if it does not agree with your version of the truth?" Dowling asked.

"Ye can crucify Christ upside down as far as I am concerned," the priest answered. "The way Saint Peter was crucified in deference to Jesus. Ye can marry Mary Magdalen to Jesus. Do what you like but it will not change the faith of the true believers. They have seen it all already from child abuse to refusal to ordain women. If you tell the truth, tell things as you see them even if I or the community do not agree with you, I will not complain. You are welcome to this neck of the woods."

Nicólás Dowling stood up and shook hands with the priest who said "Sorry, I didn't even offer you a drink or even a cup of tea, I was so wrapped up in the conversation that I forgot my manners."

The film maker laughed. "At least you didn't give me a fiver to buy my own tea in the local shop when you thought I was a beggar"

CHAPTER THREE

"The Three Migos" they called themselves after three Irish international soccer players who were nicknamed "The Three Amigos" back in their parent's time. The father of two of the young people involved constantly talked of a trip he had made to New York to watch the team in a world Cup many years earlier. There were actually four members in the teenage band the young people had formed even though they tried to deliberately confuse the world by insisting on calling themselves "The Three Migos." It would sound good if they were ever to hit the bigtime, it was also a nod to a book all of them had enjoyed in early teenage years. Alexander Dumas "The Three Musketeers" which were actually four people when Ahos, Porthus and Aramaist included the legendary D'rtangan.

Aisling and Eoin were brother and sister and their next-door neighbours were Eithne and Alan. Their youth had been spent into and out of each other's houses and they had become firm friends. Despite the changes that had come during teenage development they were still close to each other and were sometimes thought to be members of the same family. They had steered clear of romantic entanglements with each other, while being sometimes withering about choices any or all of them made from time to time with different members of their classes at secondary school.

The Migos enjoyed playing pranks on neighbours especially at times like Halloween. While some people of their age smashed turnips and heads of cabbage on the roads, the Migos got around to a different type of disruption they heard their own families talk about. The took farm gates from their hinges and moved them to other fields. They used a JCB to pick up beer barrels and place them on top of police cars. They sneaked into the local church and set the Angelus bell ring every hour of the night. They did not boast of their achievements and often left other young people to take the blame for their actions. They got away with many pranks because they were seen as sensible young people who were more interested in music than anything else.

Fr. Éamonn Ó Sé had some doubts about them. He remembered the time they served Mass some years earlier and the strong smell of altar wine he used to get when it was their turn to serve, but he had no proof that they had been sipping from the bottles. He remembered the fascination that Aisling and Alan especially had with the electronic bell and how it worked, but he had no proof of that either. He understood that one of the worst things a priest could do was to accuse someone in the wrong, or even worse speak from the altar about to criticise something relatively harmless. It would get attention alright, but it would alienate a lot of people.

He remembered the words of an ageing Parish Priest in a parish in which he was sent to practice his sermons while still a deacon many years earlier. He still did not know was the older man joking or being serious when he proclaimed to Ó Sé and his colleagues. "Denounce them lads. It is the only thing they will listen to." Down through the ages of clerical domination of their parishes, few things stood out as terrifying as being "read from the altar." There was no going back from that, especially in the case of women who were targeted for being pregnant and unmarried.. That virtually became the unforgivable sin in a religion supposed to be about love

The Migos had started their own music group and they came together on a regular basis in a small chalet close to one of their family houses. It had been built many years earlier to accommodate tourists, but as the years went by that particular source of income was no longer needed because mothers especially were able to go out to work as their children got older. The young "Amigos" wanted to create their own particular music in the manner of The Beatles in Liverpool or U2 in Ireland. They were young and confident enough to set themselves such high standards. They spent hours practising and refining their own songs. As the evenings passed they were more likely to turn to the next prank they would play on unsuspecting local people.

"We should be able to play some major trick on that crowd that are coming to do a film about Jesus," Alan said. "I would like if we could take a snobbish crowd like that down to size, like the stunts we played on the priest and the Angelus bell he was so proud of."

"I would not be too keen on that kind of thing," Aisling said. "The priest was good to us when we were serving Mass. He is not the worst."

"We are talking here about having a bit of fun," her brother Eoin said "We wakened people up with the angelus bell in the middle of the night, but nobody was injured. No one got a heart attack and died. It just gave them a bit of a laugh."

"So what if we had the bells ringing," Eithne commented. "Sure most of the old people are half deaf anyway, and they block their ears with cotton wool when they are going to bed."

Alan had a suggestion "We should crucify someone for the craic. Isn't the film they are making supposed to be about crucifixion? If we could get one of the actors on his way home scuttered from the public house, we could tie him to a bit of a cross for the laugh."

Aisling was not too sure about that "Are you really talking about getting hold of one of the casts and nailing him to a cross? To die. Like Jesus?"

"I am not talking about a hammer and nails job. I am not that stupid. That would be pure murder. But we could tie him to a cross with masking tape or something simple like that It would be a bit like Houdini in old pictures. It would go viral all around the world."

"If it was done to one of our own relations instead of one of the actors," Eithne said, "nobody could pin it on any of us. As far as I am aware it is a serious crime to kidnap someone. Someone or more of us could end up in prison. The police would not see it as a prank, so let us think hard before doing something like that."

Aisling had her own theory "It would be a lot more sensible to look for parts as extras in the film. At least we would get paid and we would get to know a lot of the actors and actresses"

"You always had your eye on making money, Aisling." Eoin said.

"What is wrong with that?" was her reply.

"I am not finding fault with earning a few bobs. In fact, the best prank of all would be to skin a few of them by selling them minerals and sandwiches while the filming was being done. Or we could offer to sing a few songs or play music for them."

Alan strong his fingers over the strings of his guitar "The Migos are getting bearded to be apostles for the weirdoes."

Aisling put her hand to her face before saying "Eithne and myself will not be growing beards, thank you very much, but I am sure both of us would like to get parts in the drama they intend to film. You would not know who would notice us. Hollywood, here we come."

"There would be a lot more fun in crucifying someone. Symbolically, I mean," Alan said. "That would really put the cat among the pigeons, if not the pigeon among the cats."

"Hands up everyone who wants a part in the film," Eithne said as she counted "One two, three, four Migos. Who is going to speak to that guy that is in charge?"

"Why don't the four of us go?" Aisling asked. "Strength in numbers. We could bring our musical instruments to show that we mean business."

"They hardly had guitars and banjos back in the time of Jesus," Eoin said.

"Was music even mentioned in the Bible?" Eithne asked.

"Weren't there angels singing at the first Christmas?" Aisling asked.

"Surely they had Christmas carols," Alan suggested.

"No way," Eithne said. "We are talking two thousand years ago here."

Eoin wondered "What is the point of bringing my guitar so?"

Eithne asked "How do we know that it will not all be done in modern dress and musical instruments? Don't they often do that nowadays when they are trying to talk an old story for a modern age?"

"What have we to lose from talking to the guy in charge?" asked Alan. "If we don't get parts we can throw a few spanners in the works and upset their applecarts by crucifying someone like we said."

"You have crucifixion on the brain," was Eoin's comment.

"Some people are turning against the film crowd already," Eithne said. "I heard my Mum tell my Dad that Mary from the Mountain is dead against it being filmed."

"Fuck that one," Alan commented. "I don't know if she realises yet whether the world is round or flat."

"We are related to her," Eithne reminded him.

"Sorry about that," Alan said, "but being related to someone does not mean that they are not boring or stupid.."

Eithne stuck up for her relative. "She is not the worst. Not one time did she come to visit in our house that she did not bring sweets to us. I will never forget that."

Alan crunched up his face as he spoke in a peculiar accent "That's her alright. Sweets for the children and then she goes on to backbite everyone and everything. She still thinks that nothing has ever changed since life first began."

"Will you ever give over and pick on somebody else?" Eithne answered him. "What we need to do now is to put on our best manners and try to persuade that little man they call 'the devileen' to give us parts in the film."

"We will be as gentle as angels in the stable singing for the baby Jesus until we persuade him to give us parts," Aisling said. "When is anything like this to be ever acted out in this place again?"

Eithne agreed with her "By the time anything like this happens in this area ever again, we will be away at university, or working later on. We will never get this kind of a chance again."

Alan changed the subject with a juicy bit of local gossip. "They say the old guy that is in charge of the film is banging Margie from the Post Office. Should we raise that matter when we go to see him?"

"I doubt if Margie is so stupid as to be with an old codger like that," Eithne said. "Anyway, I doubt if blackmail would work on someone like that."

"That is what the lads at school are saying," was Alan's reply. "Believe it or not, there is seldom smoke without fire."

"I'd say the lads that are saying that are just jealous," said Aisling. "There isn't one of them that wouldn't get in her pants if they had half a chance. She is a fine-looking woman."

"It sounds like you fancy her yourself," commented Eoin playfully; "I hadn't realised you were like that."

"I am not into grannies," Aisling said. "I am not into anyone for that matter. I have more for doing with my time."

"Such as?" Eoin asked.

"Playing music and putting up with the likes of you."

Eithne commented "I haven't seen the old guy Margie is supposed to be having it off with. They say he is as ugly as the devil himself but he has a prick on him like a donkey."

"Who said that?" Aisling asked.

"It must have been Margie. Who else would know?"

CHAPTER FOUR

Margie from the shop and Nicólás Dowling lay side by side in her bed as they drew deep breaths as if they had just finished a marathon. They were laughing even louder than they were breathing.

"Wow," Margie said. "What is just after happening?" She looked at her watch. "You have been going like the clappers for the past half an hour. It's the best fuck I have had in my whole life.."

"Is that what you say to all the men?"

"Men of your calibre are fairly scarce around here."

"You sounded like you were enjoying it?"

"I was pretending, of course. You know yourself the craic?"

"You were crowing like the cock in the morning."
"The cock was all yours," Margie said. "You were unbelievable. How on earth did you keep it up?"

"Practice, Experience."

"Viagra, I would say, but I am not complaining. I will have a pain in my insides for a week."

"A pain of pleasure, I hope," said Dowling "If I have anything to do with it."

"You might." Margie laughed. "If you are lucky." She reached between his legs "I will say this much for you. They don't call you the little devil or the diabhailín as we say in Irish, for nothing, it never occurred to me when you came into the shop for the first time that we would end up like this."

"I knew it the first minute that I looked at you."

"You knew what?" Margie asked.

"I knew that you were not getting the satisfaction from life that you deserve. The joy that a woman of your age and beauty deserved,"

"That is a load of bullshit." Margie kissed him. "I didn't think a professional in the film industry would be interested in a small fat woman like me."

"You are extremely attractive. I like a woman with a bit of flesh on her bones, and you have just the right amount. Skin and bone do not appeal to me."

"Have you fucked many skeletons?"

"Too many, and there is not much satisfaction to be had from doing so."

"You have been around the block a good few times is what I gather from that."

"I gather that it was not your first time either," Dowling said.

"You don't know anything about me."

"I know more now than I knew as I watched you dealing with great care for your customers in the Post Office. That appealed to me as much as your good looks and your sexual chemistry."

"You are a complete bullshitter," was Margie's reply.

"All I wanted at that stage was to find somewhere to stay."

"You would think the hotel would be the ideal place for a gentleman like you. A big knob from the city like yourself?"

"That is where the actors, actresses and film crew will be staying. I need to be at some distance from them or it will all be about drinks and reminiscences of past film, not to speak of theatres, dramas and who said what when. I am here to work and staying here will give me a different perspective."

"Is that what you call it?" Margie joked.

"I need space. Away from the well named 'madding crowd.'"

"So is this what is known as the casting couch?"

"You can have the part I mentioned before if you want it. The strong woman who stood up to Jesus and asked where was his bucket for the living water. I can coach you if you are interested."

"You have coached me already if I can put it like that, but it is probably better not to put the scarlet woman in the actual film."

"The Bible is actually full of strong women, stronger than the church ever gave them credit for."

"So you have read it all?" Margie asked. "It is a long way from the Bible to what we have just been at."

"It is no length at all. It is all about the human condition. There is more about wedding and bedding, not to speak of bedding without wedding in the Bible than a lot of holy Joes and Marys would like to admit. The story of the women taken in adultery which led to Jesus saying 'Let the one without sin cast the first stone.' That was left out of Bibles at one stage because clergy were to admit that Jesus said such a thing. The powers that be in the church have a lot to answer for, and it's not just about child abuse and stuff like that."

"So the people in the Bible wouldn't mind what we were at?"

"Some would, some wouldn't. There were always narrow-minded people in society then and now. But human nature always finds a way."

"Tell me again about that woman at the well that put Jesus in his box."

"So you will play that part?" Dowling asked.

"I will think about it when I find out all about it."

"I will print out a page about her for you to look at, and you can make up your mind about it then. Even before we came together I thought of you when I saw you in the Post Office. 'A feisty bit of stuff,' I thought, but a kind one. I must be a good judge of character."

Margie elbowed him gently in the ribs "Flattery will get you nowhere."

"It has got me everywhere already, and I hope that it will again. Soon."

Margie and her companion discussed the part of the Samarian woman at the well for some time, and especially her riposte "You don't have a bucket..."

"Do you think Jesus was used to being spoken to like that? Or was he the kind of bloke that would get scandalised about a simple little thing?"

"They talk now about bucket lists," Dowling said, "but that woman's reply was probably like music to the ears of Jesus. Here was someone not putting on an act for 'The Great Man' because she didn't have a clue about what or who he was. It must have made his day to find someone who was not deferring to him."

"You seem to have gotten to like Jesus?"

"Why wouldn't I? He was a great bloke. Some would say that he still is. It is not his fault that the church turned out the way that it did. That is not to say that there is no good in the church. Many great charitable causes have been inspired by Christ and the church..."

"Tell me one of them," Margie asked.

"Take the Saint Vincent De Paul Society for instance. A quarter of the people in this country would go to bed hungry without them."

"That is charity. People should not have to humiliate themselves to ask for help, especially in this day and age. That should be the Government's job." Margie said.

"I fully agree with you, but until that happens how many children will go to bed hungry." Nicólás Dowling answered.

"So there is nothing in the proverbial bucket but empty promises and high faulting notions?"

"I don't know. I would like to prove whether or not there is sense or reason in religion, and in particular in the one we are probing in our film. Was there ever anything substantial in the bucket? As soon as I begin to think I understand it, something always throws me off the scent.."

"What kind of stuff throws you off?" Margie asked.

"I called to see that priest that lives over the road today. It is not that he said anything that stands out in my mind, but I was sitting there looking at someone that has spent his life in a certain way because that faith caught him by the short and curlies in his youth. Christ took a grip on him and he has not let him go since. That made me think that this is no pretence. There must be something real to it."

"So that is what gave you the hard-on?" Margie joked.

Dowling laughed. "I will be calling to see him every day if that is the case,"

"Sorry for interrupting your train of thought, but I could not resist. I am beginning to think that you and he are birds of a feather, that you are both hooked in different ways to the same search for truth."

"Obsession of different kinds. I was thinking as I looked the priest in the face?"

"Is he in it because he is too old and tired to get out of it?"

His train of thought was interrupted by Margie rubbing her hand around his belly, kissing him around his neck and on his lips. Nicólás sat up in the bed and swung his legs out across the edge and on to the floor. "Would you mind if we were to take this up another time. I have a serious phone call to make?"

"And fuck you too," was Margie's reaction.

"It is just something that I need to do," Dowling said.

"Tell her I was asking for her," was the sarcastic reply.

"Tell who what?"

"Your wife, I suppose, or boyfriend or some other fucker, I suppose."

Dowling was pulling on his trouser. "There is no wife or anyone else of that kind in my life but I just remembered that there were certain things I need to attend to with regard to this film, actors I have to see, payments I have to make. We have had a lovely couple of hours together, but certain things have to be attended to before nightfall. I will see you then and hopefully take up where we left off."

"And fuck you too," Margie said as he headed towards the door. She lay back against the pillows and wondered had all his flattery to do with getting a comfortable place to stay so that he would not be under pressure in the hotel. "If any man needed to pay for his pleasure, it is this one," she thought as she drifted off to sleep.

CHAPTER FIVE

Fr. Éamonn Ó Sé went about his priestly duties in the usual way with the visit Nicólas Dowling had paid him or anything to do with the film that was to be made in his parish far from his mind. For him, the holy communion visits to the old or sick of the area was his most enjoyable and uplifting day of the month. The First Friday of the month was the day on which Roman Catholic clergy paid such visits and Fr. Ó Sé knew none of them for which it was a chore. His parish sat between mountain and sea and while the population was relatively small there was a lot of driving to be done between houses, many of which meant negotiating narrow country lanes, some of them high up on the side of the mountain. The faith of people was what marked out such days for the priest more than anything. Despite pain from rheumatism and old injuries not to speak of coughs, colds and flu, most people were in good humour as they welcomed not just the priest, but the eucharist bread which represented the body of Christ himself. What struck the priest most on such visits was the fact that those people who had most reason to complain, complained the least.

Those monthly visits often sent the priest down long memory lanes as people he had known in other parishes in the previous thirty years returned to his mind. He saw them again in the eyes of his mind and imagination. He remembered the old woman dying of cancer whose last request was for her dúidín or clay pipe. When the pipe was lit by her daughter, her life seemed to rise from her body in a cloud of smoke. It was probably the happiest death he had observed, although there were many more who slipped away quietly, their peaceful passage helped in no small way by pain-killing drugs which were among the great blessings that medicine had brought to people's lives.

Many changes of that kind had come during Fr. Ó Sé's own lifetime. In the early years he had heard and seen a number of people die roaring. It brought back memories of one of the cruellest curses he had ever heard. "May you die roaring," and he felt that there were few things worse you could wish on anyone. There were fears at the time that drugs would lead to a kind of mercy killing, and some doctors seemed to fear that they could actually be accused of murder through palliative care, sense and compassion gradually put paid to that kind of fear and stoicism, so a time had come in which most people were able to die without too much pain.

As he passed a particular house, now closed and starting to show the effects of wind and weather, the priest remembered the man who had sent him a valentine card "from Jimmy and the ducks." The blue eggs of the same ducks had featured on many a breakfast in his presbytery table. It gave him the opportunity to tell one of his jokes, that he was quacking up because of all the duck egg. That would be followed by the observation that duck eggs were less harmful than others because they had less cholesterol. This would be followed by the killer line. It is probably a quack that said that.

In the eyes of his mind, Fr. Ó Sé saw the woman who challenged him about wearing a beard at a time when such a fashion statement was neither popular nor profitable. "When are you going to get rid of that old goats' beard?" she asked.

He had pointed to statues of Jesus, Saint Patrick and Saint Padre Pio. "Did you ever see a saint without a beard?" he asked.

She had pointed to the pictures and statues around the church of the Blessed Virgin Mary, Saint Teresa and in more recent Mother Teresa. "Those have no beards," the old lady answered. "And are you trying to tell me that they are not saints?" The glint in her eye told him that behind her apparently stern face was her own kind of humour.

Story followed story as he drove around.

A man in his nineties whom he was anointing with last rites told him of a woman who sent for the then local priest in the middle of the night to anoint her very frequently. Before he returned home she would ask him the same question every time "Am I going to die tonight, Father?" He would reply with some kind words to put her at her ease. He used to encourage her to send for him if possible before nightfall as the mountain roads were narrow and winding and dangerous. Little heed was taken of that advice and it was even later on a dark and stormy night that she had sent for him again. When the woman was sitting happily by the fireplace asked him about the possibility of imminent death "Will I die tonight, Father?" He answered "Not tonight, but I would be very worried about the time after that" She never sent for him again and she eventually outlived him.

As he got older the priest wondered did he tell the same story to the same people time after time, either in his sermons or ordinary conversation. If he did itself, they probably inadvertently had their revenge by telling him old stories from their own family backgrounds. Many of the same stories were told in different areas with different people named in them. One of the stories he heard from many different sources while he was a student in Maynooth seminary had to do with the arrival of what was known as AI in different parts of the country. A similar story seemed to have emerged in every townland in Ireland. This particular AI did not refer to Artificial Intelligence but to Artificial Insemination.

That was the time in the nineteen fifties when the work of the local bull was usurped by men who delivered bovine semen in canisters to impregnate cows and heifers without the benefit of a bulleen balls. Similar stories emerged from all over the country, the woman phoning from the Post Office for instance, asking that a little head ford "bulleen" be sent out as their cow was coming into heat. That story was embellished by the AI agent being told "There is a basin of water and soap in the barn for you to wash your hands, and a nail on the back of the barn door to hang your pants," Even a bull would have considered that to be a 'cock and bull' story."

As he drove about on his pleasant duties to the elders of the parish. Fr. Éamonn Ó Sé's thoughts turned to the swarthy television producer who had visited him with what seemed like a courtesy call to the local shaman. He wondered what influence would this retelling of the story of the passion and death of Jesus Christ have on the local community. Would it come as an eye-opener to many people with regard to their traditional beliefs? That could hardly be a bad thing if the story was told without prejudice. Was anything likely to disturb what used to be known as "the faithful" anymore? They had seen bishops become fathers, mass servers abused sexually, Banks crashing, thousands homeless with little hope of help. Even the national television service was racked in scandal.

Much of what happened in the wider world seemed to wash over the local community as far as the local priest was concerned. Life went on, birth marriage for many people still, death. The rhythm of the seasons. There was no great sign of poverty in their coastal community, but little sign of wealth either. People got by, raised their families, sent their children to school and university if at all possible. After all the years of emigration a small circle of people were coming back from England and the United States to work from home. This had become possible because of the introduction of broadband and other online services.

When he had finished his parish rounds and other regular duties for the day, Fr Ó Sé sat into his big comfortable armchair to watch his favourite television soap-operas. This was his favourite pastime as the years went by and he felt too old for any kind of sporting activity other than his daily walk. This helped clear his mind before an evening Mass or some other spiritual exercise. A walk by the sea which lapped against the boundary wall of the church at high tide always reminded him of the line from an Old Testament Psalm "Near restful waters he leads me to revive my drooping spirit."

The "soaps" revived his drooping spirits in a different way as far as he was concerned, this was the Shakespeare of modern times. Drama for the masses as opposed to the often stereotyped and snobbish drama of the theatres. There was nothing as such wrong with them apart from ticket prices and the "more intelligent than thou" atmosphere that prevailed in many of them. The soaps tended to be looked on with disdain by many who seemed to look down their noses as they watched them all the same as an amusing pastime.

Fr Ó Sé was in no doubt but that the soaps have helped people to come to terms with issues like homosexuality, racism and social snobbery. Would same sex marriage referenda in Ireland have succeeded without them? The small screen had shown the public that such issues were not really a threat to anyone, not least his own church that had its doubts and questions for biblical reasons. The primacy of love in the teachings of Jesus Christ had assured this particular priest at least that these issues were not a threat. So had the powerful reaction of parents and siblings to the recognition of difference that had stigmatised sons, daughters, brothers and sisters until then was no longer a threat to their very existence.

Its pleased Fr. Éamonn Ó Sé as a priest and a Christian to praise the soap dramas because they had helped develop what he would call the attitude of Jesus Christ more than that of the official church and bring it to his parishioners. He had ad been told by some local people that it had been said in the local public house that he as priest had arranged Mass times in a way that would allow him watch the "soaps." That had brought a smile to his face as it was clear to most people that such programmes were repeated so often that anyone could find time to watch them.

He remembered a time about twenty years earlier when he was working in a different parish and the American soap, "Dallas" was all the rage. He had listened to an Irish language programme in which a number of older women had been invited to take part. The presenter had tried might and main to get them to speak out and condemn the goings-on in that particular drama, but there was no complaint from any of them even though they were all staunch Roman Catholic. They laughed at the presenter's efforts to make them condemn the programme. "What is it but a bit of fun and a great way to pass a while of a night? Isn't it a pity we did not get the chance to have a bit of craic like that ourselves when we were younger?" The priest wondered would the reaction locally be to the film that Nicólás Dowling was about to make about the passion and death of Jesus Christ?

CHAPTER SIX

Nicólás Dowling had arranged a meeting in a private room of the local hotel to interview the man he had picked to play the part of Jesus in his film. He had never previously met the man but he had seen the relatively young Irishman in various BBC dramas mainly of the police variety. He was about the right age for the part and the growth of a beard and moustache would enable him to look like Jesus did in traditional holy pictures. As the story was to be filmed in Irish and English at the same time, he wondered if Tadhg Ó Maoldomhnaigh as he called himself would have enough Irish to play the part. That could be rectified of course with a voiceover, but it would not be quite the same as natural speech. He would soon find out, he thought, as the man he had chosen to play the part was coming through the doorway.

They shook hands and introduced themselves formally, even though they had previously spoken by phone or contacted each other by email. The younger man had already started to grow a beard on which Dowling complimented him. "You look just like the man himself?"

"Do I?" he answered with a smile, "or is it that he looks just like me?"

"You have passed the first test," Dowling answered. "I like your accent in both Irish and English."

"I am a bit rusty after ten years in England."

"You will have Irish spoken all around you here in the Gaeltacht. You will take it in your stride in no time at all. I will take you up to the room I have booked so that we can have a bit of privacy as we talk. There are people in the bar most of the time so it is difficult to find a bit of peace to talk without interruption."

Maoldhomhnaigh laughed. "I hear that you have some strange methods when it comes to acting, but I was not expecting to be invited to a bedroom straight away. Or is it there you have the proverbial casting couch?"

"You haven't heard half of it yet," Dowling assured him. When they reached the room, the actor was asked to lay down on the floor on his back with his arms stretched out at both sides.

The actor looked a bit doubtful. "You mean now?"

"On your back. Flat out."

"What is this about?"

"Lie down and you will soon find out," was Dowling's answer as he took a couple of pieces of wood from the bag he was carrying, as well as a hammer and some large nails. "Close your eyes now and tell me later what feel when you hear the noise of hammer on timber..

Tadhg lay down with his arms stretched out in the manner of Christ on his cross. Dowling started to drive nails into the pieces of wood and he continued to do so for a few minutes, before he asked "Now, what do you feel?"

"Do I need to stay down here?" the actor answered. "Flat out?"

"Sit up or stand up now. Just tell me how you felt when you heard the sound
of hammer on nail."

Maoldhomhnaigh rose slowly to his feet. "I felt nothing at the beginning, but I felt a strange kind of peace coming over me then."

"Good," Dowling said, "but why peace when you are supposes to being nailed to a cross?"

"I was actually having a bit of a rest," the actor answered.

"Are you taking the piss?" asked Dowling. "I thought you realised you were getting into the part for the crucifixion of Christ?"

"That is exactly what I was doing," Maoldhomhnaigh answered. "I am literally flat out because in the previous twelve hours I have been betrayed. I have been sold for thirty pieces of silver. Peter has said he does not know me. Pontius Pilate has mocked me and literally washed his hands of me. I have been scourged, spat upon, kicked and humiliated. I have had to carry a cross up the hill, falling three times in the process. And then I get to lie down. Why wouldn't I have a respite for a second? Things can hardly get any worse. That is why I can draw breath for a moment,"

"I like that," Dowling said. "That is a good start."

"You mean that I have the part?"

"Let us put it like this. You are in the running. I can see that you have read your bible and read it well, but it is the feelings that I am after, the noise of the hammer, the nail going through the flesh, teenage Roman soldiers who have never handled a hammer in their lives all hit and miss as they try to drive a nail."

"Is it any wonder?" Tadhg asked "that Jesus remarked that they did not know what they were doing?"

"How would you feel about a crown of thorns being driven into your head?" Dowling asked.

"Don't you worry. I have had that headache, but it was from too much to drink too often."

"Being facetious is of little help to us," the film producer said.

Tadhg sounded a little peeved "OK, so it's a bit of a joke. What I mean is that I have experienced that pain or something like it for whatever reason, I know the fucking feeling."

"That's good."

"What's good?" Ó Maoldhomhnaigh asked.

"It is good to hear you getting irked. Feeling the feeling as we say in the trade. Pain needs to reach the marrow of the bone before we really feel it."

Tadhg grinned. "You keep being a pain in the ass and I will have even deeper feelings. I am doing my best here."

"As am I. It is not personal. If I need to shock, I will shock. It is my baby and I will play it the way I like. They used to call it the greatest story ever told, which seems like a bit of an exaggeration now that we have seen everything from 'Star Wars' to 'Barbie.' But it is a gripping story."

O Maoldhomhnaigh raised himself on an eyebrow. "Even though we know the ending?"

"We only know the beginning and two thousand years of trials and tribulations, wars, schisms, forced conversions, great hate, great love, children abused, lies told, fortunes made and lost, great art created, great minds destroyed. We could just call it 'A bit of everything' but that would not get in the crowds in the way that blood and guts can."

"Just as well we are only telling a small part of the story," Tadhg said.

Dowling looked the actor in the eyes. "I need you to get you into the character fully and completely. You are Jesus, not infant Jesus meek and mild, but Jesus the carpenter with hands hardened by physical work. You have learned your trade from your father, Joseph. You know far more about timber and about a hammer and nails than the youngsters from the Roman army whose job is to nail you to the cross. You could buy and sell them with your skills. The hit the nail with one blow of the hammer and the next one lands on your wrist. Feel the pain."

"No wonder the man himself remarked that the soldiers hadn't a clue about what they were doing."

"That's it. You have the gist of it now. That is what I am looking for, that each actor would go into their character and think it through, whether it is Jesus or Mary, Judas or Pontius Pilate, Peter or Mary Magdalene. You will need to inhabit the character, imbibe it, live in its sandals from now until the cameras start to roll in a couple of weeks' times."

"A thought struck me," the actor, Tadhg said. "Could it be that Joseph and Jesus made crosses for the Roman army as part of their trade and that Jesus was far more aware of how well or badly a particular cross was made than the ordinary person did?"

"Now you are thinking in character," Dowling replied. "But would it be unpopular or possible, not to speak of profitable for them to be making crosses for the Roman army?"

"They might have no other choice as carpenters. I'm sure the same cross would have lasted for years, polished with sweat and blood from the backs of crucified men, and women too, maybe," the actor said.

"Are you telling me Jesus might have made the cross he hung on himself?"

"It is thyself who sayeth it," Tadhg said dramatically. "It would certainly a new angle to an old story."

"Hoisted on his own petard," Dowling said with admiration in his voice.

"I don't know what a petard is," his companion answered, "but it fits the bill in this regard. I wonder did he get thirty pieces of silver for making his own cross, as well as the thirty Judas threw back at those who betrayed his boss?"

"You are going too deep into the characters now," Dowling joked. "Next thing you will be claiming that Jesus died a rich man."

"I doubt if the poor man had two sheckels to rub together."

"He didn't because Judas was minding the money and he had popped his clogs before Jesus did." Nicólas Dowling smiled. "I hope he is not listening, Jesus, I mean."

"Don't go all soft on me now," Tadhg said, "and go all superstitious."

"Acting is the most superstitious trade in the business, as you well know. Not much faith, but lots of superstition."

"I am dying to find out if I have got the part of Jesus?" Tadhg asked..

"No guarantee yet," Dowling answered. "There are a couple of other potential Jesuses to interview yet. You will definitively have a part if you want one but I have to be fair to everyone who are in for the major jobs."

"I need to work on my carpentry so."

"And other skills. The part of John who was the only apostle to go as far as the cross along with Mary the mother of Jesus is an interesting one."

"Wasn't he supposed to be gay?" Tadhg asked.

"It is said, and he probably was. Have you a problem with that?"

Tadhg shrugged his shoulders. "Of course I would prefer the part of Jesus, but there are times when work is scarce and basically any job will do."

Dowling said "Keep thinking. Keep imagining the part of Jesus. You are close but I have to be fair to everyone."

CHAPTER SEVEN

Margie the shopkeeper lay in her bed stark naked as she expected Nicólás Dowling to join her when he returned from interviewing actors in the local hotel. She was tired after a long day's work as well as all that had transpired between herself and the man who was her houseguest. He had left her side with such haste earlier that she had little time to think of why he had done so as she went around her daily business in shop and Post Office. Margie had not been with a man for a long time before the previous night, and he had certainly awakened pleasure and feelings she had not experienced for a long time.

Her husband had been like that at the beginning when she had first come to the area to learn the Irish language. She had got part time work in his pub and it was not long until they were together day and night. They had married in haste when their child was on the way but their lives were shattered when their baby was stillborn. Her husband left with the next girl who had come to work in the Post Office and bar and she had not heard sight or sound of them since. There were rumours he had been seen in Australia with another woman. It would not surprise her if he was to return some day as he still owned the business. In the meantime, Margie got on with her life and spent every penny that came through the tills in case her estranged husband ever returned and looked for money.

One lesson that her life experience had taught Margie was to take in Irish language students in summer holiday times, and share her bed with some of the finer specimens who were unlikely to ever forget their working holidays. They certainly learned more than the local language and were generally grateful for the experience. But they were just boys whereas her lodger the previous night was undoubtedly a man of many skills who did not need to be taught anything. If anything it felt that it was from pornography that he had learned his skills. He sought experiences that nobody had sought previously, but she ended the night feeling both shattered and unsatisfied. Despite that she looked forward to similar and possibly even more pleasurable feelings later that night.

Margie fell asleep unknown to herself. She had a dream that her husband who had been known locally as Seamus the Post were fighting over her. The contestants were out in the yard, naked to the waist, fighting bare fisted but no matter how hard they hit each other, neither drew blood. It was then that Margie noticed Seamus drawing a knife from his wellington boot. She screamed and awoke from her nightmare covered in sweat. She tied a dressing gown around her and made her way to the room that had been booked by Nicólas Dowling even though he had not slept there the previous night. The door was locked.

Noises could be heard from inside the room. "The bollocks," Margie said to herself "He has brought some old bitch home with him and he is really rubbing my nose in the dirt now. Under my own roof." It was almost against her will that she knocked on the door of the guestroom. She realised immediately that Dowling was snoring. She hurried back to her own room but no sooner than she had done so she heard the film maker emerge from his room. "What is going on around here?" he asked, between sleeping and waking.

"I heard some strange sounds," Margie said. "I thought someone was after breaking into the house."

Dowling's head was swaying from side to side as if he had just emerged from a drunken dream. "I didn't hear anything strange," he said, "but it felt as if someone had knocked on my door. I was sleeping deeply because I had a long day of interviews and a few drinks afterwards."

"You must have had a right tear of drink?" Margie said, trying to keep their conversation going so that he might come back to her bed and they would forget whatever had come between them earlier in the day.

"I had a few drinks alright, but it was the interviews that had me worn out altogether."

"Was it even worse than the interview you and I had earlier?" Margie asked.

It seemed as if their passionate coming together the night before had been completely forgotten. "Do you mind if I go back to bed now. I am flaked out and I have a big day's work ahead of me tomorrow."

Dowling closed his door and Margie heard the key being turned in the lock. She returned to her own bed seething with anger. She wondered why she should be surprised and angry that Dowling had not joined her in bed, even if it was just to sleep. They were not a couple. They were not partners, she told herself. Why should she expect anything from him? They had their fun and they should leave it like that, although it smacked of the old phrase "Have your fun and run." He had awakened feelings that Margie had ignored for a very long time.

"I need to get back to living a life," she told herself, "rather than just going through the motions in shop and Post Office." She thought of one of the senior students at the Irish college who had shared her bed while working part time in the shop. A nice young man who was awkward in bed and inclined to shoot his load far too quickly. But at least he did not just run away as soon as he had his oats as the old saying used to put it. She could do with such company now, she thought. Margie tried to recall the names of other students who had shared her bed, "Marcas, was it? Or was it Beartla." They tended to morph into the same young hunk in her memory. "I will have to jump on poor old Tom Dharach one of the days," she told herself jokingly, "while he is on the way home from Mass and he comes in for his pension. I would surely kill him and would end up accused of murder by shagging."

It was the voice of Nicólas Dowling that wakened Margie the next morning. "Is there any chance of a bit of breakfast?" He entered her room without knocking, all dressed up and ready for the day. "Have I got up too soon?" he asked.

"I'm on it," she answered, feeling shameful because of the stale odour in the room. "There are cornflakes on the table, milk in the fridge and I will get on with a big fry straight away."

"I wouldn't mind one bit hopping in there beside you," he said.

"A pity you didn't do it last night. You had your chance, but it is too late now."

"Why is that?"

"Are you not looking for your breakfast?"

"I could think of an even nicer kind of a breakfast," Dowling answered.

"I have a breakfast to cook, a shop to prepare, the post will be coming into the Office. I have my face to put on. Let me have some space to ready myself. To put on some clean clothes."

"You didn't need clothes the last time I was with you."

"That was another day, another night. There are more important things to be done. You will have to deal with your hard-on the old-fashioned way, if that is your problem I have to get on with my life."

Margie prepared breakfast for both of them in a professional way. She did not want to give the impression that she was an easy touch. As far as she was concerned at this stage, her previous encounter with the film-maker had been a mistake. She would keep her distance from now on.

CHAPTER EIGHT

Fr. Éamonn Ó Sé was not long dressed in the early morning when a young woman in what seemed like her early thirties knocked at his door. He seemed to have a vague recollection of having seen her previously. Even in a remote parish he would see quite a few different people, but this woman's accent suggested that she was not from the area. She held out her hand in greeting before telling him who she was "Edel Nic an tSaoir is my name," she said. "I am a journalist for a small magazine with a growing reputation and increasing coverage all over the country. Have you heard of the 'Cúl Le Cine' organisation?"

"I can't say that I have," the priest answered, "but then as you can see, I live in a remote area, and I don't get out much," he said, half-jokingly.

"We were set up to push back against the growth of anti-clericalish, anti-Catholicism and anti-religion trends in Irish society. As I am sure that you are aware secular sectarian bigotry in our country that is far more vicious and threatening than religious sectarian bigotry ever was."

"As you can see," the priest answered "I am old and grey, tired and overworked like most clergy of all denominations in Ireland. Our numbers have halved in twenty or thirty years, so I do not have the opportunity to keep up with every trend or jump on every bandwagon. I feel that I should apologise for not having heard of your organisation, even though your face seems vaguely familiar to me."

"No apologies needed. I have been interviewed on a number of occasions in the national media, so you may have seen me profiled there or in the magazine section of one of the national newspapers. We are a Catholic organisation set up to challenge the media in particular for their constant denigration and in some sassed mockery of our true religion."

Fr. Ó Sé was wishing he was somewhere else, anywhere else in the world rather than to have to face some kind of an inquisition about religion in what was supposed to be his area of influence. "We are so far from the hotspots of the media and influencers of the world that such matters have neither come to my attention or caused me any trouble. I belong to the 'live and let live brigade'. If someone wants to mock or the belittle us, so what? Our religion was mocked from the very beginning, and we seem to have managed alright What has Jesus got these times between all of the Christian religions? About two billion followers?"

"Oh, you of little... I won't say faith, or you would not be in this job if that was true," Edel said. "Our religion is crashing all around us, and you say that you have not even noticed."

"I have seen the drop-in church attendance. I would be blind if I hadn't, but I am long enough in the tooth to know that does not mean a collapse of religion. Look at the funerals. Look at the christenings. Look at the first holy communions. Look at the majority of weddings. There is a lot of faith still out there."

"Don't be fooling yourself, Father? How many holy communicants would you have if there were not the show-off dresses and suits? Not to mention the outrageous first communion monetary handouts? It is an industry more than a religion at this stage, and a failing industry at that."

"So that is what brings you to our little neck of the woods?" Fr. Ó Sé said. "To save our souls in this little enclave on the edge of the world?"

"I am here to challenge the makers of the film about the 'Passion of Jesus Christ'." Edel bowed her head after saying the name of the Lord. "It is high time for you father, as Christ's representative on earth, or at least this part of the earth, to speak out and stand up for 'The Faith of Our Fathers.'"

"If anything, it is even more the faith of our mothers, to their credit, than of our fathers. You can hardly expect me to condemn something I do not know anything about. That film could be the answer to many of the failings that you find in our religion at present,"

"It is the work of Satan," she answered, "the work of the devil because that Nicólás Dowling that is making it has no religion, nor have any of his staff, as far as I am concerned."

"Perhaps he will find religion," the priest answered. "This place could be his road to Damascus. When he called here a few days ago he seemed to have quite an open mind."

"You mean to say you spoke to him?" his visitor asked.

"I have never turned anyone away from my door." He tried to be witty. "Didn't I let you in half an hour ago. Forgive me for my lack of manners. Would you like a cup of tea or coffee?"

"No thanks, Father," Edel said abruptly. "I am disappointed that you are so innocent."

"I was never accused of being innocent until now," the priest said with a wary smile. "After more than thirty years in the cloth as they used to call the black soutane, I can assure you that innocence has not become my middle name. I have seen too much of life and death and a lot of what happens in between to be accused of innocence."

"It is not an accusation, Father, but you are hardly naive enough to think that Nicólás Dowling will not have you hanged drawn and quarter on stage and screen, not to speak of in the Dublin media."

Fr. Ó Sé felt ready to grind his teeth, but he felt a little cynicism might have more of an effect. "I heard of a bloke once who was actually crucified for his beliefs. I suppose he was naive and innocent too."

"You are being facetious now, Father. That crowd is here to stage a vicious attack on everything we believe in. Do you not read the Dublin newspapers, or watch television? It is all completely and utterly against God and religion."

"I felt Dowling had an open mind when he called to see me," was the priest's reply. "I am prepared to give everyone a chance. He told me he was trying to find out the full truth about Jesus after all those centuries, and I can see no harm in that. Our religion has survived OK until now from what I see. It has ups and downs, scandals and successes. Nothing in this world is perfect."

Edel did not seem to be listening. "You should have told him to read his Bible," she said, "if he wanted to find out the truth about Jesus. What else would he say except that he was seeking the truth? That he was trying to knock Jesus and the church off the rails?"

"If he was to say that itself, what would I be supposed to do about it?" the priest asked. "Are film makers not free to make films about whatever they like?"

"Nobody is entitled to take the mickey out of Jesus Christ or make a mockery of his church," Edel said defiantly.

"Are you talking about some kind of fatwah, as Muslims call it? What is your solution?"

"I am not that stupid," Edel answered bluntly. "But nobody has a right to attack our God, not to speak of Mohamed. We don't have hate speech legislation for nothing, although in practice it seems that we do. How many cases of that nature have been taken so far?"

Fr. Éamon Ó Sé said quietly "Jesus was mocked and spat on long before now and in fairness, he hands his followers got over it. You know yourself what his answer was. 'Forgive them because they don't know what they do.' In other words, get over it. A small film made here on the edge of the world is unlikely to upset an applecart. We have years of experience in ignoring bullshit."

"It will be the work of Satan from start to finish," Edel said, "and you are the only person in Ireland capable of putting a stop to it."

The priest laughed out loud as it was the last thing he expected Edel to say "I wish that I had the kind of powers you think that I have. Even if I did have such powers, how would I be expected to stop Dowling's film?"

"You could denounce them from the alter, father. I am sure you would have the support of the community if you pointed out the damage that crowd are likely to do to God and his holy church."

"I have no doubt but that it would do more harm than good. That film, like most films will be completely forgotten in a matter of years, if not weeks."

Edel came back strongly "What about the film 'The Life of Brian' that made a mockery of religion long before I was born? It still raises laughs and gives people an opportunity to mock Christianity."

"It made some people, maybe a lot of people laugh, but how many people lost their religion because of it?" the priest asked. "It may have helped people who were looking for excuses to mock religion as the 'Father Ted' television series did later. On the other hand, I think the bit of fun helped many people to be less hung up on peripheral details of religion in the years that followed"

Edel shook her head slowly from side to side as a mother might have looked at a wayward child. "You have a lot to learn father. You take too much for granted while your church bleeds to death and you are doing nothing about it."

"You are beginning to sound like Sir John Barbarolli, the great musician," Fr. Ó Sé said.

"Who is he, or what has he to do with anything?" Edel asked.

"He was training a young musician to play the Viola and he became so frustrated by her efforts that he declared. You have God's gift to humanity between your legs, and all you can do is scratch it."

"Begging your pardon, father, but what has that to do with anything? Apart of course from being rude and vulgar?"

"Your expectation that I can cancel the making of Dowling's film sounds like the musician's belief that the young woman could play a musical instrument when there is no proof that either would be a success beggars' belief. I do not have the skill or the power, not to speak of the inclination to attempt to stop that film in its tracks."

"If that is what you think, and ignoring your crude reference to a woman's private parts, I think you are mistaken, and the coming weeks are likely to prove it for worse more than for better.."

The priest made another effort to explain his position. "It is not those who are outside the faith that are likely to damage it, because they don't care one way or another. It is insiders like me, priests, nuns and brothers who have created the scandals that have nearly sent the church to the wall in recent times. It is the enemy within that has created the difficulties, not the journalists of television producers or film makers."

"Are you talking about yourself personally now, or the clergy in general?" Edel Nic an tSaoir asked.

"That is precisely what I am talking about," was his answer, "but at the same time I am not going to confession to you, because no doubt you would give me a hell of a penance. But of course, I feel guilty about all of the abuse that has happened and the fact that more people had not spoken up about it while it was being perpetrated. Was its innocence or self-preservation? Who knows for sure? We were on pedestals in the eyes of many people, 'God's representatives on earth' as the old people used to say and we did not have the guts to destroy that image in the name of truth."

His visitor shook her head, seemingly more in sadness than in anger as she replied "Your eyes and those of your colleagues are closed to the vicious attacks that are constantly being made on our church at the present time. They are at least as bad as those that were made back in penal times but no one seems to have the courage to say it like it is. It is all a 'temporary little setback,' as one of your bishops called it. The lifeblood of the church is draining away and your crowd just whistle while Rome burns."

Fr. Ó Sé could not help himself reminding her that the old quotation was that "Nero fiddles while Rome burns."

"You have just illustrated my point," Edel answered. "You just play around the edges and correct grammar and quotations while ignoring the obvious."

The priest answered "What you call attacks are for the most part legitimate questioning of the church's history and failures down through the centuries. Of course, we have a lot to answer for, but we are searching for those answers so that we can tackle and overcome our faults."

Edel shrugged her shoulders "It looks like I am wasting my time talking to you, father. I am not going to change your mind about anything."

It was the priest that broke the silence that hung like a fog in the room for a while "Why does your organisation, your group call yourselves 'Cúl le Cine?' if you don't mind me asking. I know what the words mean but what do you mean by it?"

"It was not me that named it," she replied." But I fully agree with the title. As you probably are aware it means turning your back on your own people, and that is exactly what is happening in our church at the present time."

"What if people genuinely do not believe?"

"They are jumping on bandwagons, hunting with the hounds and running with the hare; They have no backbone, no courage, no understanding of what their forefathers and mothers went through to hold on to their religion."

"If anything," the priest said, "I see people of many religions and cultures being accepted into this country and society."

"We will be the laughing stock of the world when we have a black church, when religion is only black or brown or yellow and the progeny of those who fought the enemy with thunder, fire and sword no longer believe in anything."

"Does that not sound a bit racist?" the priest asked.

"I am not finding fault with the blacks and the browns. Our peoples spent their lives supporting 'the black babies,' while a statue of a black Saint Martin stood on the mantelpiece in almost every home. My problem is with the white Irish turning their backs on thousands of years of Christianity."

"We had a lovely christening here at Midnight Mass last Christmas," Fr. Ó Sé said, "a Swedish girl whose parents had moved from Bosnia years ago. So, the movement into and out of the church is not all one-way."

Edel gave a slow handclap. "Bully for you, father. One in and a thousand out. That is exactly what is happening in your church. Do you think God removes the gift of faith from those who are baptised? No, they give it up, walk away..."

"As is their right," the priest interrupted.

"That is why so many leave, because it is easier to go than to stay. They have neither the courage or the strength to face difficulties and to follow the Son of God in the road he has laid out for all of us. They turn their backs not just on their religion, but on their culture because that is what is fashionable at the present time. Most of today's youth are softies without any depth. We need to harden them up to face real life."

The priest shook his head from side to side in as kind a way as he could, while letting it be known that he did not agree with the views of his visitor. "Everyone out of step but our Edel."

She replied with words of Saint Paul "If God is for us, who can be against us?" She spoke in a pirated way "If all that was left in the world was the courage of my convictions, and my willingness to stand up for my faith, that is enough."

"I consider myself a follower of Jesus Christ too," the priest answered quietly, "the Jesus who was kind, merciful, understanding, open minded and open hearted, a Christ who was as friendly with the unbeliever as he was with the believer."

Edel interrupted his statement to add her own personal touch. "A Christ who was responsible as well. And though He threw the money changers out of the Temple. Because they had the house of God turned into a marketplace."

"I admire your fire," the priest said. "I had that about me once. A long time ago, I must admit. Nowadays I feel that mothing is black and white. We have to come to our own conclusions that try to allow for everybody."

"That is precisely what is wrong with our church," Edel answered. "That is why you will not stand up to that crowd that are going to make a mockery of Jesus Christ and his church in your own backyard, your parish, your homeland."

Fr. Ó Sé smiled ruefully "I enjoyed our chat, but I feel that you and I are not going to agree about the film, about which we actually know nothing. I recommend that you go directly to the producer, Nicólas Dowling and make the arguments you have made to me. I cannot stop it. He can, so he is the person who should hear your views which you have put very articulately, if I may say so."

"I may very well do so," Edel answered, "seeing that you do not seem up to it. But it is writing about it I will be at the beginning. I am a journalist, all the same. I will tell the truth as I see it, the truths I have spoken to you already. I will need to write too about your mealy-mouthed reaction to my comments and your refusal to stand up to Nicólas Dowling and condemn his film from the altar. At the same time, I will refer to your courtesy and your willingness to listen to my point of view, even though you rejected it out of hand," Edel formally shook hands with the priest, thanked him for his time and made her way out the front door.

The priest felt glued to his chair and he chided himself for not showing his visitor the courtesy of being escorted to his door. For the first time since he had heard of the film being made in his parish he had a feeling that all hell was about to be visited on him and his parishioners.

The sounds of the sea could clearly be heard half a mile from the shore as rocks and stones rolled against each other in the in what seemed like boiling waves. Although the "Migos" were not practising their music in sight of the sea, the stirring of the waters could be heard day and night. As they took a break from their practising their tunes. Eithne remarked "Wouldn't it be lovely if we could include the sounds of the sea in our next album?"

"What noise are you talking about?" her brother, Alan asked as he farted loudly. His friend Eoin laughed but neither of the girls were impressed.

"You are gross," his sister Eithne said.

"Are either of the two of you going to ever grow up?" Aisling asked. "There is nothing funny about that kind of messing. And we all have to put up with the smell as well as the noise."

"What noise are you talking about?" Eoin asked Eithne. "Do you mean the noise from the sea breaking on the rocks?"

"That is a noise that would make a lovely backdrop to a

tune. They say it is a sign of a change in the weather," Eithne said

"You are only saying that because you were listening to the weather forecast," Eoin commented. "You know absolutely nothing about the weather."

"I know as much as you do."

"And that is sweet fuck all," Eoin got back to thinking about music. "What instrument would be able to capture the songs of the sea."

"It will come down to trial and error, I suppose. We can experiment. Lay down one track over another until we get it right."

"That would be alright on one of those old CDs Dad and Mom used to have." Aisling said "Tape the sea and sing a few numbers on top."

"But what would we do in a live performance?" Eithne asked.

"Bring everyone down to the shore," Eoin replied.

"Don't be facetious," his sister snapped. "For someone who thinks that he knows it all, you know nothing."

Alan suggested a way forward "Arguing will get us nowhere. We do not have to solve that problem immediately. We can work on it, think about it, see how some of the great musicians dealt with it. It is not the end of the world if we don't manage to work it all out today."

"The sea and the roar of the sea is part of what we are, where we come from," Aisling said. "That is what has formed us as people, as musicians. We could not even get away from it if we wanted."

"Has anyone thought about what we discussed the last time we were here?" Eithne asked "Writing a song for the film they are going to make?"

"Hymns were never part of our repertoire," Alan said.

"We should have open minds," was Eithne's answer. "It is something we could bring the sounds of the sea into. Wasn't there's a story at school about Jesus being lost at sea, or something."

Aisling said "Something about his calming a big storm."

"We will pass on the magic stuff," was Eoin's answer to that.

Alan had a different approach "We don't have to go all holy God or something, but if we can get our faces or our music shown to the world in that film, we will be on the world stage."

"For a sad film like that they would only want old-style keening, ochón and ochón ó."

"The keen of the three Marys, maybe," Eithne said.

"Who were the three Marys at the crucifixion?" Aisling joked. "Mary from the Mountain, Mary from the Valley and Mary, Mary quite contrary?"

"What about Margie?" Eoin asked. "Is that a form of Mary as well, or is it short for margarine?"

"What about the keen of the three Migos?" Eoin asked. "I have had enough music this day. What could we do to pass a while of the evening?"

"What about study?" Eithne said as she imitated her mother's voice. "Your Leaving Cert is just around the corner."

"We have all of the weekend for study," Alan said. "We could knock a start out of someone like we used to do in the old days and show the world that the Migos are alive and kicking. People would recognise straight away who we are."

"Why would they think it was us if we don't tell anyone?" Aisling asked.

Alan said "Just let them keep guessing. Let's have a bit of fun without drawing the law or anyone else down on top of us."

"We could do something at the church," Eoin suggested. "Steal the altar wine and have a little party from the bottle. I remember how tasty it was when we were serving Mass as youngsters."

"We had our fun with the electronic bell a while ago," Eithne said, "but I heard my mother saying that the local committee are keeping a close eye on the place now. They have even put CCTV in the sacristy."

Eoin joked "That is because the priest was drinking too much wine himself."

"I wouldn't blame him," Alan said. "It was lovely when we used to have a slug of it before or after mass."

"What about Tom Dharach?" Eoin asked. "He lives alone and we could knock a bit of a rise out of him for the craic."

Aisling said "I hear that he is after buying a shotgun."

"They say that he doesn't even know how to use it," Alan said. "That is not to say that he wouldn't try and he could blow someone to pieces. I think he is as blind as a bat."

Eithne wondered "Can bats see in the dark? Maybe Tom can too."

"We could just bring him to Specsavers," Aisling joked.

Alan asked "Wouldn't it be great to capture Margie and her new fancy man on one of our cameras, and put it up on line."

"The devil has really got into you," Eithne said about her brother.

Aisling laughed almost in a shriek "It would be brilliant if we could manage it."

Eoin was wary. "They Guards would be able to work out on what phone it was filmed, or what computer it came from, as far as I know." Eoin said.

Alan suggested "We could swipe the cine camera in the secondary school, and put it out on the computer there."

Aisling suggested that was a big risk. "What if we are all caught on CCTV?" "All we need are a few black plastic bags to cover ourselves from head to toe and it doesn't matter what TV Margie has in her place" Eoin said. "We can lose the school cameras as soon as the pictures go viral all over the world."

Aisling asked "How are we expected to get into Margie's house?"

"If we go there in the middle of the night," Alan said, "I am sure we will find some corner of the curtains that have not been fully drawn." He made a little circle with his fingers and thumb "All we need is that little bit of space for the eye of the camera. Ye were talking earlier of putting our music on the map. Well we have a great chance now to put Margie's Post Office and herself on the map as well"

Eithne commented "I don't like it. It smacks of peeping Toms. I would hate to have it done to me."

"What have you to hide?" Eoin asked. "Apart from those little tits. Margie has a pair on her that would poke you in the eye."

"But is it fair to put them online?" Eithne asked.

"She doesn't seem one bit ashamed of them," her brother said, "there was she leaves them hanging out of her dress like two footballs."

"Isn't it you that takes notice?" Aisling said.

"You can't miss them. I have spent a fortune buying stamps, just to get a look at them."

"I didn't know that you were such a pervert," Eithne commented.

"Only joking," Eoin said. "Anyway, we will see. It is only a very small chance that we will find a space between the curtains. That is unless they are riding night and day and forget to close any kind of blinds. But I doubt if an old pair can spend all night in the saddle."

"You would think you were talking about horses," Aisling commented.

"It could be the horse and pony show," Alan suggested gleefully, "and the whole wide world will get to see it."

"You need to wash out your dirty mouth," Eithne told him.

Aisling had found masques the friends had used at Halloween which they carried in their hands at first as they made their way to Margie's house and Post Office. Although there were street lights there was enough shade from the trees to hide their faces and shapes which were shrouded in black plastic sacks. Eoin said they looked like big black cats as he praised the others for covering up so well. As they came closer to the Post Office they dodged from tree to tree along the one street of the village.

It was well past midnight that they approached their destination. There were lights in the upstairs windows but no blinds or curtains drawn.

"They must have been working late," Aisling suggested.

"That or else they are banging away thinking that nobody can look in," Eoin said. "What we need is a ladder. Or two of them if we can." He asked Alan to go with him to help him search the yard. They returned with two aluminium ladders.

"Those yokes will make a lot of noise when you put them up against the window sill," Eithne said.

"Not if we tie a bag around the top of each of them," Alan said. "There are plenty of empty bags on the floor of the shed." When they had the ladders ready, Alan asked "Which room you think they are sleeping in?"

"I don't know," Aisling said, "but we will soon find out." She reached for one of the ladders.

"No way," her brother said. "This is a man's job."

"It is as light as a feather," she answers. "We have one of them at home."

"I am not letting my sister fall from a ladder."

"That is an anti-feminist remark," Aisling pointed out.

"Fuck feminism," her brother whispered loudly. "You two girls can hold the bottom of the two ladders."

"But I want to see Margie and your man in action," Aisling said.

"Eoin and myself will go up first to reconnoitre. If there is anything worth seeing, we will hold the ladders for the two of you. Anyway, if there is anything worth seeing you can see it online all day tomorrow."

"Get sorted out," Alan whispered, "or next thing Dowling will come through the front door and confront us."

Eoin and Alan placed their two ladders to reach just beneath the window sills above then and with both girls hanging on to the bottom of a ladder they began to climb. Alan had a bag hanging around his neck which contained a camera while Eoin

was hoping to use his mobile phone even though he was aware that would leave him open to detection. As far as he was concerned Margie or Dowling were unlikely to show the police pictures of themselves in compromising positions.

Alan warned Eoin to freeze as he put it when one of the rails of his ladder rolled around and squeaked when he stood on it. The slowly climbed upwards after that, taking extreme care on every step. They reached separate windows of a large room in which Margie and Dowling were sharing a bed with lots of space between them.

"How long do we need to wait for a bit of action?" Eoin whispered to Alan. "They are far too comfortable for my liking."

"Get a few pictures while you can," came Alan's reply. "You wouldn't know what they will get up to after a while."

"They have probably done all they are able to do by now," Eoin said. "After all they look too old to get up to anything worthwhile."

"A waste of an evening so. Do you think we should let the girls have a look?"

"We will be in trouble if one of them falls off a ladder."

"Why don't we just make up a tory for them and pretend we saw more than we did? They won't know the difference."

"They will if we don't get anything on camera," Eoin said.

"Sssh," Alan said. "Dowling is going to the jacks, I think."

"I hope he hasn't heard us whispering like two fools."

Alan remarked "Maybe Margie has a dose of the runs as well. She looks like she is about to get up."

"Maybe we are going to get a bit of action at last."

"Keep your head down," Alan said, "in case they see some movement at the window and we are fucked."

"At this moment I wish it was them who were fucked so that we could get out of here. Hold on. Get your camera lens just above the bottom of the window. We might catch something yet."

When they peeped again Dowling and Margie were lying side by side propped up against the pillows. They seemed to be just having a chat after waking up, but Eoin noticed something else. "I think she is pulling his wire. The dirty bitch. Make sure we get that on camera."

"No fucking way," Alan said. "She is taking it in her mouth."

"The bloody bitch. It's worse than bloody porn."

"The whole world will be looking at it tomorrow," was Alan's comment. "Who would believe it? In our neck of the woo"

After their exertions Margie and Nicólas Dowling lay back on the bed from which they had kicked off all of their clothes, breathing hard, smiling and laughing at each other. It was then that the film producer put a finger to his lips to indicate that he thought he had heard someone talking outside. As he glanced towards the windows he was shocked by what he saw. Faces that looked like clowns at first glance. For the first time in his life he wondered were there such things as ghosts. Was he hallucinating after the alcohol he had drank earlier? He made an effort to draw Margie's attention to what he had seen by pointing towards the windows. By the time she looked the faces had vanished.

"What is up with you?" she asked.

"Did you see the fuckers?"

"Did I see what?"

"The faces at the windows?"

"Have you lost your marbles, or what? By the way you have a fine pair of apples, or is it oranges down there. They tasted a bit more like figs, I thought."

Dowling was not listening. He was at one of the windows looking out to see could he make anything out in the eerie darkness. It was then that he made out the figures of four people giving what looked like the two fingers to him across the street. He angrily pulled down the blind.

"Don't do that," Margie said from the bed. "I hate it when the blinds are pulled. I love to see the moon from the bed."

"Do they have something like Halloween at this time of the year around here?" Dowling asked.

"Why do you say that?"

"It was hard to make out what they were at but there were four people in what looked like some kind of drag waving at me from across the street."

"Were they young or old?"

"I have no idea. It was too dark but there seemed to be some kind of shiny stuff reflecting in the lights."

Margie went to the windows but there was nothing to be seen that was out of the ordinary. "Are you sure it was not a rick of the light?" she asked.

"Do you take me for a fool?"

"Of course not, but with all that religious stuff that you are reading up for the film, you might be having some sort of a hallucination? You know how some people see the Blessed Virgin or moving statues when they are big into religion."

"Do you think that I am stupid? This was real," Dowling answered bluntly. "Now that you mention the film, they may be mounting some kind of a picket to try and stop it going ahead."

"Speaking of mounting." Her partner for the night gave Margie a withering look before saying "You are not taking this seriously."

"You are certain of what you saw?"

"They looked like four devils, each one as black as an old saucepan. They were wearing hoodies or something and seemed to have masks on their faces. Have you had a run in with anyone here lately?"

"Why are you making this about me? I am not the one here to make a controversial film. By the way I hear that there was a young woman journalist going around asking questions about you and your film. I know that she spent a long time in the priest's house."

"And you never thought to tell me about her?"

"You were the enemy at that stage, blowing hot and cold, and then you came back here bulling for the ride. I was hardly going to tell you about a better-looking woman than me when you were whispering the sweet nothings in my ear." She smiled "In both ears, actually."

Nicólas Dowling asked as if talking to himself. "How did they get up to look in the windows?"

Margie seemed flabbergasted. "How do you mean looking in the window? I thought you saw them across the street?"

"There was a face, if you could call it a face at each of the windows."

"What exactly had you drunk before you came back from the hotel?"

"A couple of shorts. A couple of pints. The usual. I had a long hard day of interviews before that. I thought I deserved to wind down a bit."

"Have you ever imagined funny stuff before now?"

"I was not imagining. I was seeing."

"And then you were fucking. Like there was no tomorrow. People do have out of body experiences from time to time."

Dowling could not resist a kind of pun. "What we had was more like an into-body experience."

"How did they get up to the windows?" Margie wondered.

"There are such things as ladders. They might have brought some with them.

On the other hand, they might have been sailing through the air with the greatest of ease like some of your saintly or religious friends."

"I don't have any friends of that kind," Margie answered, before correcting herself. "Half of my customers are what I sometimes refer to as religious maniacs. I only see them when they come in for their pensions on their way home from mass. But I have to say that they are mostly lovely innocent people."

"They would not be climbing ladders in the middle of the night?"

"They would be far too old for that. Now that I think of it there are a couple of aluminium ladders in the store at the back of the Post Office. Half the village borrow them when there are gutters to be cleaned or painting to be done. Some of the young gurriers might have got hold of them and got up to the windows."

"Have those so-called gurriers anything against you?"

"I have never had hassle from any of them. They do play pranks, here and there, ringing the church bell from time to time when they are not supposed to. Or drinking the priest's wine in the sacristy, I am told."

"Does the priest allow them to do that?"

"They obviously don't do it when he is looking, but he is a bit of a softie in many ways and he does not take little things too seriously. Naive maybe, but nice."

"So, you are an admirer?"

"No way. I am not into religion, but we tolerate each other. We have little chats when he is buying something in the shop. Nothing deep or meaningful. A nice guy, and the people seem to like him. In other words, he doesn't bother them unless he has to."

By now the Migos were back at their base, beating their drums and strumming their guitars as they often did late into the night, whether they had school the following day or not. They were winding down after what was for them, an eventful night. The main thing from their point of view was that they had some fun at other people's expense and had not been caught. Eoin and Alan were still discussing between themselves what they had seen at the windows, but were not comfortable discussing it with their sisters.

Alan tried to imitate a policeman who might be interviewing him about what happened at Margie's house. He had a pen and a small notebook as he pretended to be questioning Eoin while the girls were out. "Would you mind explaining to me why you and your colleagues known as 'The Migos' were congregating at the Post Office building occupied by the local postmistress and her lodger, Mr Darling, or is it Dowling who allegedly cohabits with her on a temporary basis while organising a dodgy film in your area?"

Eoin attempted to answer on his friend's behalf. "The only thing dodgy that I was aware of was that the alleged Post 'Mistress' was sucking the cock of the alleged Film maker, who proceeded to give her the time of her life with his alleged cock. There were no animals hurt in the making of our film which is available to watch online throughout the world this evening."

The two teenagers were laughing so loudly at their own jokes that Eithne and Aisling looked at them suspiciously when they returned from taking showers after they had removed their masks and plastic sack camouflage. "What has got into the pair of you," Aisling asked.

"All will be revealed as we upload the footage we took from the top of the ladder. Your next question may will be 'What got into Margie?' See it to believe it. The answer will be on the screen shortly."

"I don't want to see it," Eithne said bluntly.

"Me neither" commented Aisling. "What we did was wrong. It is one thing to try and have a bit of fun, another to destroy a couple's reputation."

"What reputation?" Eoin asked. "If you saw Margie with Dowling's cock in her mouth, you would know that neither of them deserves to have a reputation."

"So what?" Aisling shrugged. "It looks like everybody is doing it now."

"Are you?" her brother asked. "Is that what you are trying to tell us?"

"I am not, but it wouldn't surprise me if you are. Mam has to hold her nose when she is bringing your sheets to the laundry."

"Too much information," Eithne said.

Eoin asked the girls "When did the two of you turn into holy Marys?"

"We have principles." Eithne said.

"Principles? Do you mean the school principal?" Eoin winked at Alan as he addressed the girls. "Are you gone all lessie? Riding the Principal, and maybe riding each other as well because I don't see you showing any interest in boys?"

"Shut up," Aisling said. "What we do is none of your business. And if you want to know, we like boys, but not tramps like the two of you that would go up on a thorn bush to get your holes."

Alan winced exaggeratedly. "That would be a thorny ride."

"Why don't you try it?" Aisling said, "because it is the only ride someone as gross as you are likely to get."

"Jealousy, jealousy," Alan said, "just because nobody would look at two bitches the likes of you."

"Look at your sordid porn pictures," Eithne commented. "It is as near as either of the two of you is likely to get to the real thing."

Eoin lifted up the camera that had filmed at the window of Margie's place "Sit down and have a look, girls. It will bring the juice to your pussies and teach you how to live."

"Come on, Aisling," Eithne said. "We are going home."

"You will be missing a great piece of ass on screen," Eoin said.

"The two of you are disgusting," Aisling said as they left. "Just grow up."

"Is this going to get us in serious trouble?" Alan asked Eoin.

"I can't see how, but I tell you one thing. Margie and her mate will be in a lot of trouble tomorrow morning."

CHAPTER NINE

In the woods, Nicólas Dowling had arranged a meeting with the actor he had chosen to play the part of Judas in his film. He had gone there ahead of the actor and tied a piece of rope to one of the lower branches of a large tree. When Óran Breathnach arrived to meet him, they spoke for a while about projects in which they worked together in previous years as well as actors that had shared those experiences with them. Eventually, Óran asked "What's with the rope? Are you thinking of hanging me or something?"

"You have got it in one," Dowling said. "It is not here to hang you but to hang Judas Iscariot. That is who you are for the next few weeks. You can start by putting the rope around your neck."

Breathnach looked at him curiously. "You are joking? Are you going to choke me? If I fall with that around my neck, I could be a goner in a few seconds."

"The other end is not secured to anything. I just want you to feel that you have betrayed your best friend with a kiss for thirty pieces of silver, and now you hear that he is about to be crucified. How does that make you feel?"

Breathnach started to laugh. "I'll tell you how I feel. I have some ready money in my own or in my purse that I didn't need to steal from the communal kitty. I am going to throw a party for the rest of the lads. Get a few birds to fuck and have a bit of life without bloody do-gooding."

"What are you thinking about Jesus of Nazareth?"

"Fuck him. He has ran out of road as far as I am concerned."

"Get serious," Dowling told him. "This is not a bit of fun but the remaking of a film that has gone down in history as 'The Greatest Story Ever Told.'"

"But I don't believe any of it," Óran said. "The way I see the whole episode is as a kind of runaway train that went off the tracks and turned a mountain into a molehill. The local Jews just wanted to toe the line. The last thing the Romans wanted was to turn him into a martyr. It did help what is called the spread of the gospel that the Roman Empire was so well organised with roads and waterways reaching out all over Europe. Jesus was just a pawn in the whole affair until it all exploded."

"How do you mean exploded?" Nicólas Dowling asked him.

"It always reminds me," Breathnach said, "of the Irish Easter rising 1916. It was an insignificant two fingered salute to the British Empire that was a damp squib until the leaders were brought out and shot. That got the genie out of the bottle and there was no going back. In the same way if Jesus had been let go by Pontius Pilate, as that poor man had planned, there would be no Christianity. The Nazarene would not even a footnote of history at this stage."

Dowling shook his head admiringly. "That is very heady stuff, but what choice have we except to generally follow the story as it has been written for the last two thousand years. Does this mean that you are not interested in the part of Judas?"

"Is it me to turn down a plum part in a film, whatever I believe in it or not? I am an actor, a gun for sale, and what I believe in or not is irrelevant to the project. On the other hand, I have second thoughts about the lot of it. I am almost afraid that Jesus will grab me by the balls and suck me back into the church. As a onetime Catholic, I understand how hard it is to turn your back on what you were brought up with, but as I no longer believe, what can I do about it? From the point of view of truth, from the point of view of conscience, I am torn to pieces. Some people find it easy to leave all that stuff behind them, but not me."

Nicólás Dowling gave him a gentle mental push. "Not Judas either, I suppose. That is why he reached for the rope. Was he between two minds? Or three?"

"Who knows?" Óran said lightly. "Maybe he just did it for the money and here we are creating a conscience for him."

"The rope was probably his conscience," Dowling shrugged. "It is not for us to put the genie back in the bottle, but to see all sides of the story. Or the stories as the case might be."

Breathnach suggested that it was the writers of gospels that had really hanged Judas, not literally but metaphorically. "He was in no position to fight back or to explain. They just put the boot into an emotional and stressed man who ended up as so many people do in this day and age when all other options seem to have disappeared. It was something far deeper than money that led to his suicide."

"And are you going to tell me what that was? In your opinion?" Dowling asked.

"Fucking faith, the root of so much evil and so much good.. We don't seem to be able to live with it and we don't seem able to live without it.."

"I thought you said you gave it up long ago?"

"What did someone call it?" Breathnach asked. "The hound of heaven. It keeps gnawing at your arse for the rest of your life."

"You are between two minds," Dowling said. "Just like the rest of us."

"I thought that you jacked it in a long time ago."

"What do you think that I am doing here? Making a film about fucking Jesus because I cannot get away from him. The fucking hound. Am I to assume that you will accept the part of Judas, whether you believe in any of it or not?"

"I am often accused of trying to have things both ways, to run with the hare and hunt with the hounds. If there was no Jesus, we would have had to invent him or her or it. Or nothing. Something to hang on to. I was wondering even as we talked whether Judas felt that he had seen through Jesus. All he saw when he looked was someone he could see through. A scarecrow. A star that had burnt brightly before falling to earth. He had believed in the hype and then the hype had all melted away like snow."

"A good point," Dowling said, "but they didn't have the kind of hype makers and hype builders that we have now in terms of worldwide communication."

"They had the same thing but they just called it word of mouth. What brought the crowds out to the desert to see John the Baptist, or his cousin Jesus after him? Hunger. Hunger for news. Hunger for faith. Hunger for excitement. Hearsay is more powerful than radio, television or all the other gadgets on the planet. Word of mouth is still stronger than any of them.."

"Despite all the hype, almost everyone had turned against Jesus before he died."

"What would you expect of a great communicator except to turn it around with the magic of death?" Breathnach joked. "Things were down to the wire on Calvary's hill when he had hardly a friend left in the world."

"It was not the death so as much as the resurrection that swung it for him."

"What was its Brendan Behan said about resurrection?" Breathnach asked.

"Remind me, I have heard a lot of his famous comments but I am not too sure about that one."

"As far as I remember it had something to do with a new political party. They were looking for a slogan such as "From the cradle to the grave." Brendan topped all of the suggestions with the immortal words. "From erection to resurrection."

"I vaguely remember hearing that many moons ago, but never thought it would be raised while discussing the Jesus story."

"I have a feeling that even Jesus would have a laugh at that one," was Óran's answer.

"It looks like our Jesus was a bit of a softie. He was hardly able to win an argument, but we are still talking about him a millennium or two later."

"The biggest mistake the man made as far as I can see," Breathnach answered, "is that he believed his own hype when things were going well at the beginning, water into wine, feeding the five thousand, supposedly raising the dead. How could anyone follow that? As soon as he got around to spreading what his real faith he started to lose all his followers. He was well aware of it himself when he said 'Unless you see signs and wonders you will not believe.'"

"You seem like a man who went for it all, hook, line and sinker at one stage." Nicólás Dowling remarked. "You seem very well informed."

"We had an old teacher at National school. Or at least she seemed old to me. She would gather the small children around her desk like a mother hen surrounded by her brood. She told us simple versions of Bible stories, and that was how I got hooked on Jesus. This was some bloke, Water into wine. Picnics in the desert for the masses, but the best of all was the raising of a widow's son from the dead. That blew my mind altogether. For all the wrong reasons, of course."

"What reasons?" Nicólás asked.

"I was hooked when the story said that Jesus had touched the bier, as the kind of coffin was caused. The only beer I had ever heard of was from the porter barrel that my Father and his friends tapped at my grandmother's wake. The foam from the Guinness shot up and hit the roof of our kitchen. I imagined the widow's soon shooting up to our ceiling like a jack-in-the-box.

This Jesus is one cool dude I thought to myself, although I probably did not know terminology like that at the time."

"A pity you were to lose him later," Dowling remarked.

"Maybe you could blame that same barrel of porter, more than blaming Jesus. I hit the bottle as soon as I went to University and although I managed to barely qualify later on, most of my time had been dedicated to drama and the bottle, or in my case, pint glass. They were great years, but they were nearly the death of me."

"You became an accomplished actor. Was that not success?"

"I became a rogue and a waster. If it was not for Alcoholics Anonymous I would be a dead man now."

Dowling tried a bit of wit. "But you rose from the dead like the man himself, and here you are with a rope around your neck, ready to play Judas."

"Are you telling me that I have got the gig?"

"You know more about religion than most of the people I have ever met."

Breathnach answered "Next thing you will having me saying 'Thanks be to God,' like a good Roman Catholic."

"I can take off your halter now," Dowling said, reaching for the rope around the neck of the soon to be Judas character. "It is great to see you getting into the part in a meaningful way."

"I suppose that there is a Judas in all of us. We start off, well meaning, full of excitement, full of hope, full of confidence, full of adventure, ready to jump for joy, jump on bandwagons whether we know where they are going or not. Jackpot Jesus is held up before us and we reach for top prize. Then the trophy melts and we melt with it as we scramble around for the pieces of silver that may help us to live again, to see a prize that might restore faith in someone or something. Disappointment seems to be the biggest or is it the smallest staple in life?"

Dowling rolled the Judas rope around his hand and elbow until it made it neat and easy to carry. He handed it to Breathnach "This is yours from now on, or at least until the film is finished."

Breathnach accepted it with a smile. "I must not be ready for hanging yet."

"I suppose everyone feels that their boss is the hangman," Dowling remarked.

"Especially if they don't get the job, or the part they wanted."

"Take your rope and walk," his producer said. "It is a bit of a change from 'Take up your bed and walk,' as Jesus used to say on a good day."

"He had a lot of good days at the beginning, but he was certainly under the cosh when he was on the cross. 'May God, My God, why have you forsaken me?'"

"He was able to whinge alright," was Nicólas Dowling's answer to that. "How did he think of a word forsaken unless he was planning for it to be repeated for the following two thousand years?"

"It was part of a psalm he had probably learned in the Synagogue when he was a child, but things were pretty desperate when he was having a go at his God." Óran Breathnach said as they picked their steps through the long grasses of the wood.

"I think God is of the opinion the best kind of prayer of all is 'Go on. Have a go at me.' I love it."

His companion laughed "God must be laughing at the two atheists in the wood spending all of their energy talking about him and putting words into his mouth."

"I think his real followers are actually the atheists. Most of us have a love/hate relationship with him, but we seldom forget about him for long." Dowling continued "The bloody believers just have to bless themselves, say their prayers and all is well in the world."

"There will be great craic on Judgment Day," Óran suggested. "I am sorry for all the poor holier than thou's who will be getting a boot in the arse."

"If there is judgment, it is or should I say it should be person by person, day by day, your charge sheet shared between yourself and the man or woman above, as we say for feminist and politically correct reasons. I think for instance Judas would have come out better from judgment than some of his old mates. Some of the so-called saints never seem to have been called to account for their own carry-on."

"Which of them are you referring to?"

"All of the Apostles really, except John who had enough guts to turn up beside Mary at the crucifixion. The rest of them were abject cowards. They denied, they ran. They hid. They shouldn't believe it when he allegedly turned up in the Upper Room after his resurrection."

There is a good story about that," Dowling said. "It is about Jesus turning up at the Upper Room, risen and glorified. There was a party going on inside with sounds of music and smells of good wine. Peter was in shock when he came to the door. "We never expected to see you again," he said. "Judas came in for a bit of money and we were having a party."

"So, the all-saints were not all saints?" Óran asked.

"It is just a story told to lighten the mood after the trials and tribulations of Jesus. The Christian view is that all of the saints were sinners at one point in time, but it would be claimed that all of the apostles redeemed themselves by martyrdom in later years.."

Óran Breathnach remembered "There was an old Parish Priest down our ways who had been a professor in Maynooth seminary but he was put out on grass later in life. When people would remark after a funeral of someone recently deceased had been 'a saint,' he was won't to reply. A saint alright, but like a lot of so-called saints, a bit of an old shite." People loved him so he could get away with saying anything.

Nicólás Dowling got back to business. "Speaking of Judas again," he said "Do you think he really was stealing from the purse, or was that said to draw down opprobrium on him? What does that say about the likes of Luke, the doctor and writer and his gospel, for instance? Was he just putting in the boot to really bury any little bit of a reputation Judas had left after his suicide?"

"I suppose we can forget they were all human even if they were 'so-called saints?' What is the old line 'He who is not with me is against me.'"

"The way Jesus himself put that line is 'Those who are not against me are for me,'" was Nicólás Dowling's answer to that.

"It is hard to believe that they were all friends at some stage."

"How do we know? We take it that is how things were, but can you ever have a group of people without differences and jealousies? I know Paul was not there at that stage, but himself and Peter had some raging rows in the early days of the church, and it was not Peter the anointed leader who came out on top but the little gurrier from Tarsus. And of course, James and John sent their 'Mammy' at one stage to look for the two best jobs in his kingdom for her darling boys."

"That smacks of a mother's love alright" Óran said. "It is a nice human touch to the bitching and backbiting."

Dowling asked as they left the wood "At what stage do you think that Judas realise that he was getting fed-up of Jesus and his teaching and he wanted out?"

Óran Breathnach thought for some time before answering. "I would guess that it was when Jesus laid into the Scribes and Pharisees and accused them of hypocrisy and being like whited sepulchres. That was like calling the Roman Catholic Cardinals a bunch of bollockses."

"And what would be wrong with that?" Dowling asked, tongue in cheek.

"It is thyself who saith it," Breathnach answered in mock religiosity. "But you know yourself that people are likely to react strongly if their leaders are being attacked, whether it is in politics or religion, despite knowing that they are imperfect human specimens. There is an element of 'They might be imperfect, but they are ours.' I would say that was what cut to the heart of Judas and set him on another and a different path."

After leaving the wood, the two man's thoughts drifter from their religious discussions to how the trees that had been set as part of a millennium project had grown and flourished in the meantime."

"Whatever about matters of faith. Whatever about Jesus and Judas these trees will be flourishing for many years to come," Óran said.

Nicólas was somewhat less sanguine. "With wildfires flourishing more than trees in recent years, I have my doubts. Maybe we should be concentrating more on environmental questions than on Gods and sinners."

Nicólas Dowling sounded as if he was talking to himself. "Remember the question in a poem we had a primary school? At a time that forests were being decimated in Munster. 'What are we to do without timber?' It felt like the end of the world. We could ask now what are we to do without religion? We will have nothing left to argue about."

"Don't worry," Óran said "It will be a weight off our backs. But you are right. Some of us would have nothing to talk about even though we don't believe in any of it. Or do we, unknown to ourselves? I was only wondering a while ago why Judas did not go to Jesus with his worries and anxieties. Or was Jesus so full of himself and his own worries at the time that it was difficult to approach him?"

Dowling had his own take on the matter. "Maybe Judas did approach Jesus and that he was told God the Father would look after him and that he had nothing to worry about. We often forget that these blokes, the apostles downed tools to follow Jesus. Did they still have contact with wives, girlfriends or family. What pressures were on them to bring home more fish? Put more food on the table? Act responsibility. The loaves and fishes, not to speak of the water into wine had not lasted very long."

"The last supper story gives the impression that Jesus knew exactly what Judas had in mind," Breathnach said, "and he as much as told him to go out and do his damnest."

"I have sometimes wondered was Jesus looking for martyrdom at that stage," Dowling said. "Not unlike our own Padraig Pearse who was fascinated by the Jesus story to the extent that his Easter Rising in 1916 was just that, a blood-letting that was foolish in the extreme even though it led eventually to what we might call a limited Irish freedom."

Óran asked "So you think that it was not just Judas that was suicidal, but Jesus as well?"

"I don't think he was suicidal in the sense that he was trying to kill himself. It is really the notion of sacrifice I am talking about. Remember the slaughter that was going on in Flanders and Passchendaele at the time. Pearse was not the only one willing to go to his death. Every young man who was dying at the western front was following some stupid rabble-rouser or other."

"The war to end all wars," Óran remarked. "The religious sacrifice in Jerusalem that spawned such religious upheaval. And we still love the bastard, even though we pretend that we don't."

Dowling shook his head. "God's own little bastard. Poor old 'Saint Joseph' was the real martyr in all of that stuff.."

"God as the cuckoo in the nest," Óran said "Have any of our great theologians ever thought about that?"

His companion laughed. "We have come up with more theology since I put that rope around your neck earlier today than all the theology pumped out by Maynooth's priestly college in the past two hundred and fifty years."

"I think we should take a bow," Breathnach nodded his head dramatically in the direction of Dowling.

"Let us leave the bowing until we get back to the bar," was his answer. "We have done a good day's work today."

By now they were back on the main road feeling the relief that came from walking on solid ground rather than in the wood or the grass pathways. They walked for some time in silence. It was the actor who broke the silence. "Was there ever a pair setting out to make a film about Jesus that were as cynical as we are?"

"If we are not cynical, we are dead as artists and film makers," was Dowling's reply. "We have established quite a while ago that neither of us is a true believer as they say in some places. It is our job to be cynical. Or are we to allow the great communicator, the great so-called saviour to suck us into his clutches in the way the spider catching the fly?"

"Are we overdoing the cynicism, though?" His companion asked. "Are we turning the son of God into a devil from start to finish?"

"I hope the trees of the forest have not been listening," Dowling said, "or we will be getting our walking papers from this place sooner than we think. We might be pushing it a bit to suggest Jesus is a devil when we don't believe in either of them, God or devil." He gave a little laugh. "It looks like I am the real devil in so far as the woman who provides me with digs is concerned."

"Have the two of you got up to a bit of devilment together?" Óran asked, "or why should she call you a name like that?"

"She is some bird that one, A great bit of stuff but she has a quick tongue."

"You mean she talks a lot," Óran asked.

"Tongues can do more than talk," was the vague reply.

"Gentlemen do not talk."

"Since when were you a gentleman? So, spill the beans?"

"Let's say, she knows how to treat a man."

Óran put a note of wonder in his voice "You mean, breakfast in bed?"

"Not just breakfast."

"Am I a cynic or do I hear wedding bells? Or is it something else that is ringing?"

"I have offered her a part in the film,"

Óran asked "What part? Mary Magdalene?"

"The woman at the well. A strong woman who put Jesus in his box to some extent. More about that later."

CHAPTER TEN

Edel Nic an tSaoir visited a number of houses in an effort to see out the mood of the local community and their opinions about the film that was to be made in their midst. It seemed to her that local people had little enough interest in the project other than that is was something that might create employment in the area for a short time. In the longer term it could mean that tourists would be attracted to the area in the way that "The Quiet Man" or "Ryan's Daughter" had done in the past. If anything, people seemed to feel nothing much could go wrong in the making of a film about their "Saviour" as they saw it.

Tom Dharach always removed his flat cap in respect whenever there was mention of Jesus at any time, and he did so again in his small kitchen when Edel spoke of "the Lord."

"Isn't it a wonderful thing that a film is being made here in our own parish about our Lord and master, the Son of God who was sent on earth to save us."

"A lot depends on who is making the film," Edel answered.

As she looked at Tom's face she imagined that he was looking at one of those old holy pictures that were common in many houses in the twentieth century.

Tom said "I am looking forward to seeing a lovely homely film that will raise our minds and hearts. I am sure that it will start from the stable in Bethlehem and with him ascending into heaven to send the Holy Spirit in his place."

"What about if there are things in the film that annoy you?" Edel asked.

Tom laughed. "It is hardly going to be one of the old kissing films we had to watch years ago when all we wanted to see was a good lively cowboy and Indian film with lots of action."

"I am not talking about that," Edel said, "as much as the suffering and death of Jesus that you can see in the stations of the cross in most chapels. It is one thing to see it in a picture on a wall, something else altogether if you are looking at scourging and crowning with thorns, never mind being nailed to a cross."

"Of course, that would upset me. But I see that in my head every good Friday when the story of the passion is being read out by three or four people. They make a great job of it. I have to say and they really make the story come alive. As you and everyone else knows there are harsh things in life that none of us like but we have to face up to them. We hate to think of Jesus suffering and the pain it brought to his holy mother, but we know that in the long run it helped to save us all."

Edel pressed him "But if they put things on screen that we don't like or don't agree with?"

"We don't like scourging. We don't like an innocent man being nailed to a cross, but we know that it happened. We can't whitewash it like you might do to a stain on the wall of a barn."

Edel tried to be as subtle as she could without upsetting Tom. "What if they bring Mary Magdalene into the story?"

"What if they do? Wasn't she a friend of Jesus? Didn't she wash his feet with her tears and dry them with her hair? Not to speak of anointing them with perfume. He must have had the sweetest feet any man ever had. Fair play to the woman. God bless her."

"But she had been with a lot of men?"

Tom did not take the bait. "What is wrong with that? I am surrounded by women when I collect my old-age pension. We have the bit of banter and great craic altogether. Banter at the counter, Margie from the chop calls it."

"I don't think the same Margie is such a shining light in this village from what I heard" Edel said. "I think she is a bit of a Mary Magdalene herself."

"I think Margie is the nicest looking woman I ever saw in my life," Tom said. "It lifts my heart to see her face when I go in for the pension. It is a pity I am not forty years younger."

Edel commented under her breath "She lifts more than men's hearts from what I hear."

"I missed what you said there," Tom answered. "The old ears are not what they used to be."

Edel Nic an tSaoir did not say much for a while as she slowly sipped her tea. She felt at home with him in his small kitchen despite her failure to grasp what she meant with regard to Mary Magdalene. This must have been the holy and wholesome Ireland that the great leader Eamon De Valera spoke of in a famous address often ridiculed in particular for the line "homely maidens dancing at the crossroads," What was wrong with that kind of Ireland? Here was Tom, an innocent abroad in the twenty-first century in many ways, but a man who knew what he is and what he stands for. LGBT+ issues would not keep him awake at night. Here was at least one man who was highly unlikely to turn his back on his Catholic past.

Looking around at the clean but sparse room, Edel asked "Do you even have a television set, Tom? Or is it in your bedroom?"

He smiled. "The bedroom is for sleeping in, the kitchen for eating. I prefer the radio. You can see the pictures in your head, I wander down to the hotel from time to time to watch the odd match such as an All-Ireland Final. All the news is on my little transistor radio, the first and only one I ever bought, and the sound is still as clear as a bell."

"Are you fond of music?" Edel asked.

"I do the odd step here in the kitchen to a 'Stack of Barley,' or a 'Siege of Ennis.' Music likes the heart."

"Faith and music must keep you going."

"Where would we be without the faith?" Tom answered, "And we have a great priest. The poor man is running off his feet, doing the job three of them used to do once. He gives nice talks from the altar. You would think it is Jesus himself that is talking sometimes. He is very easy-going really. And he says the Mass good and quick, not the way some of them were long ago."

"I don't like short Masses myself," Edel said.

"I suppose there can be too long and too short," Tom said.

"If you had a cow calving or a sheep lambing up in the field, you might be inclined to tell a priest to hurry up," was Tom's answer to that. "Our priest is never in a big hurry. He says what is needed to be said and does not hang around all day. We like that. And he can be funny too. He might say the collection basket is his best friend, or something like that, but he is not a greedy man."

"Has he said anything about the film they are going to make here in the next few weeks?"

"He did welcome the visitors to the parish, as he put it, even though I don't think that any of them went to mass. Not that I saw anyway. But 'live and let live' is our priest's motto."

"Live and let live," Edel repeated aloud. "Live and let die. That is what the church is doing at the moment. Not bothering their... I won't say it. All is well so long as it doesn't bother anyone else. Has the phrase 'standing up for what you believe in' been completely forgotten? She answered her own question. When people don't believe anything, they have nothing to stand up for."

"I have lost you there Miss, or is it Mrs?" Tom asked. "What did you say your name is again?"

"Edel. Not a very common name but I was called after a very saintly woman that my mother, the lord has mercy on her, had a lot of time for."

"Where would we be without the saints?" Tom asked, more for the sake of conversation than anything else.

"There are not a lot of them about anymore," Edel answered," with their live and let live and don't bother anyone points of view. Whoever said the whole world is in a state of chassis wasn't far wrong."

Tom repeated the words "state of chassis" to himself before asking "Is that one of the United States of America. It is a long time since I finished in the National School at the age of fourteen and I have forgotten a lot of my geography." .

"It is just a line out of a play," Edel said, "although I would not be surprised if was true of some American States. To get back to something you said about the priest's motto, 'live and let live' do you think that he has no problem with the film that is to be made here one way or another?"

"How would I know?" Tom asked, as he appeared to be getting agitated. "What stop you to ask him that question yourself?"

Edel rose to go "Pardon me," she said. "I have kept you too long. I am a devil for the questions. One more thing. Now that I have mentioned the devil, do you believe in him yourself?"

"Why wouldn't I believe in him? Isn't he tempting me day after day from morning until night."

"What kind of temptation? Like he tempted Our Lord in the desert?"

"Pardon me," Tom said, "but those are things I would not be able to tell anyone while there is a young woman in the company."

"It is just between me and you and literally the wall."

Tom answered "While I am drawing the pension for three years and seven months, the devil tempts me every day, more than once sometimes with thoughts of women, some of whom are not half as attractive as yourself. You could be the one I will be dreaming about tonight. I am a disgrace to the known world."

"I am sorry I bothered you at all with that question," Edel answered, "but that was not what I was really talking about. I was thinking about what you might see in a newspaper or a book, or even in the new film they will be starting soon, thoughts that might disturb you or turn you against God"

"I beg your pardon," Tom said, "but I will leave all that to God to sort out."

Edel encouraged him "If everyone was as good as you, there would be no need for devils or hell. She looked at her notes as if seeking a suitable final question. Tom got in his question first "Is there something about this film that is being made that you haven't told me? You seem to have a lot of doubts about it?"

"It has been suggested in my office that the people working on it have their plans made to attack God and religion and it seems that most if not all of them have no religion at all."

"Have you told this to the priest?" Tom asked, a worrying look on his face.

"I told him but he didn't seem to believe me that or he didn't care."

"If it is good for Father Eamon Ó Sé, it is good enough for me." was Tom's answer. "He is our leader, God's representative on earth, a man who knows the Bible from back to front. There is not a week goes by that he does not praise Jesus and all he did on earth. Only the other Sunday he described him as God's captain of our parish team, and we are all winners because of him.."

"He seems to be turning religion into a football or a hurling match."

"It is just his easy-going way of getting a point across."

"Is there a referee at this match?" Edel asked sarcastically.

"Of course there is, our man in the sky. God himself." Tom laughed at his own joke. "God might send Jesus to referee a junior match, with the holy spirit as one of the umpires behind the goal."

"It's great that people like yourself and the priest are able to joke about something so serious, but does it not make a bit of a mockery of religion?"

Tom looked down at the back of his hand. "God and ourselves are like the fingers of that hand. We all look different but we work together.

Edel gave a kind of nervous laugh. "It almost sound even if it is completely stupid. Was it Father Ó Sé that told you that in a sermon?"

"I thought of that myself," Tom said proudly. He surprised Edel with the question "Did you ever think of joining the nuns?"

"I must say I thought of it for a moment but not for long. There is hardly anybody joining religious orders now. Why do you ask?"

"You seem very interested in God and religion. It's a pity woman can't be priests. People would go to Mass to look at you because you are fine and handsome and what you would have to say would draw them to God."

"All recent Popes have ruled out women priests and what they say goes as far as I am concerned. There are plenty of other callings available to God, and standing up for your faith is one of them."

"You might be a priest in the next life," Tom said airily.

Edel looked at her watch as if she had another appointment shortly. "I have one more question if you don't mind. You were talking about how good your priest is at telling a story. Is there any really good one that stands out in your mind?"

Tom Dharach started to talk as he had just received an invitation to give a lecture "I am about to tell you about a priest that worked in this parish long before Fr. Éamonn Ó Sé took over in more recent times.. The priest in question had a habit of putting names on children he was baptising that were not the names parents requested when asked what name they wanted their child called. He would say 'Get away out of that. The child deserves to be called after some great saint, not some kind of a local hero that lived near the holy well.' They had no choice except to call the child after the saint proposed by their Parish Priest. In case their poor child would spend eternity in limbo. As a child was often baptised at the time the day after being born in case it might die without the sacrament, the poor mother would be unable to attend as she was still recovering from the childbirth."

Edel glanced at her watch "Is this a long story," she asked, "as I am due for another appointment before long."

Tom continued with his story as if he was in danger of running out of words and forgetting what he was talking about. "There was this particular man who brought his daughter for baptism before the second mass on a Sunday while the people were gathering for that ceremony. The Parish Priest was not satisfied with answers to the questions about their faith he had put to the parents and godparents for the child, so he sacked them and put two schoolteachers in their place. At least ye know something about the faith, he said, not like those other idiots." The priest then proceeded to address the child's father "With what name will I baptise this child?" "Elizabeth," he answered. "Why in the name of God would you want your daughter called after the Queen of England?" Tom clarified that he was talking about something that occurred in his youth, so it was Queen Elizabeth the first the priest was talking about.

Tom took a moment to draw his breath before continuing "I will give you a name," the big Parish Priest said, "a name that will stand to your child in this world and the next. I will call her Attracta."

By now Edel Mhic looked like she would prefer to be anywhere else in the world except where she was, but she did not want to hurt the old man, Tom Dharach who continued with his story. When the baptism and the mass were over, the child's father want home to his wife, who asked him when he went in the door. "How things went in the church." "Alright," he answered, "but I don't know what name the priest gave the baby." "What kind of a fool are you," she asked, "that you can't think of the name of your own child? Go back to the priest and find out."

"That was a bit harsh," Edel said as she tried to hurry the story.

"We were living in a different world at that time," Tom answered, "and that was not harsh at all, because a lot of the priests were like that. They ruled the roost."

"Did the man find out the babies' name?"

The poor man went back to the priest to find out, and the first answer he got was "What kind of a fool are you that doesn't know the name of his baby girl?" The father went home with his tail between his legs and his wife asked had he found out the name, he answered "I don't know, but it sounded like tractor."

"At least the priests don't seem to have that kind of power now," Edel said.

Tom answered "The way you were talking a while ago, it looked as if it was that kind of priest you wanted in this country. It is the easy-going priest we have now that we like, live and let live..." He paused for a few seconds "Not every priest was a tough nut then either. There were two or more of them in every parish at the time, and there were soft ones as well as hard ones."

"Tell me about one of the nice ones before I go," Edel said.

"I think I have talked enough, and you are bored out of your mind."

After checking her watch, Edel held up five fingers. "Five minutes. I really have to go then as I have other appointments."

"I am talking of a man who was a pure saint even though a lot of the other priests thought that he was silly. He would come into the school and tell us stories about Jesus. Lovely simple stories that I remember to this day. When I heard talk of something Jesus said long ago, it is in that man's voice that I hear it nearly seventy years later. Father Tommy. God's gift... That is all I can say. So don't be too hard on the softies like our Father Eamon."

"You would have made a great one yourself," Edel said. "You have both the faith and the gift of the gab."

"Can the gift of the gab get a person into Heaven?"

"They say that arguing with God is the best kind of prayer. I hope it is because there are times I think he has lost his marbles."

"I wouldn't be inclined to insult him myself," Tom said, "because I am not that far from the pearly gates."

Edel half embarrassed him with a parting hug that brought a smile to Tom's face.

CHAPTER ELEVEN

"Do you think I am some kind of a cow that you have to bull night and day?" Margie asked when she awoke to a number of different smells, a mixture of body sweat, alcohol and Eau de Cologne. Nicólás Dowling was standing naked by her bed and it was immediately obvious that he had a particular idea in mind.

"Get on with it," Margie said. "Get it over with. I need sleep."

"That is passion killer talk. You will put me off my stroke," Dowling answered.

"A stroke is the very thing you will get," Margie said. "I am certainly not able for you. Where are you hiding the viagra, by the way? No man can perform the way you do. Find a hole in the wall," she said. "I have to be up early."

"It will all be over in a minutes."

"You would not know a minute if you saw it. Whoever invented the words hammer and tongs was surely thinking of you."

"Can I just lie beside you and hope for the best?"

"Are you a baby or something? Hoping for the best is what has you the way you are. Just go and have a cold shower."

"What about a hot one and you can join me?"

"Go on then, but don't be all night."

"I can't do anything when you are in that kind of mood."

"Don't so. Give me a break. Go pull your wire."

"Wait until you are desperate."

"I was never desperate in my life except for sleep right now." Margie said.

"Just go fuck yourself," Dowling said angrily.

"That is exactly where you need to go."

The film producer started to laugh and Margie asked "What's so funny?"

"I just remember what fellows used to say when I was at secondary school. Some bloke would ask did you want to get your hole, and if you said yeas you were told to just put back your hand."

"Good night," Margie said tiredly.

"It was not as good as I hoped for, but you can't win 'em all. Goodnight yourself," he said fairly gruffly.

Ten minutes later Margie asked "Are you wanking yourself off?"

"I thought you were asleep. Let finish the job in hand."

"How can I with you pulling tug-o-war with yourself?"

"Help me out here," Dowling said "and you will get to sleep then."

"Let it go and I will finish it for you in seconds."

"You have such lovely hands," Dowling said when he had got the relief he desired.

"Never ask me to do that again," Margie said as she turned away from him.

"I didn't ask. You offered."

"Shut the fuck up and get to sleep."

Some minutes later it sounded as if Dowling was talking to himself. "Isn't it strange how doing the dirty helps someone to fall asleep?"

"I know now why some women murder their partners," Margie said, "because they won't let them go to sleep when they desperately need to sleep." She suddenly sat up in the bed and said "Let's talk."

"You mean now? I thought you were tired. I certainly am", Dowling said.

"Let's talk for half an hour and I bet we will sleep then when we have cleared our minds."

"I would try anything that might work at this stage." Nicólás Dowling said. "What do you want to talk about?."

"Your film, Jesus FN Christ."

"I have been talking about that all day. I need a break."

"A pity about you. You have kept me awake until now."

"What do you want to say?"

"I haven't a clue what I want to say, she said. "It is your project, your baby. Do you know what I think?"

"Spit it out. But I hope it does not come between me and my night's sleep."

"Religion must be the most complicated subject on earth. I think one thing. You think another. A born-again Christian in the Southern United States something else again. Then there are the millions who have not the slightest interest in religion, except to moan about it or condemn it as the opium of the people."

"The film is getting a grip on you," Dowling said with some satisfaction. "You are thinking deeply about it. I will be looking forward to hearing your opinions again and again as time goes on."

"I wonder what Mary and Joseph were thinking as they lay on the straw of the stable in Bethlehem listening to their baby breathing." Margie said.

"You shouldn't be thinking thoughts like that. Wasn't Mary a virgin according to the stories. She was hardly lying back smoking a cigarette after having it off with Holy Joseph."

"If Mary and Joseph were as holy as they say they would not even have thought about sex and is there evidence that Joseph was gay? That would have solved a lot of problems."

"Now you are flying it," Dowling said. "You thought of something all the great theologians and scripture scholars even thought to mention. I should raise my hat, or raising something to you."

"All of those points would have been raised years ago if women were allowed or encouraged to study theology years ago. Those are the very questions they would have had at the tips of their tongues."

"Joseph could have become a champion for the gay community if that is the way he was.." Dowling wrote a quick note on the back of a picture next to the bed.

"Fuck you," Margie said. "You have ruined my Padre Pio picture."

Dowling looked at the picture "Don't tell me that you go to bed with a picture of Padre Pio next to you?"

"Why wouldn't I?" She asked. "It's a free country."

"You are a young free minded feminist woman. A woman of this day and age."

"Doesn't free thinking include the idea of being open to anything?" Margie asked.

"I thought you told me that you have no religion at all."

"I don't believe in much of it, but what is to stop a person having a picture of someone people call a saint as a bit of a shoulder to lean on now and again?"

"You are one funny bird," Dowling said.

Margie laughed. "Would it have put you off your stroke if you realised in recent times that Padre Pio was one of your bed companions?"

"It would just have given me a stroke instead."

"If you knew would you have thought that he was looking at you? And if he was itself it might have taught him a lesson. That he should try and understand everything and everyone in the world. On the other hand, I have little doubt that many of the world's Catholics put more trust in Padre Pio from a health point of view than in the Jesus on whom you are basing your film."

"How do you know?" Dowling asked. "How could you know when you don't darken the door of any church or meeting house?"

"Because I work in a Post Office and bar. I talk to a lot of different people from morning till night. I talk to the pensioners on their way back from mass as well as the teenagers who are trying to escape from going to mass despite of their parent's efforts. I talk to young and old. People open up to me because quite a few have no one else to talk to from one end of the week to the other."

"You were trying to sleep a while ago," her companion said, "and I couldn't shut up. It's you that can't stop talking now. Would you mind if I went back to my own bed for the rest of the night? I have three or four serious interviews with actors coming up tomorrow."

"Wait here between myself and Padre Pio," Margie teased. "There won't be one more word out of me for the rest of the night."

"No funny business," Dowling said, "or I will have to cancel my meetings."

"Not a word. Not a stir," Margie said and her bedfellow soon drifted off to sleep. Margie turned this way and that without waking him. She eventually reached her hand between his legs and caressed him awake and they made passionate love after which Nicólas Dowling immediately fell asleep...

Margie's thoughts turned to a time when she was obsessed by church and religion in her youth. Her father just about tolerated talk of all that was holy but her mother attended all kind of religious services as well as flying off with neighbours to international church shrines such as Lourdes and Fatima. Margie had even learned to play simple hymns on the church organ. She wondered what her customers who thought she was a lost cause at this stage would think if they were to find her playing the organ and singing religious songs in the local church. "Maybe I will surprise them some Sunday," she said to herself as she eventually drifted off to sleep..

CHAPTER TWELVE

The local Parish Pastoral Council was called together at the request of its chairperson, Mabel Ui Chionnaith. It was one of the committees organised in every parish to assist the work of clergy as their numbers plummeted not just in Ireland but in most of the Roman Catholic world. Those parishes lucky enough to have a priest at this stage were sharing a priest with a neighbouring one or two others. Generally speaking those new arrangements were a success as they led to much more and better participation by the laity, and lessened some of the extra burden on priests.

Many such changes and improvements in church structures has been planned and promulgated by the Vatican Council half a century earlier. Some parishes had taken to such moves like ducks to water, but people in many parts of the worldwide church choose to leave what they felt was working for them alone. What did they have priests for? Many people thought, if the laity were expected to do the work. As clergy numbers decreased dramatically at the beginning of the twenty-first century, the new situation propelled most parishes to bite the bullet and share the workload with men and women of faith, although the idea of woman priests in the Roman Catholic church was kicked to touch again and again.

Mabel Ui Chionnaith had spent ten years as a nun in a religious order as a young woman and she left the order with a broadminded attitude to religion. It was whispered that she was pregnant when she left the order but there was no proof of that among the general public except that she married what had been her childhood sweetheart quite soon after leaving the order. They had six other children by the time they reached their forties, and the words that "they must be at it hammer and tongs making up for lost time" were frequently used as their young family grew.

"What would this parish be like if she was still a nun?" an old man had asked in the hotel when he was told she was pregnant for the seventh time. "We would have a very small population here except for the two of them." Fr. Éamonn Ó Sé saw Mabel as a great boon to the parish and he was delighted when she was elected chair of the Pastoral Council. It was not that she would always agree with his points of view but she had a broad understanding of religion.

Mabel opened the meeting by announcing that it was being called at the request of four of the elected members. She suggested that they would leave the minutes of the previous meeting until the following month, with the Committee's permission of course, as this was to be an emergency meeting to discuss the film about the Passion and death of Jesus Christ that was planned to be made in their parish in the immediate future. "Some members of the parish and the public feel that it is unsuitable, and I call one of them known to all and sundry as Mary from the Mountain to begin the proceedings."

"I don't need to explain why we are hers," Mary began, "as the making of this film is the talk of the town, if not the talk of the parish." She turned immediately to the priest "What do you think about it, Fr. Ó Sé?"

This came as a surprise to the priest. While he knew why the meeting was called, he did not expect the antagonism in Mary's voice. He found himself stuttering as he began to say that he saw that making a film on that subject was an honour to the parish community.

Mary from the Mountain asked the priest directly. "Was it you that invited that crowd of atheists to make that film here?"

"I knew nothing about it, any more than anyone else until it was announced on the radio."

"Did you give them permission to come to this parish?" Mary asked bluntly.

"I have no authority to ask any film company to do anything," was the priest's answer. "I don't own the place and I have no authority to invite or to refuse permission to anyone. It is still a free country, thanks be to God."

"Do you admit that you entertained the chief producer of the film, Nicólás Dowling in your house for most of an afternoon?" was Mary's next question..

Mabel Ui Chionnaith as chairperson cut in on the discussion. "This is not a court of law, Mary, and the priest is entitled to talk to anyone he likes. How do we know that he wasn't giving confession to Mr Dowling?"

Mary from the Mountain gave a sarcastic laugh. "I would say that he needs to

confession alright if we are to believe all we hear about himself and his fancy woman."

Mabel Uí Chionnaith, as chairperson that she had no evidence that there was anything untoward about the film that was proposed to be made about the passion and death of Jesus Christ. If I had such evidence, I would be the first to oppose it. We need to take a balanced view and not rush into criticism or condemnation without a shared of evidence.

Tom Dharach who was one of the senior citizen's representatives on the committee seldom spoke in public but he took this opportunity to say that he could not imagine that there would be anything to complain about in a film about the "death and resurrection of our saviour," as he put it. That is exactly what I told that nice young good-looking woman who called to see me the other day. Edel was her name and she was a bit worried about the film, but I told her she had nothing to worry about. What could go wrong with a holy and wholesome film?"

Mary from the Mountain had a different view "I was talking to Edel myself because she came to see me as a member of this committee. She knows things about the film and the crowd that are making it that the rest of us do not know. She called it the work of the devil just as contraception and divorce and gay marriage and all that LGBT+ stuff is. Edel works for the Catholic Action newspaper in Dublin. I would give a lot more notice to what she has to say than I would to that dark little devil that is trying to foist his film on our community."

"That is very different to what Tom Dharach told us about her," Mabel Uí Chionnaith, the chairperson said.

"Tom has an eye for the women," Mary answered, "He always had. I even fancied him a bit myself before I went to America, but I knew he would always be more married to his mother than he would to me. He obviously fell hook, line and sinker for Edel and didn't even hear what she was actually saying about the little dark devil with the beard."

"Is it you that she is talking about?" Tom asked the priest who was sitting beside him.

"My beard is far from being black now, Tom. After all the years.."

Mary from the Mountain overheard their loud whispers and clarified what she had in mind. "The little black devileen I am talking about is Nicólas Dowling whose proposed film we are here to discuss."

Mabel, the chairperson warned people should be careful about what they said in case would draw the might of the law on themselves for libel or slander.

"Are we to have censorship now on top of everything else?" Mary from the Mountain asked. "Soon we will not even be able to open our mouths, but nobody is going to shut my mouth. I am the one speaking the truth about the threats to our community while the mealy mouth members of this council or whatever it is called are sitti ng on their hands and saying nothing."

"Nobody is trying to censor anybody Mary, but people can easily draw the law on themselves in this day and age." Mabel said lightly.

Mary directed her next question to Fr. Éamonn Ó Sé. "What did Dowling say to you, Father, about his film when he spent some hours in your parlour recently?"

"We talked generally about life and religion. Nothing too serious, but as you know private conversations should be kept private."

Mary gave a little guffaw before asking. "Are you telling me that the dark devil came to you to hear his confession?"

"If he did itself, Mary, it would be bound by the seal of confession."

Mabel intervened from the chair. "We are getting away from the point now."

Maty was outraged. "While our priest is hiding behind the seal of confession, he is being closeted behind the skirts of the nun that is in the chair."

"I am no longer a nun and have not been for many years," Mabel said.

"Once a nun, always a nun," Mary said, "even though you have spent all the years since on the broad of your back making babies. Sure, this parish would have died out long ago if you were not here to populate it."

"Now Mary, there is no need to insult anybody."

"So, it's an insult now to tell things like they are?" Mary from the Mountain said.

Mabel stood up abruptly and announced "I think that is enough for tonight, unless someone who has not spoken until now wants to raise a point."

A retired schoolteacher in his eighties gingerly raised his hand. "Would there be any sense in inviting this Mr. Dowling who seems to be the centre of attention to a public meeting about this proposed film?"

Tom Dharach chimed in "Why not?"

Mary from the Mountain proposed "I would like Edel Mhic an tSaoir to be invited also, to provide balance and tell the other side of the story from a Christian point of view."

Tom Dharach suggested "Wouldn't it be better to ask our own priest, Fr. Éamonn Ó Sé to do that?"

"We have enough live and let live as we are," Mary from the Mountain said "It's time to get back to the old rugged cross."

"We need time to reflect before anything is decided," Mabel Ui Chionnaith said as she closed the meeting.

CHAPTER THIRTEEN

Micheal McLeod was among one of those Nicólás Dowling had called for interview for the part of John The Baptist in his film. As a big strong bearded man Michael reminded the film director of medieval pictures of John he had seen in Italian paintings. He had a powerful voice as would befit a character living rough in the desert preaching and teaching as well as calling some of those whom he hoped to convert "a brood of vipers."

The Bible told the world that the Baptist's diet was "locusts and wild honey." He had never actually seen a locust in his travels but did not think much of the ones he saw in books or magazine. The "wild honey" stirred old memories of Nicólás and his family disturbing red bees in the hayfields of his youth. They tore the little honeycombs apart with glee to suck out the sweetness. The one thing that softened the character of the Baptist in Dowling's mind was honey like that he himself had licked from his fingers in those bygone days. That and the rough breaks John the Baptist had been subjected to in his lifetime.

The film producer laughed when he saw the actor with a sheepskin tied around his waist in an effort to get into the character.

"Nice miniskirt," Dowling said.

"There is no effing way I am going to wear this shagging sheepskin around my waist for weeks," McLeod said.

"It might not suit out in the desert at fifty degrees heat," Dowling said, "but it would good when you would be out dancing with Salome."

"It is not the skin of a sheep or anything else I would need if Salome was in my arms before they chopped off my head."

"Don't worry," the director said. "You will be wearing something much more suitable out on the bog than what you would have needed in the desert. By the way what did you think of John the Baptist as a character?"

"A strong man, a strange man, an odd man, a man who was badly treated, made a fool of really."

Dowling told him "I want you to live in his sandals, to get inside his skin between now and the time that part is to be filmed. Read the scripture. Google him. Ask questions. Look up encyclopaedias. Leave no stone unturned."

"I would much prefer to be in the skin of John The Baptist than in this old sheepskin," McLeod said, as he discarded that piece of clothing and stood before Dowling in his underpants, his powerful physique showing an athletic body which had been shaped in a gym.

"Cover yourself up," Dowling said laughingly, "or it will look like the two of us were having it off out here in the bog. I don't feel like being burned at the stake by those I hear are rising questions about the film already."

"One thing I have discovered already about the Baptist," McLeod said, "is that he was the first to point out exactly Jesus was, or was supposed to be."

Dowling was not too sure of what he meant. "You are telling me nobody else had copped on to the fact that Jesus thought he was the son of God."

"Precisely. I know he was a cousin of Jesus, but as far as I can see it was he that put words on the answer to the big question 'Who is this guy that feeds the hungry in the wilderness, makes water into wine, seems able to raise the dead or an odd one of them at least?'" It was John who pointed the finger "This is the lamb of God. This is the guy to take away the sins of the world."

"And this is the leader who will help us kick out the fucking Romans" Dowling said. "More people were interested in that than in the vague promise to take away the sins of the world."

"Was that really the reason John The Baptist's head was knocked off?"

"The thing was that it was pure pettiness that led to his death. A promise, a vow from Herod to his wife's daughter, the most needless death that was ever recorded, the death of a good man for bloody nothing. A head on a dish for no reason other than a stupid promise."

"It gives a whole new meaning to losing your block was Nicólás Dowling's attempt at black humour."

"Pure stupidity," McLeod said. "It was the old lady's fault and Herod's weakness from start to finish. Salome had no inkling of what it would lead to until it was too late, or that is the way I see it anyway."

"It looks like you were seduced by her too."

"So was many a writer, such as Oscar Wilde.."

"It is in your hands now," Dowling said, "You have to deal in it in your own way, your imagination, your take on the subject."

"You are saying that I have the part?"

"You are the picture of the John the Baptist, or John the Bastard as one of my classmates used to call him when we were preparing for first communion many moons ago. Think of yourself as the Precursor," his director said.

"Has that something to do with cursing?" was the actor's slick answer..

"The Precursor was the old Biblical term for the one who comes before, the way John came before Jesus and set him up as what he called the lamb of God."

"Set him up for the cross rather than the chop poor John got?" McLeod said. He joked "I wonder what would happen if I was to baptise you, Nick?"

"The heavens would open, as before, I'm sure, but for a different reason. By the way while you are baptising in the river all you will have to wear is something like a child's napkin."

"Fuck you," the actor replied. "You are joking, I hope. For all I know the Baptist might have been up to his neck in saltwater and nobody could see his napkin."

"We are not talking saltwater here but Jordan water as clear as crystal so there will be nowhere to hide if your napkin falls off."

"Don't leave me too long waiting in the river," McLeod said, "or I will be in brass monkey territory, not like Jesus in nice warm water with no hurry on him when he was baptised.."

"You are beginning to get into character now," Dowling said.

"Edel?" Óran Breathnach said just after he had paid for a packet of cigarettes in the Post Office shop. "Don't tell me that Edel Nic an tSaoir is here, alive and kicking?"

"Oscar?" she said. "What has you here? I did not recognise you with the beard."

"Right man, wrong name?" he replied. "Óran Breathnach. Long-time no sees obviously since we starred together in the drama group at college."

"I think 'starred' is a bit of an exaggeration," she said as she shook his hand. "Óran of course. It must have been more than fifteen years ago."

"Are you as wild now as you were then?" Óran asked.

"Me wild? I was never wild in my life."

"You never missed a party back then, but to your credit you were the life and soul of many of the same parties."

"You are making it up," Edel said "Or were you drunk all of the time."

"Have you lost your memory or what? You could not be that forgetful, and I am not forgetful either."

"Students were always like that," Edel answered, "but sense comes with age."

"So, you are not hiding what a party girl you were at the time?"

"What I mean is that you are probably mixing me up with someone else who spent a lot of her time on the town. I used to out alright, but not that much."

"Are you living around here now?" Óran asked.

She pointed to the bottle of water in her other hand. "Wait until I pay for this and we can have a chat." Edel looked at Margie behind the counter as if she was checking her out in a serious way before explaining to Óran as they moved away "I am here really to see this woman because I have heard of her reputation. It looks like the film producer Nicólas Dowling and herself are having it off as people used to put it."

"I didn't think people talked like that anymore," Óran said.

"Talked like what?"

"Talked as if they had a problem with someone's private life? You of all people?"

"What do you mean by that?" Edel asked frostily.

"You have been known to put it around in your time."

"That is a very insulting thing to say," Edel answered. "I doubt if you kept your own weapon in your pants all of the time.."

"Nobody did, in so far as I remember."

Edel changed the subject "What has you in this neck of the woods?"

"I have a part in Dowling's film. John the Baptist actually. Are you in the film yourself? As Mary Magdalene, maybe or Mary the mother of Jesus? Have you discovered virginity in your middle age, or is that possible? ha joked."

"That is an awful thing to say," Edel answered.

"Can you not take a joke anymore?" Óran asked. "Whatever happened the Edel Nic an tSaoir I used to know and love?"

"There was never any love lost or found between the two of us."

"You are getting forgetful again. You probably gave me more pleasure than any other woman ever did."

"You are losing your marbles as well as your mind," Edel told him.

"You and me have a bit of history. Even if you continue to deny it."

"You and I?" Edel sounded incredulous.

"You were putting it around at the time and I took my chance like a lot of others. No big deal. Everyone was doing it. It was like going for a burger and chips but a lot more fun. Cheaper too which helped a lot when all of us were broke. Do you remember the freezing night that some of the lads broke up the banister of the staircase in the place we were staying to put in the fire and keep us warm? The parents were landed with paying the tab at the end of it."

"I remember no such thing," Edel said as if she had never heard the likes of it in all her born days.

"You were there. I remember it well. You and a couple of other girls rewarded us for getting a fire going and warming up the place.."

"Is this your idea of a joke?" Edel asked. "I could sue you for slander or libel or something like that?"

"Sue away for all your worth, but you will have to get a few heavies to take out the witnesses that were there. You wouldn't have a leg to stand on. Not that I am saying that you were footless at the time."

"You are still mixing me up with someone else. Some shameless bitch and there were plenty of them in the college at the time."

"It was no big deal," Óran commented. "It happened. We got over it and grew up in so far as we did. But they were great times. And we staged a couple of great dramas. Didn't we get to the all-Ireland Drama Festival?"

"Didn't we win it?" Edel said. "I remember that alright, but not the other stuff. At the time I think I was the only woman in the world that played a part in Waiting For Godot?"

"As far as I know that record still stands," Óran said, "but I might be wrong.
Didn't Beckett himself, Big Sam write to congratulate you?"

"That as they say was a bit of an exaggeration."

"But don't change the legend," Óran advised her laughingly.

"We all had great imaginations at the time," Edel answered.

"It was not all imagination, but in some ways a lot more than imagination. We
lived lives that our fathers and mothers never got to achieve. We loved, we laughed, we fucked as it there was no tomorrow. We were all on a high. We were actually high most of the time. Even at the lectures. We were like rabbits in headlights, like rabbits inside and outside their burrows. Fucking was the new heaven and we left the old religion behind us without as much as a second thought."

Edel shrugged. "That was then and this is now. I am certainly a different person than I was at college, and so are you I suppose if you are playing the part of Saint John The Baptist in Dowling's dirty film."

"What makes you think it's a dirty film?" Óran asked.

"I have done my research and I know that Dowling has neither faith or morals."

"So he is just like we were twenty years or so ago. Can people not change?"

"They say that leopards do not change their spots."

"I must admit that I have changed my sports a few minutes ago. It is not John the Baptist I am playing in the film, but I did not like to admit it, it is actually Judas."

"Some difference," Edel said, "but a part is a part, and there was a time, I suppose that we were all glad to get a part in any drama."

Óran asked "What part are you playing in the film yourself?"

"I am not actually in the film," Edel replied. "I am here to disrupt it and destroy it if I can. So Judas, are you proud of your new name?"

"I have probably been called worse before. It's a job. Everyone needs thirty pieces of silver from time to time."

"You are admitting that you are just doing it for the money?"

"I presume that you are getting paid for what you are doing too," Óran said. "What is it again? Trying to destroy the film before it starts? You must have some reason for doing that?"

"You say that you are doing it for the money? Do you not care at all about the damage that it is going to do to people's lives?"

"It is only a drama. Like a soap-opera on television. Of course, some people will be upset, especially believers, when they see your man being nailed to the cross. It is not as if most people do not know the story off by heart already. What harm can a bit of drama do to anyone? It might even open minds"

"I am told that his Dowling is completely and utterly against all form of religion, and Roman Catholicism in particular," Edel answered.

"Have you spoken to him? Have you seen his credentials? Have you watched any films he has made already? Have you checked him out at all other than listening to hearsay? I see him as a serious artist, He has told me that he is actually searching for the truth, and if he finds it in Jesus, he will be the first to say so."

"Pull my other leg," Edel said. "He has his mind made up. Why else has he come to this remote place? People have seen through him in the capital. He just wants to take advantage of the natives."

Óran Breathnach laughed. "I would advise you not to use such a prejudicial word as natives around here. It is pure nineteenth century hate speech that was used to speak about the indigenous Irish in this part of the world. It went down in history along with what American Africans call the N-word, or Irish travellers call thinkers."

"People everywhere should be allowed to say what they mean without bloody political correctness coming into it," was Edel's answer to that.

"Keep up that kind of talk and you will be leaving town sooner than you expected."

"I say what I mean and I mean what I say."

Óran looked at Edel as if he was trying to make out whether she was serious or joking. Her face reminded him of the student he had known and had sex with many years earlier "Do you know I could still fancy you?" he said. "You haven't changed a bit, except with the wool you are trying to pull over my eyes. All this right-wing stuff that is a long way from the Edel I used to know. And love if I may say so."

"I have seen the evil of my ways," she said quietly, "and changed for the better."

"Are you talking about some kind of a religious conversion? Has it taken you from one extreme to another?"

"I was never off my trolley to the extent that you claim to remember."

"We were all in the same boat, living it up, ready to die young and make beautiful corpses, as they used to say."

"I hated myself for the way I was at that time. I eventually saw the light, found my religion again and here I am fighting sin every inch of the way."

"And sin, you tell me, is called Nicólas Dowling?"

"I am here to try and stop him in his tracks before he does any damage," Edel said. "Born again might not be the name for it, but I am not the girl you used to know."

Óran Breathnach replied "I was in the hotel last night and I did not notice any enmity between the locals and the actors who are here to take part in the film. There was music and dancing and an all in all lovely atmosphere."

"Were those involved buying drinks for the natives?"

"Natives" is a hate word."

"Lets' agree to differ."

"I was not counting but it seemed as if a round or two was on the house, and everyone got their own after that."

"There is your answer," Edel said. "They are trying to buy off the community with alcohol."

"People are not as gullible as that," was Óran's reply. "If the local people were against us it would be perfectly obvious."

Edel had her own theory. "There was a meeting of the Pastoral Council going on in the hall at the same time and from what I hear it broke up in disarray."

"What is a Pastoral Council when it is at home?" Óran asked.

"A group elected by people of the parish to help the priests especially since they became scarce. They usually have their ears to the ground more than the drunks in the pub."

Óran Breathnach said "Nicólas Dowling told me he was talking to the local priest and he did not seem to have an issue with the film being made here in the parish."

"That is something that people who do not practice their faith do not realise," Edel said. "There was a time when a priest could call the shots, but that day is gone. The clergyman is just one among many. Things are more democratic even in the church than they used to be. Everyone has their say at those Pastoral meetings and they often say things that a priest does not like. I heard that the priest and some of his cronies on the council came in for a bit of stick at last night's meeting. From people who did not want to have their faith undermined by Dowling and his gang."

"What exactly is your own role in all of this?" Óran asked Edel. "When I met you earlier on I thought you had something to do with the film because you were an actress when I knew you. So, you are a journalist now for a right-wing Catholic newspaper?"

"We don't use labels like right-wing or left-wing or middle wing for that matter."

"A lot has happened in this country since I went over to earn a crust in London, I would not be back now either if Nicólas Dowling had not sent for me, but I am delighted with the chance. He only asked me because he thought I was the picture of Judas Iscariot."

Edel shrugged her shoulders. "I suppose that there is a bit of Judas in all of us. None of us really knows what we would do when things get tough."

"Have you any plans for tonight?" Óran asked. "Would you have any interest in coming to the hotel for a few drinks?"

"I have not had an alcoholic drink in years."

"There would be no pressure on you to drink alcohol. Half the country is off because of breathalysers and stuff like that. And there are some really cool non-alcoholic drinks now."

"I have an appointment with a woman that was at that meeting last night," Edel said. "A formidable lady known locally as Mary from the Mountain. I may step into the bar if the meeting does not last too long."

"I will be there until closing time," Óran answered. "You can bet your life on that. It would be nice to have a chat for old times' sake."

Edel laughed. "A real Irish date – I'll be there if you are."

"If it's a date you want?"

"My dating days are long over," Edel said.

"You mean you are married?"

"Far from it."

"You have joined the nuns?"

"I work hard. I earn my night's sleep"

Óran laughed. "I will see you if I see you.."

Nicolás Dowling brought back Tadhg Ó Maoldomhnaigh for another interview for the part of Jesus Christ in his projected film. As far as he was concerned the part was Tadhg's for the taking but he wanted to see him in action as an actor before he finalised the role. Nicólás knew already that Tadhg was a fine actor but he tended to be lazy if not kept under pressure by a director. It was well known in the business that Tadhg was fond of a drink, and he was known to go on stage from time to time when he was a bit tipsy. He was able to carry that in a less serious role than that of Jesus, but a drunken "saviour" was more than observers would accept. Dowling felt that he had no option than to insist that Tadhg would not drink alcohol while the film was being made.

They went through what they had rehearsed earlier, Tadhg stretched on a wooden floor with his arms spread out, the noise of hammer on nail echoing through the room. Tadhg sat up and put his hands over his ears.

"Straighten out your arms," Dowling roared at him. "You are like an old fool out in the bog on a sunny day with nothing to do."

Tadhg sounded shocked. "Take it easy. My head is splitting."

The director laid on the sarcasm "Alright Jesus. We won't crucify you until you get over your hangover."

"I need a hair of the dog to get over last night," Tadhg said. "Would you mind if I had a brandy and port?"

"You will be for the high road if you don't give up the drink until the film is made. Lie back now and listen to the noise of the hammer. How would you feel if you had a crown of thorns on your head at the same time?"

"That is exactly how I feel right now. You know I'm not elfin Jesus," Tadhg said. "We had a great night in the bar last night and drank a few too many. We are paying for it today."

Dowling shook his head. "I don't know if this is the part for you. How are you to look on the cross with that big porter belly on you? Have you ever seen the likes of it on any crucifix in your life?"

"I will give it up," Tadhg said. "I will start jogging. I will do exercises. I will do anything to keep the part of Jesus. Many actors crave the part of Hamlet. Or Lear. Or your man in the Scottish play that it is a curse to mention. I have craved the part of Jesus all of my life. I just want to do it once. I would be happy to die after that."

Dowling laughed. "But would you rise on the third day? OK. The part is yours if you do what you say. Give up the drink until the filming is done. Do some of the exercises you promised. Don't overdo it. We could live with a slightly pregnant Christ on the cross. That would appeal to the feminists. If however, I get one sniff of booze off you, you will be Judas and Óran Breathnach will Jesus. You will have a part because you went to the trouble of coming here, but it will not be the part you crave unless you so what I say."

"One last request for the condemned man," Tadhg said. "Would there be any chance of one brandy and port and I will be ready to rise from the dead after that."

"No chance," Dowling said. "You can choose between Jesus and Judas, between drunk and sober. Let me know tomorrow."

"I am more like Judas than Jesus," Tadhg said, "but if giving up the jar to play the part of Jesus is what I have to do, that is what I choose. It is the bigger challenge and I will be ready to tackle it from today on."

"You are one of the best actors in Ireland," Nicólás Dowling told him. "You have your chance now to prove it. It's up to you."

"Just call me Jesus from now on," Tadhg said, "and I won't let you down. That is a promise."

"Play it as you feel it," Dowling said. "No need to go over the top. No need to make water into wine, or wine into water for that matter. Just be yourself and be Jesus at the same time. I will leave it to yourself to work it out."

"How do you see Jesus?" Tadhg asked his director.

Nicólás Dowling stood with his eyes half closed as if he was trying to look inside his imagination. "I see him like a bloke who goes to the Casino. Everything goes right for him at the beginning. He can't lose, can do no wrong. He is like Midas with everything turning into gold. Gradually the wheels begin to fall off his wagon until he is eventually left like a scarecrow on a hilltop cross with birds of prey hovering ready to tear flesh from bone."

"I like the image of the scarecrow," Tadhg said, "and not just one scarecrow but three of them on the hillside, not to keep the crows out of the spuds like the scarecrows we used to have in the garden long ago. That picture of three crosses on a hill with three very different men hanging on them was burnt into my imagination as a child, three failures sharing Calvary while the shouts of their hangmen and women echoed in the evening air. Come down from the cross and we will believe in you."

"A waste of a life but not of a death, it seems," Dowling said.

Tadhg continued "And then there were those brave women. A little huddle of Marys And John later known as the Evangelist whom many people see as a bit of a girl himself, even in De Vichy's painting. They were the real heroes of Calvary. Themselves and Veronica who had the courage to wipe the blood and sweat from his face. Not to speak of Simon of Cyrene who was hijacked to help him carry his cross."

"Do you think John was a bit of a ladyboy?" Nicólas Dowling asked. "He went on to be quite a writer, especially the poetic stuff at the beginning of his gospel. And he lived a great long life."

"I would say that he dodged a bullet in one way by having the guts to turn up along with the Marys at the foot of the cross. All the others were martyred according to the Bible, but John survived even being thrown into a vat of burning oil. He might have been the first saintly hamburger if he had not been pulled out in time. Mary the mother of Jesus seemed to have a soft spot for him, maybe because he was the youngest. Or maybe because he was gay. So what? He had more courage than all of the big brawny fisherfolk put together. By the way have you got someone for the part of John The Evangelist yet?"

"Not yet, but I saw a young handsome teenager, I would say in the Post Office yesterday evening when I was putting letters in the post. Maybe he is too young for the part. Maybe his parents would not allow him in the film, as is their right. But he does have the face of an angel and a bit makeup could add a few years. He was the picture of someone who would be at home in a Leonardo Da Vinci painting."

"Don't let Margie find out you are fancying young fellows," Tadhg joked.

"Margie is not my boss, nor would she want to be."

"I hear she used to like young teenage boys herself."

"Where did you hear that?" Dowling asked.

"In the place in which will not hear any more gossip," Tadhg said, "because I will be staying out of the bar from now on."

Nicólas Dowling was inquisitive still. "Was Margie's husband younger than herself?"

"I haven't got a clue. I was told that she took a couple of students that were working for her to her boudoir, where she gave them lessons. They learned more than the Irish language in their stint in the west."

"How did you hear that?" Tadhg asked.

"Wasn't I a detective in that soap-opera on the BBC? There are ways and means of getting information out of people and none of them are better than buying drinks for them in the hotel bar, a place in which all the rumours surface, whether they are true or false. None of it matters a curse to me, because I will not be drinking or carousing again until the film is made."

"It's no skin off my nose either," Dowling said, "even though he sounded a bit shocked at what he had heard."

Tadhg Ó Maoldomhnaigh sounded as if he walking to himself. "I heard Jesus Christ being referred to on some radio programme yesterday as the Almighty judge of the living and the dead. It is going to take him a long time to sort out the truth from the fables and the tunours."

"It is on this life we will be concentrating in the film," Nicólas Dowling said, as if he was in a hurry as well as somewhat upset by what he had heard about Margie. He touched

Tadhg's shoulder as he got up to leave. "Stay away from the wine juice, good man, and you will make a great Messiah."

"I will be a wineless wonder, which is more than Jesus ever was."

CHAPTER FOURTEEN

Fr. Éamonn Ó Sé took a day off in order to get away from the storm brewing in his parish about the film that was to be made about Jesus Christ. "A pity that themselves and their film didn't stay a million miles away from us," he hold himself as he drove in the direction of the city. He hoped that he would return a few days later with a clear head and the weight of the world lifted from his shoulders. He knew from the years he had ministered to communities on Atlantic islands that a short break would do him good, that everyday problems would not seem so insurmountable as they did before he left home.

The priest regretted that he had not learned to play golf as many of his colleagues had done in their youth. It was a game for people of all ages unlike football, hurling, rugby, or basketball from which most players retired in their mid-thirties. When he thought back on his young and more radical days he knew that he had seen golf as an upper-class affair, at least in his part of the country in which it was played mainly by professional people such as doctors, bankers or teachers. He had wanted to see himself as part of the working class in the image of French worker priests who had inspired him when he was younger.

The fact that Fr. Ó Sé had spent most of his priestly life in the highlands and islands of the west coast of Ireland meant that golf courses tended to be far from his place of work and in many cases there was little place to hit a golf ball before it would come to rest against one more stone wall. By the time he had got a parish on the mainland, he felt that he was too old to swing a golf club. As the years had gone on he became more aware of the question of clericalism, the king of closed which many of his colleagues seemed to inhabit. It was not that there was not great fun and camaraderie when a group of them got together, but it increasingly came across to him as a closed shop in which child abuse had unfortunately thrived without question from any authority, church or state.

Many priests seemed to live in their own comfortable cocoon side by side with the harsh realities of life they had to deal with in times of trouble, death, diseases such as cancer or Alzheimer's which had become such a scourge particularly as people tended to live longer. Many of the clergy had traditions of lake fishing, fouling, cardplaying and the aforementioned golf. There seemed to be an element of trying to be part of the better off classes about them, part of the professional classes such as doctors, vveterinary surgeons, bank staff and senior police officers. They would seldom be seen in places in which many of the public congregated such as public houses. They seemed to belong to a particular caste of the kind you would hear about in places like India.

It did not surprise Fr. Ó Sé that such observations were made in the many investigative reports that were published in the wake of child abuse scandals. It was as if invisible walls had been built between many of the clergy and the communities they served. There seemed to be a reticence on both sides, the clergy who had chosen what was ostensibly a life of sacrifice and self-denial and a public which revelled in so far as it could in celebration and enjoyment, in sport and recreation as antidotes to the harshness and difficulties of life.

That said, most priests were held in high regard in their parishes because they were there for their communities in times of trouble, of sorrow as well as joy. They were there to bless the new born with Baptism, salute their growth with Holy Communion and Confirmation, ask for inspiration at times of serious college exams, bless the weddings even of those who had drifted from their family faith. Some clergy were brave enough to risk the ire of church authorities by providing blessings for gay marriages. As he drove along Fr. Ó Sé smiled to himself as he thought of what a mixed bunch he and his fellow priests were. In many ways the mirrored the mixed bag of disciples chosen by Jesus Christ to be his first followers. A mixed bag from Peter to

Judas, swaying from the highs of transfiguration to the depths of depravity, denial and betrayal.

Parish life lived in different areas, mainly by the ocean reminded the priest of the movements of the sea and constant changing of the tides. There would be quiet times as most times actually were in areas of scattered population. But there were also storms close to hurricane force at times in both weather patterns and in daily life. This was true of both island and mainland. There would be unrest in island communities because of the lack of facilities such as piers and landing places, ferries and their failure to sail often enough. Mainland storm would have more to do with land and factories, employment or the lack of it. Coastal communities always seem to feel they were not getting a fair crack of the whip from central government, but every community everywhere probably felt the same.

Disputes on land or sea had always disturbed Fr. Ó Sé because people became divided and drifted apart as each person or group had its own strong feelings on a particular issue. He had always stressed the Biblical teaching to "love your neighbour as yourself." He was well aware that this was a lot easier to say than to do. He put emphasis especially on the "as yourself" part of that quotation as much as on the "love your neighbour." Selflove was especially important at a time in which self-harm and suicide had become far more common than in his younger days.

There was a time in which Fr. Ó Sé spent his weekly day off in the company of fellow priests who had shared seminary life with him in Maynooth College for seven years of their lives. One of them had since left the priesthood, another had become a bishop while a third lived more than fifty miles away at the other end of the diocese. They seldom met any more due to their workloads, but just thinking about them brought to mind a night they had shared with others many years earlier. A party had been arranged in what was once a parish house in the centre of the city from which clergy were being moved into more suitable accommodation.

One of the "historic" aspects of the old house was a line of holes along a wall about a foot from the ground. The poor state of the building that had served the area for more than a hundred years could have been summed up by those holes in the wall. They had been made by a priest with a shotgun shooting rats from his bed during scary nights when rat poison had failed to keep the "monsters" away. That was one of the many memories toasted on the night.

Priests who had worked from that building in their youth had gathered from all over the diocese. A neighbouring business had provided a barrel of Guinness. Plates of pig's feet known as crubeens were passed around and eaten with relish, nobody caring any more about what fell on the floor as the house was listed for demolition. Songs were sung and stories told. Looking back on it now it seemed like the end of an era. Numbers of priests had plummeted in the meantime. The child abuse scandals as well as those that had to do with mother and baby homes, illegal adoptions, Magdalen Laundries had all come to light. Fr. Ó Sé remembered sending altar cloths, albs and other church items to the laundry in a Magdalen home in his earlier years as a priest without batting an eyelid as he had known nothing of the background of such institutions. He had often wondered how many present and future politicians had done the same in their innocence. Innocence many of them had forgotten about as they condemned such laundries on the Parliamentary floor of Dáil Éireann. A copy of a manifest from any of those laundries would make interesting reading for among others Presidents and political leaders who had once had their shirts washed three....

As he drove along Fr. Ó Sé reflected that he was happy though times he had joined former colleagues on days off were no longer part of his life. What he needed more than anything now was rest on such occasions, a break from being on constant call for parish duties, some of which were serious, others a hangover from past practices that were no longer really necessary. His Pastoral Council were well able to fulfil such duties, though there were some people who would still ask

"Where is the priest?" when a local farmer or his wife might turn up to lead prayers.

As far as he was concerned the best thing any bishop could do short of ordaining women priests was to have trained members of the church council available to anoint those who were sick or dying in cases of emergency. This was an area that hung heavy in the mind of any priest away from his home. The nearest priest in country areas could be up to twenty miles away and called out at the same time to administer to someone in his own parish. Fear of "dying without the priest" hung heavy in the minds of many older people. Very few people would be happy to be told by phone by their priest "I have an appointment with myself today so you will have to send for someone else."

"What an odd bird I am." The priest told himself. "I am driving away from my own people just to have a break from them, and heading into a crowded city just to be on my own." He felt that his cravings were those a youngster would have on a day out, a burger and chips, with tomato sauce on top, a newspaper to read while he was eating.. "That is peace to me," he told himself.. He thought of the Bible stories of Jesus heading out into the hills to pray and to get away from it all. He smiled to himself. "And the poor man didn't even have a feed of potato chips to satisfy his hunger.."

The Atlantic Ocean was to Fr. Ó Sé's right side as he drove towards the city, islands on which he had spent much of his life to be clearly see in the few seconds on which he took his eyes off the road. Traffic was in nearly full flow, so he was being extremely careful, as he was more used to meeting a car every ten minutes or so in comparison with the city traffic.. Those years spent on offshore islands held some of his best memories because they were so different from mainland life.. Some of his colleagues felt the same about their first parish postings, probably because life was so different from the life they had "endured", some would say, in college.

"There was so much to learn on the hoof" as a young island priest travelled by canves curach with three men rowing from one island to another, seas that looked mountainous to a young man whose only sea journeys had been by ferry to England in large ships. It had taken him a while to realise that the waves and the troughs between them were not unlike the hills and valleys a person might find on a country road. It was then a mountainy wave would rise up, as high as the local church and threaten to swallow a man and his crew. The men on the oars took it in their stride of course, or whatever passes as a stride on the sea. He soon learned that if his crew were not frightened, he did not need to be either.

    The strong faith of the people in his various parishes had impressed the priest greatly. Not every weekend crossing between islands for Sunday Mass was a life or death situation but many of them were. Each household on both islands took turns to ferry the priest across. Some islanders were excellent oarsmen, because they earned their livelihoods form fishing, while others farmed the land and only took to the oars a couple of times a year, in the mackerel season for instance, or to bring the local priest from island to island. In practice only, the best oarsmen took the priest across on a bad day, lesser boatmen paying them in kind with a lamb or a calf as a reward for their risk.

    The dispute about the film that was coming to the boil in his parish reminded the priest of disputes that had occurred on some of the islands on which he had worked in earlier times.. Disputes about co-operatives which had been set up to enable governments to bring electricity and running water to the local population. There were disputes too about ferryboats, piers and other infrastructure. These were not the priest's immediate problem of course, but it hurt him a lot to see a divided community.

    Disputes sometimes harked back to times of poverty and famine, rights to seaweed or fishing. Families and individuals seemed to take sides along traditional lines, with the question "Which side are you on?" often hanging heavily in the air. To answer "I am not on anybody's side" could lead to even more opprobrium and the suggestion that a person did not care. To suggest that a priest should always be neutral dug an even deeper hole, as that led to the question "Do you not believe in anything?" There were usually no winners, no losers in such situations.

    To make matters worse local radio stations would tend to take sides with one group or the other. Things came down to propaganda at that stage, and which side had the best spokesman or woman. After appealing to his congregation one Sunday to pull together for the sake of the community, one radio station accused him of taking sides. When Fr. Ó Sé denied this in a weekly newspaper article, he was accused of abusing his pulpit in the church as well as his newspaper article. This the priest described as "lazy journalist." Solicitors letters were quickly coming through his letterbox from half a dozen journalists accusing him of libel.

    Luckily enough a barrister who was a regular visitor to that particular island took up the case and offered to represent him in the High Court if necessary. The accusers never went ahead with their threatened action. The priest was careful to tape any programmes from the station that referred to that island as well as interviews with local people broadcast on air. He quickly built up a dossier of questionable comments that would help support any case he might have against "lazy journalism" on that station. As his voluntary barrister put it "The arse quickly fell out of that particular case, and nobody made a quick or easy buck from it."

    The years slipped quickly by and anytime he now visited the island for a wedding or a funeral he was welcomed in a way that showed no hard feelings from people who had given him stick in the old days for not taking sides in a dispute. Other such disputes and distractions had come and gone in the meantime. He had a better understanding now than he had as a young man. He felt that island and coastal people were the most politicised people in the country, not in matters of party politics but in fighting their causes without fear, even if there was favour. It would probably the same with regard to the film that was a matter of dispute just then, but would probably be long forgotten in twenty or thirty years. One way or the other, he told himself, "I will not let it bother me until I get back to the parish. Things always have a way of working themselves out."

As Fr. Ó Sé sat in Supermac's restaurant licking the juices from his fingers that held a bun burgher, his thoughts turned to what seemed now to be two separate tribes living side in his parish, the staunch believers and those whom religion seemed to have passed them by. He remembered a time in which there were discussions about what was known as "the Two nation theory" with regard to Roman Catholics in Northern Ireland who tended to be Irish Nationalists and their neighbours mainly of Presbyterian or Church of Ireland background when see themselves as British sharing the same country. His parish now reminded him of that in microcosm.

It was normal and natural that some or even many people should shift from their faith, the priest thought. After all who had ever really seen God? Who had ever seen anyone rise from the dead? He laughed to himself when he remembered the man who had dug a grave so deep to allow for other family coffins in the future that he had disappeared from view more than six feet down, and had to be hauled from the grave with a rope. "That is as close as I have ever got to the resurrection," he thought. He had no problem with those who abandoned the faith of their ancestors particular in the light of the many scandals that had occurred in his own church. It was with those who had a hatred of religion that he had problems.

Those were the ones who put "Big" into bigotry, Fr. Ó Sé thought. They tended to be far more vicious than sectarian bigots had ever been and they had free in from media to peddle their wares. OK, so churches had got a free run for a long time, and things were levelling up at last. "Am I turning into Edel Mhic an tSaoir?" he asked himself, after criticising her and her group founded to take on those who had rejected the religion of their ancestors. "I have not gone that far yet," he told himself. "I need to take a grip and accept that it is a free country, a free world, and people can do what they like and believe in what they like."

He thought of the English poet and clergyman, Francis Thompson who described himself as "the hound of Heaven," sniffing out people who had lapsed and bringing them back to their faith. Some people did drift back in their later years. Others chose different religions or humanism to satisfy needs and there was nothing wrong with any of that. Religious bigotry had lived on in many a subconscious after the Great Potato Famine that had ravaged the country in the 1840's. The word "souper" had been a term of abuse of those who had accepted food mainly from well-meaning Protestants. The fact that it was seen as a form of proselytism lived long in the folk memory and was an insult still thrown at families who had accepted the "soup" to stay alive.

What did Shakespeare say about "what a tangled web we are" the priest asked himself with regard to the many different religions and aspects of them. Would the world be a better place without any of it? The Soviet Union and others including China had fought long and hard to side-line faith, but had not succeeded to any great degree. Despite all the cock-ups that had occurred in his own religion a big majority of Roman Catholics choose to have their children baptised, have first holy communion and confirmation. To all extents and purposes, they allowed them fly the religious coop after that, and as far as he was concerned that was a healthy thing.

There had been criticism some years earlier when Irish President, Michael D Higgins had released a Christmas message in which there was no mention of the faith that was professed as part of that feast and festival. As the years went by people were impressed to see the same President, then in his eighties, attend the Roman Catholic funerals of four young people killed in an horrific car accident as well as a family of two grandparents and their grandchild killed on the roads a short time later. The respect shown by the Head of State endeared him to even those who had criticised him years earlier.

There was a big difference in terms of bigotry between the local and national media in Ireland in so far as Fr. Ó Sé was concerned. He himself wrote a regular column in a local newspaper which was read weekly and apparently enjoyed by thousands of people. They were sometimes heavy and faith filled, more often light-hearted and easy-going as in the article in which he confessed to be suffering from desert deprivation because Evening masses prevented him from attending wedding receptions and he missed the sweet desserts. He had written articles for magazines under the headline "The Curate's Ego," which were widely popular, but try as he might he was never given a sniff of publication by any national newspaper or magazine. "Bigotry?" or "not good enough?" Decide for yourselves.

He sometimes wondered did journalists for some of the so-called and self-styled top newspapers were asked to publicly announce their rejection of religion before being hired, as so many seemed to do so in their earliest articles and "pieces." It was not that there were not good people working in journalism but many seemed to use every opportunity they got to distance themselves from religion. The situation in Ireland differed greatly for instance than that in the United States in which Presidents and wood be Presidents sowed God into almost every speech. Many Irish politicians in contrast went out of their way to an almost pathetic degree to avoid any mention of God.

The priest spent some time in a good bookshop to try and find interesting and challenging reading before bedtime as it always helped him to sleep by taking his mind off parish or personal problems. He avoided the bigger shops and supermarkets as he preferred to do most of his shopping in Margie's shop and Post Office nearer to home. He constantly urged his parishioners to shop local and support local enterprise, so he felt that he would be a hypocrite if he shopped anywhere else. He remembered the priest in the area in which he grew up telling his congregation that he had bought a piece of steak which he had to boil and roast in an effort to make it edible, and "all it was good for eventually was to make half soles for my shoes." He himself would never be as colourful as Fr. Tommy Gibbons, his long-time inspiration as a clergyman..

By the time Fr. Éamonn Ó Sé was driving home towards a setting sun which slightly blinded him while the colours that surrounded it brought much joy, he felt that the problems that had weighed on his shoulders earlier in the day had eased. There were still problems to be dealt with as many that might never be solved from a faith and religious point of view. He could see now that he was no longer duty bound to intervene in matters to do with the public. That was not going to stop him from bringing his parish community together as best he could. In order to promote peace and contentment, "Blessed are the peacemakers," Jesus had said. The best peace making sometimes involved standing back to allow people to find their own way. "I'll leave them to it." He told himself.

CHAPTER FIFTEEN

Óran Breathnach went for a walk with Nicólás Dowling on the beach, without saying much and stopping from time to time to skim flat stones out across the top of the water. Childhood habits die hard.

"You came close to being promoted the other day," Dowling said, "from being Judas the traitor to being the son of God himself." He explained how Tadhg Ó Maoldomhnaigh had come in with a hangover one morning. "He is on his last chance, and I would like you to be considering the part of Jesus as well, in case I have to switch you from one job to another."

"That will put me into a head spin," Breathnach said, "because I have just psyched myself up to be an enemy of Jesus. I have dug deeply into the part of Judas, and that is where I would like to stay, if possible."

Dowling kicked a pile of seaweed along the beach as if he was taking a penalty on a football pitch. "I think, I hope, I nearly pray that Tadhg will stay sober, but I need to have another option if he goes on a tear again."

"We will all do our best to keep him on the dry," Óran said. "We will take him for walks in the wood, and help him to prepare for his part."

"He is a lovely man and a great actor," Dowling said, "but he does have a problem with the drink."

"Don't we all.?" His companion said, "some more than others. I think he needs company and conversation more than anything. That is what's draws him to the pub. Talk. Slagging, having a bit of fun. I think he could have that without going near the pub if we put our minds towards helping him. Walks like this for instance would help a lot. But he would not have the kick that alcohol gives."

"The kick in the balls, you mean? The shakes. The shivers. Maybe we could get him on to the non-alcoholic stuff. There is a lot of that in bars nowadays."

Dowling did not show much confidence in the man he wanted to play Jesus. "Once a drunk, always a drunk."

"Says the man who is able to sink lots of pints?" Óran told the story of a publican he knew who would give lemonade to a particular customer who always wanted more of the whiskey who normally drank himself to oblivion until the barman hit on his master plan. "He gave him red lemonade after he had a couple of whiskies."

"He would need to be a bit stupid if he did not recognise the difference in taste," Dowling said.

"The landlord used to tell him that it was American whiskey he was giving him, and he would be so delighted he would proclaim. Isn't that American whiskey mighty stuff?"

"If Tadhg does not stay sober," Dowling said bluntly, "I will be needing someone for the part of Jesus. Water into wine is one thing, but American whiskey would not fool our Jesus character.."

"So, you would want me to be your Jesus?"

"I might just do Judas myself. I'm told that some people in this community sees me already as the devil incarnate."

"I haven't been talking to many people," Óran said, "But I don't detect any enmity towards you or anyone else in the cast."

"It is the old cailleachs, the old biddies, the keepers of the faith that you would need to talk to in order to hear the full story." Dowling said.. The two men walked on without saying much apart from commenting on the clear air and what a nice place it was for people to live far from crowded towns and cities.. It was Óran who drew their thoughts back to the film. "Have you got anyone yet to play the part of the Virgin Mary?"

"I hear that virgins are a rare breed nowadays," was Dowling's answer to that.

"Thanks to you, I suppose, and people like you," Óran laughed.

Dowling asked "Are you thinking of someone for the part of Mary yourself?" He continued "I have been thinking more of the big male parts until now even though I have a woman in mind for the strong lady Jesus met at Jacob's well."

"I was talking to the journalist Edel Nic an tSaoir a couple of nights ago,"

Óran said "She is big into religion and a fine-looking woman."

"Do you think that is a contradiction in terms??" Dowling joked. "Good looking and religious? They say that about Mary too, I suppose." He thought for a moment "Where did I hear that girl's name before?"

"She might be a bit over the top. She works for a Catholic newspaper and she takes no prisoners in an argument. A bit right wing in her views but well able to articulate them."

"You fancy her?" Dowling asked.

"I knew her a long time ago when were all young and wild, but it seems she fell over heels for Jesus and all that stuff. Anyway, if she had a part she would have to follow the script like everyone else."

"I presume you have fucked her in your time?"

"A gentleman does not tell."

"That is as good as telling me you did," Dowling said. "What would a right-wing Catholic activist know about acting?"

"She acted in the Uni. As far as I know she was the first woman to ever play a part in 'Waiting for Godot.' They say Beckett himself was chuffed. I was on stage with her and we actually won the Universities Drama Festival that year."

"I gather that was not today or yesterday."

"She would still be younger and maybe better looking than Mary was when Jesus was crucified."

"This is not going to be a Lovely Mary competition," Dowling assured him.

"It would be an insult to Mary to have an ugly duckling playing her."

"Didn't the ugly duckling turn into a goose? Or was it a duck?"

"A seen as far as I know, but none of that is mentioned in the Bible."

"It would be no harm to have a look at her, I suppose. By the way is she paying you to get her the part?"

"Quite honestly I only thought of her when you asked me about a part for Mary. I would be surprise if she was even interested seeing she described you to me as 'a devil out of hell?'"

"I love compliments," was Dowling's answer to that.

"She probably wouldn't touch a part with a bargepole."

"Once an actor, always an actor was the Director's answer to that."

"I would think that she has too much respect for the Virgin Mary to even think about taking the part," Óran replied.

"She would have the opportunity to play it her way. And if she was with us she could hardly be against us at the same time. You say she wasn't so tight arsed in her younger days?"

"The life and soul of the party. She put herself around in more ways than one, but weren't we all like that at Uni?"

"I was never at Uni," Dowling said. "I was a child actor and I have been in drama all of my life. Where did you and this Edel meet again?"

"Here in the local Post Office a couple of days ago. I had not seen her for ten or fifteen years."

"Do you think she came here secretly looking for a part in the film?"

"I know she came in an effort to blow the film off the rails and to send you all home with your tails between your legs."

Dowling smiled "So you put your own tail between her legs yourself?"

"Between you and me my riding days are over," was Óran's reply. "There are too many complications involved."

"But you would jump up the first chance you got?"

"Are you telling me to actually have a go at her?"

"I am sure you have always wanted to do a virgin?"

"There is no need to be so bloody crude," Óran said. "I may not have any religion left, but I am not depraved enough to have a go as you put it at the Blessed Virgin Mary."

"I am not asking you to do anything you don't want to do. Just to keep her onside. We do need a relatively good-looking woman for the part, and a bit of intrigue or even hostility is always welcome on the set. If we are going to have a Mary, why not have a Mary with a bit of fire in her belly?"

"So, you want me to suck up to Edel?"

"I never mentioned sucking. Let the baby Jesus in the manger do that. Just draw her in. Mention that the part of Mary is available if she wants to be in the running for it."

"She will eat you for breakfast, and spit you out," Óran said.

"Once an actress, always an actress."

"I never expected to be used as a pimp," was Óran Breathnach's reply to that.

Dowling looked him in the eyes with his own beady eyes as he asked "What do you think Judas would do? And that is your part, in case you have forgotten."

"Fuck you," was the actor's answer to that. "You really do know how to manipulate a man. Why don't you ask the crazy bitch yourself? She will tell you where to stick your bloody part."

"You will ask her," Dowling told him, "or I will be telling you where to stick your part."

"So, it's all blackmail from top to bottom?"

"People have to work for their parts. It's not blackmailed. You know this Edel. I don't. Do it for me and the film, like a good man."

"I will speak to her," Óran Breathnach said. "I can't promise anything else. She has a mind of her own."

"That is the kind of woman we want. A feisty bit of a bitch." Dowling's next words came as quite a shock to Breathnach. "There is no better way to get a woman under your power than to nail her. I thought you would be aware of that at this stage of your life."

"If you had your way, you would probably nail her to the cross and have a woman Jesus to set the cat among the pigeons."

"That has been thought of too," the Director replied, "I am talking more of a subtle kind of nailing."

Breathnach was disgusted "Are you talking rape here?"

"What kind of an idiot are you?" Dowling asked. "You need to be able to draw her in, to seduce her, to fuck the living daylights out of her until she is hardly able to stand up, to get her to the stage that she will do anything for you, to get her to the stage that she is not able to refuse you anything."

"That is just another kind of rape," Óran said. "Is that the way that you have got Margie from the Post Office under your spell?"

"I haven't a clue what you are talking about." was the Director's answer to that accusation.

"The dogs in the street know what I am talking about."

"The dogs in the street," Dowling answered. "I hate that phrase. It is an insult to the dogs in the street. It doesn't matter what the dogs in the street know or don't know, because we cannot understand the barking language. Dogs in the street, my arse." He walked ahead angrily. "What about the bitches in the street?"

"Are you talking about Margie?" Óran asked. "People here like Margie from what I can see. The older people, the pensioners seem very fond of her, and they are delighted that she is getting her oats."

Dowling stopped suddenly in the middle of the road. "What do you mean getting her oats?"

Óran continued with his own train of thought. "People are afraid she might leave the area if she had nobody to share with."

"Who she shares with or what she shares is nobodies' business but her own," Dowling said.

"Nothing stays hidden in a small village."

"What people don't know they will imagine," Dowling added.

"They don't need to imagine what they see on their screens or on social media. That was where your reputation was made, when neither of you drew the curtains in the bedroom."

"What are you on about now?" Dowling asked.

"You are the last man I thought would be shy about having a fling no matter who was watching. That stuff that was shown on social media having it off with Margie. Many of the old Irish heroes actually became famous because of such exploits."

"What exploits are you talking about?" Dowling asked. "It is hard to follow what you are saying some of the time."

"To use your own word, you rightly nailed her and the pictures are there to prove it. There is no need to be shy about it.

Many a man would be boasting about having it off with one of the finest women in the place."

Nicólás Dowling shrugged his shoulders "I was not aware that you knew about that, and I thought it was old news by now. I was hoping it would not affect the making of the film or turn off the community. On the other hand, if there are people out there who look on me as some kind of a hero, who am I to complain?"

"In some ways I am surprised that there was not more about your heroics in bed with Margie," Óran said

"I suspect that someone had a word in the ear of the little shits that filmed it."

"Who would have done the likes of that?"

"Parents, teachers, the priest even. Communities have their own way of acting, of covering up."

"Why should they protect you and Margie?"

"They might call it 'for the good of the community.' Or they might be thinking of using it as a stick to beat us with. Most likely it is because they have a soft spot for Margie and they don't want to lose her. Anyway, it is a free country."

Óran Breathnach walked on without saying anything, with Dowling falling back a little as his legs tired. Óran Breathnach turned around after a short time and told his Producer "You are a right bollocks?"

"And you are developing into a great Judas."

CHAPTER SIXTEEN

Some members of the community came together in the local cemetery on November Sunday evening. There was a tradition of gathering for a rosary in memory of the deceased members of the parish during what is known in Roman Catholic circles as "The Month of The Dead." It is a tradition shared in many countries about which readers of South American literature are well aware. Fr. Éamonn Ó Sé had suggested to his congregation that someone other than he would lead the prayers as greater emphasis was being placed on people taking responsibility within the church. There were still some people who felt that while they had a resident priest he should be there to lead them in prayer. A compromise was reached that the priest would start the first decade of the rosary and the local people would take it from there.

It was a fine crisp November evening and it amazed the priest that so many had gathered for the rosary at a time on a Sunday afternoon that there was so much sport on television. People's respect for the dead was a constant source of wonder and joy to the priest and he knew that such services were replicated across the globe, in particular in areas of Roman Catholic culture. When the first decade of the rosary was completed by the priest, Mabel Uí Chionnaith announced the second as the priest glanced around the assembled crowd to see if there was any evidence that recent controversy about the Dowling film had any influence on his congregation. It was not that he expected to see if people of similar view had grouped together and there was an obvious spit in the community.

The only two people he observed to be standing away from the main group were Mary from the Mountain and Edel Nic an tSaoir. While unable to lipread the priest got the impression that those two were having a conversation rather than answering the prayers of the rosary. It seemed that they noticed him looking directly at them and began to answer the prayers with the rest of the crowd. When the priest intoned the final prayer in honour of the Blessed Virgin, Mary, Mary from the Mountain apologised to Edel "Sorry for interrupting you earlier while we were talking, but I saw the priest looking at us, so I switched back to the rosary."

"How would he know what we were saying?" Edel asked.

"It would have been a lack of courtesy, more to God than to the priest if he saw us chatting while everyone else was praying. Fr. Éamonn Ó Sé is not the worst. I was a bit hard on him at the meeting the other night."

Edel answered "He still has the power to put an end to the making of that rotten film, but he hasn't the guts to stand up to Dowling and his crew."

"He is not too much to blame," Mary from The Mountain said. "The clergy in general have lost their confidence because of the child abuse scandals and the Magdalen Laundries and all of that stuff.. The national media put the boot into them at every opportunity and between that and the shortage of priests, they are a shattered bunch."

"This should be the time for the clergy to be brave," Edel said, "That is what my newspaper is all about, to give their voice back to the Catholic people, and to our priests more than anyone."

"I understand that," Mary said, "and fair play to you. It is a pity that there are not a lot more like you. But if you and your paper put more pressure on the clergy they might get down off the fence and speak up for their people. I thought Fr. Éamonn Ó Sé might have used this morning's Mass to do so, but there he was with the same old story 'Love your neighbour as yourself.'"

"Should I have a word with him now before we leave the cemetery?" Edel asked her.

"There will never be a better time," Mary from the Mountain said. "He is just chatting with his parishioners and he will be ready in a few minutes."

Edel was not so sure "It is Sunday and he has had a busy day. I think I should leave him time to have a break."

"You will have no better chance than this. If he is busy now, make an appointment for later on or tomorrow. Strike while the iron is hot."

"I already have an appointment for later," Edel answered. "I got a text a while ago from Óran Breathnach, and he said it is urgent that we meet."

Mary from the Mountain seemed to have an issue with that "You mean one of the actors? What is he up to?"

"He will be Judas in the film. It is not every day a girl gets a text from one of the greatest betrayers that ever walked this earth."

"Be careful," Mary from the Mountain told her. "Next thing they will be offering you the part of Mary Magdalene or someone like that. Anything to distract you from your work as a Catholic journalist."

"Don't worry, Mary. It would take a lot to distract me. I actually knew Óran in University. He is not the worst. He probably just wants to ask me out for a drink."

"I thought you were teetotaller?"

"I haven't touched alcohol in years, so I am hardly going back to it now."

"Beware the betrayer. He could be Judas by name and Judas by nature. I would have doubts about the likes of him."

"I'm a big girl now Mary. We are two strangers who were friendly at College but have not seen much of each other since. What is wrong with a bit of nostalgia?"

"It is like walking into the arms of the enemy Having a chat is one thing. Allowing yourself to be seduced by some serpent in the grass is another."

"Serpents all have different strategies. They might want to buy me off, but two can play at that game. I might just pull the new Judas away from the fire."

"Is he married?" Mary from the Mountain asked.

"I haven't got a clue, but then I am not planning to have his babies. It won't amount to any more than reminiscences from college days in the University Dramatic Society, almost a quarter of a century ago."

Mary from the Mountain noticed that Fr. Éamonn Ó Sé had just finished a conversation with Margie from the Post Office, so she urged Edel to have a word with him before he left the cemetery. "Now is your chance to get hold of him. I wonder what he was talking to Margie about?"

"None of my business," Edel replied. "Maybe Margie has just found Jesus."

"She has enough to handle with that devil out of hell, Dowling."

Mary and Edel waited by the cemetery gate while the priest were making Smalltalk with some of the last of those who had gathered for the prayer service. As he was about to leave Mary from The Mountain apologised for the harshness of some of the things she had said at the Pastoral Council meeting the previous week. "No hard feelings, Father."

"There is nothing wrong with a bit of give and take," he answered. "It is far better than keeping things in and letting them fester away beneath the surface."

"Edel here would like to interview you, Father," Mary said, "to get your side of the story for her Catholic newspaper."

"I have no side to any story," the priest answered, "apart from letting people get on with their work. None of it has anything to do with me, really."

"It matters to the parish and the country and the world," Edel replied, "If people are making a mockery of our Lord, Jesus Christ."

"I have no evidence that is the case, Mary," Fr. Ó Sé said. "Now, if you don't mind I have been called to anoint one of our senior citizens in the Nursing Home."

"Who is sick? Father," Mary from the Mountain asked.

"I cannot tell you private information," was the priest's answer to that as he headed towards his car.

"It is always sad to hear of someone getting the last rites," Edel said.

"There are no last rites involved. I am sure of that," Mary said. "He is just trying to get rid of us in case he would have to answer your questions in the newspaper. Our Fr. Éamonn Ó Sé is as cute as a fox. Anyway, it is time for you to get ready for your date."

"It is not a date, just a few drinks."

"Don't drink too much. Fellows like that would have you over a barrel in no time at all."

CHAPTER SEVENTEEN

"Did you know that the dogs in the street know all about the two of us?" Nicólás Dowling asked Margie the Post Office as they lay side by side in her bed. "It seems that it about us and two the dogs in the street are barking from morning till night."

Margie kissed him "I do not care what people think as long as you can awake feelings like I have just had a few minutes ago. I want those feelings to last all night."

"I thought you would be in a hurry to get back before the shop closes?"

"There is someone covering for me tonight, so I am all yours. I will have all year behind the counter when the film is over and you are gone. You sure have tricks that I have not come across until now."

"I do my best," he answered with mock modesty.

"That tongue of yours is some instrument."

"Whatever gives pleasure to my lover. And I know that I am in competition with some of your young lovers from days gone by."

Margie leaned on an elbow to raise herself up in the bed. "What do you mean by my young lovers? What are you talking about now?"

"I have heard of some of the young blokes that worked for you in season's past."

"Where have you heard what?" Margie asked angrily.

"You know yourself? The dogs in the street again. Your fame has gone before you. I am not complaining. Its fact I am delighted to find that you know your way around a man's body."

"Fuck you," was Margie's answer to that. "My past has nothing to do with you. It is none of your business. Have I ever questioned your many conquests?"

"I don't give a fuck who you fucked in the past. I can see how you were able to seduce young fellows. You are one hell of a woman. I have never met a woman as knowledgeable as you are in so far as sex is concerned."

Margie was very angry. "What makes you think that it was not the handsome young men that seduced me? I am not a lump of meat. I make my own decisions, and if I decided to be with you it was purely for my pleasure, not for your fame and fortune as an actor and a director. They call you the devil around here. I didn't ever believe in a devil until now, and you are it, your ignorant bollocks."

"What do you mean by that?" Dowling asked.

"I don't think you respect me as a person."

"What makes you think that?" Nicólas asked. "I may not be the most attractive or the most romantic person on earth, but I do have a very high regard for you, more than I have for anyone else right now."

"You do, in the bedroom, but have you invited me to side beside you and have a drink with you in the hotel bar?"

"You are working all of the time, twenty-four seven. No sooner do you sit down but you are up again at your duties in the Post Office or the shop."

"I could get someone to cover for me if I was invited out, but with you it is the bed or nothing."

Dowling got out of the bed and went down on one knee. "Would Madam like to join me in the hotel bar tomorrow evening?"

"There you go again. Yourself and your 'Madam'. You have probably seen too many madams in your time. Still, now that I have seen you go down on one knee..."

"What about it?"

"I will," Margie answered.

"You will what?"

"Of course, I will marry you. Have you any plans for the honeymoon, or will it all be broad on the back in the bed?"

"I said nothing about marriage."

Margie laughed. "You look like a mountainy goat out there beside my bed. Get back in here beside me and do your duty like a man. The marriage thing was a joke but it was worth it for the shocked look that came on your face."

"It will be an honour to join you in the bar tomorrow evening," Dowling said. "I am sorry to have given you a wrong impression, but for me the bar seems like work as it is an opportunity to see my actors in action outside the realms of work."

Edel Nic an tSaoir met Óran Breathnach in the hotel bar. He was having a pint of Guinness but Edel did not accept his offer of anything but bottled water.

"You really have changed," Óran said. "You mean that you never touch alcohol anymore? Not even a glass of wine with dinner?"

"I manage fine without it," Edel answered.

"You could always make an exception when you meet an old friend."

"I would never drink and drive, and I wouldn't ask Mary from the Mountain to come and collect me."

"I could drop you off at her place later?"

"That would have you drinking and driving."

"You really have become a puritan."

"Call me anything you like. I have heard it all. I have just taken a different direction in life than the Edel you used to know."

"Well, fair fucks to you. I haven't found God myself but then I was not searching for him. Or her or whatever It is called now. It never held any attraction for me and I can't see that it ever will."

"But here you are preparing to play a part in a religious film?"

"A job is a job, and there is none better than one that takes me back to the home country now and again."

"Where is your present home? Across the water?" Edel asked.

"London, Finsbury Park, if you have heard of it. A great place for Irish Paddies in days gone by, and there plenty of the older generation there yet. It is nice to meet some of them in a bar but they can get on your wick talking about the heavy work they did all over London in the old days."

"I would love to write an article about the forgotten Irish in England," Edel said, "those who went over in the fifties and sixties and never came back or never visited their families in Ireland. What did we do to drive them away?"

"Your church might have some of the answers to that. They were all for the big families, or at least did nothing to prevent them. There was only room on the farm for one, so the rest had to go."

"Why does everyone blame the church for everything?"

"They have a lot to answer for, and that is even before the child abuse scandals hit the headlines. Many Irish people loved home but felt more at home in England, if you know what I mean. There was more freedom over there."

Edel said "It is a project I would like to become involved with, the lost Irish as I would call them."

"You could always stay at my place if you want to come over some weekend and check things out," Óran said.

"How many rooms do you have?"

"One big room actually and a small kitchen. It is big enough for me as I am working away with touring companies half the time"

"What good would that be to me?" Edel asked. "I could go over and you wouldn't be there."

"Not a problem," Óran said. "I could leave a key with the woman who looks after things when I am away."

"Thanks anyway, but I was hoping you would be there to show me the city and where I could meet some of the Irish who made England their home."

"I would love to be there when you come over."

"But you only have one bed?"

Óran shrugged his shoulders "I could sleep outside the bed clothes, you wouldn't be the first person to stay a few nights with me like that."

"Did it take long for you to find your way under the bedclothes?" Edel joked.

"I respect women," Óran answered. "I would not expect anyone to do what they didn't want."

"I must say that I always liked you in College," Edel said. "You were nice and kind compared with some of the clowns."

"I hope that has not changed."

"Would you mind if I asked you a serious question?"

"Ask way." Óran smiled "I have nothing to hide."

"Were you and I together? Sexually I mean? Back in the day?"

"You don't remember?"

"I am confused. You seemed to suggest that we were when I spoke to you before? Or were you just boasting?"

"We were all going at it like rabbits at the time. So, what? That's life when you are young. Clearly you have changed since as is your right."

"Sense comes with age, as the old people used to say."

"What was your Damascus road?" Óran asked. "What changed your attitude? Or did it happen gradually?"

"I was asked when I was being interviewed for the journalist job I have now what I intended to do with my life. I felt myself going blank. To be honest I answered with the first thing that came into my mind. All I wanted to do was to impress the interviewers. When I thought back on the answer I had given I realised that was really what I wanted to be. I didn't want to be a slut. I never did, but I had become one. I had never wanted to turn my back on my religion, but I had. I realised that what I really wanted was to be a good person, a person of principle."

"Not only were you on the road to Damascus?" Óran said, "but you were right in the middle of that road."

"I have news for you," Edel answered. "I am not a complete saint. Like anyone who aspires to being good, I have my faults and failings." She touched Óran's hand with hers. "I think that I will have a glass of wine all the same." She started to stand up to go to the counter but Óran eased her back in her seat. "Stay where you are. Red or white? There are no other choices or selections here."

"Red so. Thank you."

Nicólas Dowling, who had arrived in the bar with Margie from the Post Office, went over to Óran as he stood at the counter waiting for Edel's drink as well as a pint for himself "Good man yourself," he said to Óran. "You have got down to work straight away. This, I presume is the famous Edel, my sworn enemy, and a fine piece of stuff she is. Have you spoken to her yet about the part of Mary in the film?"

Óran was not pleased. "We are here for a quiet drink. That is all."

"You could strike while the iron is hot," Dowling said, "or maybe you have done that already."

"Do you ever think of anything other than getting your hole?" Óran asked disgustedly.

"What else is there?" Nicólas Dowling joked crudely. "Or are you one of those types who keep their tongues in their cheeks and their pricks in their trousers?"

"That sounds like you alright," was Óran's reply. "It is the end of the week and two old friends are out for a drink. Could you not leave it at that?"

"Time and tide wait for no man, and I have a film to make. You are on board or you are not."

"Is that a threat?" Óran asked.

"It is a request. Just see if she is interested in the part I have suggested for her."

"If you want her for the part of the Virgin Mary, just go and ask her. Edel is there on her own until I bring down the drinks. Or are you afraid that Margie will be jealous?"

"OK, I will have a go," Dowling said. "Back me up, if you have to."

"I am Judas, remember," Óran said sarcastically. "Selling someone out is second nature to me."

The film director went and stretched out his right hand to Edel. "Hi, I am Nicólas Dowling who is here to make a film about Jesus of Nazareth. Óran Breathnach was telling me all about you."

Edel refused his handshake. "I know who you are and what you stand for. All I can say is God help the people of this area if they allow the likes of you to make a mockery of Our Lord Jesus Christ. Not everyone agrees with you or your beliefs, not to speak of your methods. You should be railroaded back to where you came from, or if not you should be driven out to sea."

"It is a free country, thankfully," Dowling said, "and I would suggest that my project has more support than you and your objectors have."

"You have obviously not met Mary from the Mountain and the other defenders of the faith who can't wait to see the back of you. Your name and your fame, such as it is has gone before you, and as names and fames go, you stink."

"Isn't it you that is quick to judgment," Dowling replied. "You have damned my previous work, even though as far as I am aware you have seen none of it. You have condemned my film without speaking to me, without reading a script, without asking me a question. What kind of a so-called journalist does that?"

"The whole country knows what kind of an antichrist you are."

Dowling did not allow Edel to get any further. "So the whole world knows... The dogs in the street know what I and my film crew are up to." He pointed at Óran who was waiting patiently to deliver drinks for Edel and himself. "Why are you with this man who will be playing the part of Judas in my film here this evening? Why are you so much against me but not against him? How can you condemn a script without reading it?"

"OK," Edel said. "Give me a script and I will read it and let you have my opinion."

Dowling did not answer immediately "I don't have a script," he admitted. "That is not the way that I work. Actors work their way into their characters. And we see the way things are going then. Creativity is everything. We create the drama from the characters themselves."

Edel's face took on a very sarcastic look. "Now we are getting to the bottom of things. No script. No proper direction. Just hope that characters will fall into place and that everything works out right in the end. The result of all that should mean that it is Judas or Pilate or even Peter that will be crucified on the cross?"

"Don't worry," Nicólás Dowling said. "We won't be going that far. There are some things that we cannot change, the crucifixion of Jesus, for example, but there are ways in which we can create new approaches, imaginative approaches in telling the story to a new generation that do not give two fucks about God, man or the devil."

"That is a very thoughtless thing to say about the younger generation."

Dowling cleared his throat "Maybe the last thing I said came out of my mouth all wrong. What I was trying to say is that young people might put more interest in a story told in a more interesting way."

As Edel and Dowling argued in the centre of the floor while Óran stood by with the drinks, Margie from the Post Office came over and asked Nicólás "Have you forgotten all about me? I thought the two of us had just come out for a quiet drink."

The Film Director apologised and tried to introduce Margie to Edel, but both quickly told him that they had met already in the Post Office shop. "In fairness we all came out to share some peace and quiet, and here we are discussing a film that is not even made yet."

"I understood that you had a question for Edel," Óran said to Dowling.

"A question about what?" the journalist asked.

"It can wait," the film director said bluntly.

"If you have something to say, just say it," Edel said, just as bluntly.

"Would you have any interest in the part of Mary in the film?" Dowling asked, "Óran told me you were an actor, or do they still say actress? in College."

"You mean Mary Magdalen?" Edel asked. "Typecasting again? Is that your game?!"

"I am talking Mary, the mother of Jesus," was Dowling's answer.

"You can't be serious? Are you trying to buy me off?"

"Well?" Dowling asked.

Edel looked him in the eyes. "Well what?"

"Would you be interested in the part?"

"What kind of an idiot do you think I am." Edel answered.

Margie cut in on their conversation "I have accepted a part even though I have no acting experience and I am not involved with religion in any shape or form. Maybe this is what this film needs, a couple of strong women."

Edel looked at her with a certain amount of disdain. "Everyone knows that yourself and himself are hammering away like rabbits. I favour monogamy, chastity and decent living."

"So that makes you eligible for the part Nicólas is offering? The part of Mary the mother of Jesus, the first mother that never needed a man to provide sperm."

"Insults will get us nowhere," Óran Breathnach said.

"That bitch would bring us back to the dark ages when single mothers were locked away in mother and baby homes." Margie said "The cheek of her coming out here to stir up opposition to a film that will put this place on the map."

Edel answered with just as much venom "You and your so-called partner are on the map already because of that dirty sex-tape that has been circulating here for the past month."

Nicólas Dowling tried to ease the situation "Listen to yourselves, girls. Each of you is a strong, or should I say headstrong young woman. Think of what we might all achieve from working together."

Edel pointed a finger at Margie. "Why don't you give her the part of Mary Magdalen? Wasn't she a prostitute as well?"

Margie answered "A prostitute gets paid for sex. I do it because I love it, because I am not a miserable uptight bitch."

"You are what you are and you know it," Edel said.

Margie replied "What a joke if you were to play the part of the Virgin Mary? I heard that you put yourself around like snuff at a wake when you were in University."

Edel looked at Óran as the only person there that would have known her in college "I know now why you have got the part that you have you betraying bastard, you Judas."

Óran shrugged his shoulders "I never opened my mouth about you."

"So, you admit it?" Margie said to Edel "I was only guessing because people get up to all sorts in college. So, you did horse around? Great. It proves that you are human despite the right-wing image your little newspaper displays."

"When did you ever read a Catholic paper?" Edel snapped back.

"I read every paper that comes into the Post Office. There is plenty of time for reading when the senior citizens have collected their pensions."

"We all know that is the only pastime you have," Edel commented.

Óran touched Edel's back "Why don't we sit down and enjoy our drinks and let the others get on with their own thing?"

She sat down and sipped her drink "I don't know what to make of you. Or anyone else for that matter. Nobody seems able to escape their past. How can you stick working with that crowd?"

"A job is a job and none of us should let it get on top of us. This crowd will move on in a month or two, and almost everything will be forgotten. A few months' work means a lot in an uncertain occupation like this."

At the other side of the room Margie was having regrets that she had come out in public for drinks with Nicólás Dowling. She wondered why she had allowed herself to be drawn into the argument she had with Edel. For years she had managed to be neutral while local issues were being discussed, and here she was fighting with Edel like two fishwives in a TV soap opera. Nicólás and herself sat quietly side by side for some time, and it was she who broke the silence.

"I think that we will all regret the making of this film. It will do nothing in the long run other than create tensions that will take years to overcome."

It sounded as if Nicólás Dowling had no worries about it "It will all come right in the end. Don't worry. I have been down this road many times before. Art is never created without tension."

"There is nothing artistic about the tensions you get in a rural community," Margie said. "They take years to heal."

"Tension! Nicólás sounded as if he was talking to himself. Creativity comes from tension. Did I say that before? A great film will be brought forth from all of this."

"In the meantime, everyone will be driven daft," Margie said, "You will be gone back to your life, but my customers will be standing side by side at the counter of the Post Office without talking to each other."

Dowling looked around the bar "Is it really putting in on the ordinary people, the real people as some of the politicians used to say, the people who have their dinners in the middle of the day. The tensions seem to be coming from blow-ins like us more than between what some would describe as the 'natives' which I know is prejudicial but is the only way I can describe the locals."

"Are you calling ma a stranger?" Margie asked him. "I have been here for years and apart from a few people I feel accepted by the community."

"As far as I can make out," Dowling said, "everyone who was born here is considered a stranger. There is nothing wrong with that, but I feel that even a hundred year's residence doesn't stop someone from being called a stranger. That is normal everywhere as far as I can see."

"You mean I will be a hundred and fifty years old before I stop being a stranger?" Margie joked.

"I think people like strangers to visit and they get along well with them, but they are still strangers. That is true not just of this place, but everywhere," Nicólas said.

"You could be right," Margie said lightly as if she was tiring of that conversation.

Dowling wondered aloud "Isn't there something in the Bible that Jesus said about not being accepted by his own people."

"I don't know," Margie replied. "It is you that is making the religious film. We are in the bar now. If you wanted a religious experience you could have gone to morning Mass in the local church."

"OK, so what do you want to talk about?"

"Anything that has nothing to do with your bloody film. It is all I hear about in the Post Office from morning till evening. And at night for that matter. It is really getting on my wick. Silence hung heavily between them for a long time."

Across the bar from them Edel was drinking her wine quickly with Óran barely keeping up to her with his pints of Guinness "Are you still angry with Margie?" he asked.

"She will pay dearly for insulting me, when I get time to put pen to paper, or in my case, fingers to computer."

"Would you still be able to keep up with your journalism if you accepted the part of the Blessed Virgin in Dowling's film?" Óran asked.

Edel looked at him as if he had two heads. "You know as well as I do that was only an excuse to try and get me onside so that I will not rubbish the film in my newspaper. Who does he think he is fooling?" She said nothing for a while before she was as if thinking out loud. "It would be a great part for me to get, but I do not want to be part of Dowling's agenda."

Óran asked "What could he do with the film that could be that bad? We all basically know the story already. I am involved in it too and many more besides. We can all walk out if he goes off on some crazy tangent. He has to stick basically to the gospel story."

"So, says the man who claims to have no faith?"

"It is not about me. It means a lot to thousands and millions of people.!"

"A pity Dowling does not see that."

Óran answered "I don't think that he is here to mess up the gospel story or that he is as big an antichrist as you and many others think he is. Not only does he not force his actors to do things his way or to follow his script, he expects each actor to follow his or her own instinct. I think he could surprise you if you were to play the part of Mary."

Edel gave a nervous laugh. "It would certainly surprise him if I accept"

"So, you are seriously thinking about it?" Óran asked.

"I presume that Dowling has the last say about everything involved in the film. He can twist things this way or that to suit himself during editing. As he cuts and joins things together to suit himself."

"But what can he do that is so bad?" Óran asked "Even fucking Satan never managed to cock up the memory of Jesus in the past couple of thousand years."

"I wouldn't be so sure about that," Edel answered. "Didn't the Catholic church in this and other countries manage to fuck things up pretty badly because of child abuse and other scandals of that nature?"

"We are talking here about a small-scale film being made in a remote place on the edge of Europe," Óran said. "How much of a threat be to a religion that has a couple of million followers if you count Catholic, Protestant, Orthodox not to speak of the Bible belt in the United States, Jumping Jesuses and Pentecostals? Even the much-maligned Nicólas Dowling can hardly manage to make a complete bollocks of Christian religions worldwide."

"I suppose you are right," Edel agreed. "I suppose I could speak to my editor, but not tonight. I am tired and I suppose I drank too much wine too fast. I had forgotten how tasty it is. I better give it a bit more thought before I enter Dowling's Lion's Den."

"Non-believers made at least one great film about Jesus in the past," Óran said. "I don't think that the guy that filmed 'The Gospel of Saint Matthew' had faith. What was his name? It was a black and white film. I saw it in secondary school and it made quite an impression on me as a young fellow.. I still remember Jesus in a hurry as he went from place to place preaching and healing." Óran stopped for a moment as if struck by a bolt from the blue. "Pasolini," he said. "That's it. That was his name. A great film. Made back in the sixties, I think. Did you ever get to see it?"

Edel smiled. "I was not actually around in the sixties. Nor were you for that matter."

"Good films last forever."

"Do you think Dowling will make us famous?"

"He might, if you accept his offer."

Edel yawned "I am getting tired. I am not used to being out on the tear."

"I can walk you home to your digs," Óran said.

"I wouldn't risk it," Edel answered. "Mary from the Mountain might eat you up and spit you out. She is a formidable woman."

"And so are you. As Dowling is about to find out," Óran said.

Edel looked him straight in the eyes. "What is that you were saying the other day about one sleeping under and the other outside the bedclothes?"

"Are you coming on to me?" he joked.

"I could manage to share the bed, but not the body. Not just yet anyway."

Óran replied "Under the clothes, over the clothes, never touching the clothes and certainly not taking off the clothes. I could manage that, I suppose."

"Just for company," Edel said quietly.

"But what is Mary from the Mountain going to say when you arrive back tomorrow morning?"

"I will say that I was on an undercover mission,"

"Let's go," Óran said as both of them left without finishing their drinks. They did not make eye contact with Margie or Dowling across the room.

Margie said to Dowling "I reckon that your Blessed Virgin will not be a virgin in the morning. That's if she ever was."

CHAPTER EIGHTEEN

Tadhg Ó Maoldomhnaigh spent that Sunday working on planks of roughly cut timber with which he hoped to construct a cross capable of carrying his weight. He used a small hatchet to hack a hollow close to the end of one of his planks and in the middle of the other. He placed the shorter one across the other near to what would be the top of the cross and nailed them together with six-inch nails. He enjoyed the physical work even though he had not done anything like that for years. He gave himself a fright at one stage when his hatchet slipped as he worked and he just missed striking himself on the right shin. This reminded him to arrange his mobile phone in such a way as he would be able to reach it and make a phone call for help if that was necessary. He smiled to himself as he thought of the headlines that tabloid newspapers might use if he had split his shin. "Christ legless in the forest," or "The passion of the hatchet-man." He felt more at ease when he was finished with the hatchet. He thought of how much more at home with timber the man Jesus whose part he was to play was, "A real live carpenter."

It took some time for Tadhg to raise the cross on his back with the longer section dragging after him along the ground as he made his way up Poteen Hill. It was there that the great fire had been built many years before during a Parish Mission by the Redemptorist religious order as part of their visit to the area every four years or so. All of the instruments used in making the illicit brew called "poitín" had been gathered together during the previous week and thrown into a large pile for burning after the men of the parish especially had taken a pledge never to drink the illicit distillation again. Mass servers had been sent to the priest's house with a bucket to collect burning coals from the fire as well as a tong with which to throw them into the fire. The priest who had become known as the "cross Missioner" because of his constant ranting about poitín threw the first coal onto the pyre with the words. "Don't you see the devil rising up in the air," as the alcohol-soaked heap of discarded spirit making equipment took fire and emitted a cloud of dark smoke. Many of those present would have sworn afterwards that they had seen the devil himself rise from the smoke and flames. Others laughed because they had outwitted the preacher by supplying old and worn whiskey stills for the fire while their more up to date ones were hidden away until the mission was over.

"This bloody cross is too heavy," was the first thing that Tadhg said to himself as he pulled it up against the steep incline. "How did a man like Jesus who was battered and bruised and broken drag something similar up Calvary hill?" He had already been scourged and had a crown of thorns stuck onto the top of his head. He had lost blood to the extent that he must have little left in his system. "But Jesus was a young man," Tadhg thought, "not like a middle-aged actor like me. Thirty-three years old, they say he was, but he did have help. Simon of Cyrene. The reluctant cross carrier some might say, but the day had come that Simon's name had become a byword for someone who helps others." Tadhg had read all about the man who had founded The Simon Community in London half a century earlier. He had come across members of that organisation on one of the many recovery programmes he had tried in his efforts to give up the demon drink for once and for all. "This must be my twelfth time," he told himself. "I hope it is the last, but I have my doubts, even though I intend to stick with the pledge until this bloody film is finished anyway."

Tadhg addressed the mythical Jesus he felt he was now carrying on his back along with his cross. "Can you do anything about it? Or are you one of the good-for-nothings that promises all and delivers nothing? You make wine out of water according to the story, but what do you do for those addicted? OK, you will tell me 'Physician heal thyself.' Have I not tried often enough? Have I not swallowed cold turkey until it was coming out in my arse? Have I not faced my demons time and time again? Have I not been to hell and back nearly as much as yourself in your suffering and death? Where is my redemption? It is time you got off your high horse, your high cross, and did something for me."

Tadhg struggled on as he tried to get deeper and deeper into the Jesus character. "A man in the wrong place at the wrong time? Or the opposite, a fool who walked to his death with his eyes open? Did he even need to be in Jerusalem that week? He could have been out in the board with James and John and the rest of them, fishing and having the craic. But things had not being going well for some time before that. The crows were drifting away because he is not giving them bread and roses, bread and wine... And then there was Judas. The rumours had started that he wanted out. He felt there was sense in what the Scribes and Pharisees were saying. They had a thousand years of tradition behind them and they felt the young upstart from Nazareth couldn't leave well enough alone There were rumours that he had money problems, that he was helping himself from the communal moneybag Could Jesus not just have spoken to him? Asked him had he family problems? Maybe he was fond of a few drinks. It was not the end of the world. Judas sounded like a nice guy, an emotional guy, but he could not see any way out."

"Did any of it matter?" Tadhg asked himself. "As far as he could see most of the people he had known all of his life had drifted away from religion. OK, they went through the motions on the day of a funeral, but that was it. His mind wandered again to Simon of Cyrene. An accidental cross carrier, wrong man, right place, or was it the opposite? No matter how life was planned, it had a way of turning things on their heads. The names of Simon's sons came to mind, Alasdair and Rugus. As far as Tadhg was concerned they were names that would suit sheepdogs. Skilled dogs on the Connemara hills, more skilled than any shepherd. He had seen some in action while there was a film being made in Leenane. He would not like to admit it even to himself, Tadhg thought, but there were times he preferred dogs to people. They were not nearly as complicated, or were they?"

One thing that worried Tadhg was how he would look as he carried his cross. Would he have to do so half-naked or would

Dowling come up with a plan that would not expose him to ridicule? He had lost some weight since he stopped drinking alcohol, but his belly still hung a bit low. Still it might be a way to represent the "everyman" rather than a skinny Jesus. Maybe he could get a lighter cross for the actual "Via Dolorosa," the way of the sorrows. They could use the big cross he made himself for the actual crucifixion. A bit of slick camera work could cover up for some of his physical faults and failings. He laughed to himself as he thought of making a mockery of the whole thing by being roaring drunk on the cross. That would certainly put an elephant in Dowling's ointment.

Tadhg then thought of another plan. He placed the cross in a half-standing position against a whitethorn bush that kept it reasonably upright. He took a piece of thin rope from his coat pocket and tied it around the middle of the cross which he then eased to the ground so that he could slide it behind him on the grass. "How do I know that is was not like this that crosses were brought from place to place?" he asked himself "I could have made a fortune inventing new killing equipment if I had lived in Roman times. I will have to tell that one to Nicólas Dowling the next time I see him. He was always fond of the dark humour. He knew that he could meet him anytime in the hotel bar but that did not suit him since he stopped drinking. Temptation had to be kept at arm's length. Hard work was the best antidote to alcohol." Tadhg told himself. He ran a couple of kilometres every morning and carrying and pulling the cross would help him to lose more weight. At this particular moment, Tadhg felt that it was a cigarette he craved more than anything, so he sat down on his big cross and lit a cigarette.

Tadhg thought he was dreaming when the "Migos" surrounded him. He wondered was this a hallucination to do with giving up the drink when he saw what looked like wild animals chasing around among the fairly new trees that had been set at the time of the millennium. "I must be in the rats," he thought, but when he looked again he could see that it was people that were running around in some kind of fancy dress. "They may be just trying out their Halloween costumes," Tadhg told himself. As he looked closed, two of them seemed to be carrying hayforks, another a rope and another what looked like a shotgun.

It was obvious that the first of those who approached him had something in his mouth to disguise his speech. When Tadhg asked him what did he want, the teenage but boyish voice answered "It is you we want. If you do what we ask you will come to no harm."

"What do you hope to do?" Tadhg asked nervously. "I want you to know that I have high blood pressure and other ailments. Please do not put a gag on me."

"It is just a bit of fun," the spokesperson said. "We are here to crucify you, to tie you to your own cross. We will contact local people then so that they will see you crucified. It is a protest to let the film crowd know that we are watching them and that they can't make fools of the local community."

"Why have you picked on me?" Tadhg asked. "I am not in charge of the film."

"You are here. You have your cross with you. You are oven-fresh as people might say."

Tadhg looked at the shotgun. "Why don't ye just shoot me? It would be a lot easier than crucifixion."

Alan through his mouthful of stones tried to explain what they were about, even though it seemed he was not very sure himself. "We don't want to hurt you or to kill you for that matter, so long as you co-operate with us. We just want to mess things up a bit for that film company you belong to."

Tadhg was adamant. "I don't belong to anyone. I am just a gun for hire as you might put it. I take jobs wherever they are going or whatever they are about. Have your fun but don't leave me here to die in the wilderness."

The two young girls shrugged their shoulders but said nothing, as they had been instructed to do by Alan. Eoin had forgotten that order and he answered in his own voice. "You are not in any danger. We will let you go after a while. Don't worry about it."

Alan pointed the shotgun playfully in Eoin's direction as he put a finger to his lips asking him to remain silent. He then shouted at Tadhg. "Take up your cross and walk."

"Some of you will have to help me," Tadhg said. "It is very big and very heavy, too much for a man to lift on his own."

"Give him a hand," Alan told the others. Tadhg took the top part of the cross with the girls holding up the arms of the cross and Eoin holding the end of the long shaft. They advanced slowly, Alan acting the fool going from one bush to another and pointing the shotgun this way and that as if they were part of an army in the jungle. When they reached the place in which workmen had dug a hole some days earlier on Nicólas Dowling's orders, into which to place the "leg" of the cross.

"Leave it there," Alan instructed. "Good work. Take it easy for a few minutes." He looked at the cross and then at Tadhg before he announced. "We will tie him to the cross first on the ground and raise it up then. Or should we put the cross standing up first?"

"How can we lift it?" Eoin asked, "with the weight of that big fucker on it?"

Alan pointed the shotgun at him again "Didn't I tell you to keep your big mouth shut."

"If you ask us a question, are we not supposed to answer it?" Eoin asked. Aisling said "This stuff is going too far. This is not fun. This is cruelty. I am going home. Come on," she beckoned to Eithne.

She did not want to go against her brother. "Why don't we just tie him to the cross on the ground and send texts to the locals to come and see Jesus on the broad of his back? No way would be able to lift up himself and his cross."

Tadhg stretched out his arms "Do that so, and get it over with. I have never said no to a bit of drama."

Alan gave orders "Lie down on the cross and put your arms in the crucifying positions." He spoke then to his colleagues, the Amigos. "Tie him to the timber when the rope is divided." Eoin cut the rope into three pieces. The girls tied a wrist each to the cross and Eoin tied the feet.

Alan pointed his father's gun between Tadhg's thighs. "Is this the bloke you told me has a prick like an ass?"

Eoin shouted at him "Stop that. There might be a cartridge in it."

Alan said "Dad never leaves anything in it." He pointed the gun in the air and pulled the trigger. The noise of the blast shook them all. Tadhg thought for a moment that he had been shot and his roars and curses were nearly as loud as the gunshot. The four Migos took off in different directions.

CHAPTER NINETEEN

Edel Nic an tSaoir woke up in Óran Breathnach's bed. He was lying in top of the bedclothes covered with a blanket. As he continued to snore Edel had time to put her thoughts in order before he would wake up. She appreciated the fact that he had made no effort to join her under the sheets. At the same time, she felt mildly insulted that he had not fancied her enough to "have a go" as some might put it. To be honest, she told herself I am not sure that I would have turned him down. She liked him, but they had a lot to drink and she preferred the fact that he had been a gentleman than if he had tried his luck. The goodnight kiss had lingered while he had turned aside and started to snore. "Maybe it is just old age," she told herself lightly. Neither of us would have given it a second thought in times gone by."

She had principles of course, but sometimes principles blew away in the wind or were drowned in drink. She felt that another of her principles was under pressure since Nicólás Dowling had offered her the part of the Blessed Virgin Mary in his film. Was it some kind of a trap? "Buy me off and get me to shut my trap?" she punned in her own mind. Should she tell him to stick his offer or embrace the part and play it according to scripture. She was still in charge, she told herself. She did not have to do anything in the film that she did not want to do.

Edel felt that there was always the danger that another actress would get the part and make a mockery of Mary by it being played by a ladyboy or something like that. While she had the part, she would have the power. She could attract more publicity for her own cause if it went to that by walking away if she was put under any kind of pressure to make a mess of it. "All you want is the part of Mary," she told herself: "It may be against some principles to enter Dowling's Trojan Horse, but I would be doing it to preserve the integrity of Mary of the gospels."

"I better talk to Mary from The Mountain and others who are dead against the film," Edel thought. "The notion of subverting it from the inside might appeal to them, or it might just make the film itself more acceptable to both sides. The main thing is that it would not be a travesty, a mockery of God and religion as we know it."

Edel was pleased that she had given herself time to think things through while Óran slept. What she longed for now was that he would just wake up and she could share her news with him. He was not snoring as loudly now and there was a hint of a smile on his closed lips. "I bet that he is dreaming of a woman. Lucky girl, but what do I know? He could be married or divorced or anything. No way am I going to let him or any man break my heart."

When Óran lay on his back Edel noticed that he had an erection pushing up the rug that covered him. She barely touched the rug and he opened his eyes.

"What is that?" she asked mischievously. "The morning wank?"

Óran seemed embarrassed "Sorry. That was not planned. I was asleep."

"Maybe it has a mind of its own," Edel said.

"Maybe it is trying to tell us something?"

"It is telling us that you really fancied the woman you were dreaming about. She must be lovely?

"She is. You are." Óran answered.

"You won't fool me with that stuff. Your dream was miles away from me or from this place."

"That is where you are wrong. I fancy you even more now that you are completely out of bounds with your religious stuff."

"I am still a woman."

"There is no question about that. No way was I going to impose myself on you." Óran said.

"I thought we might have a kiss and a cuddle last night, but you choose to stay away from me."

"Didn't you tell me that you had no interest in that part of your life anymore? You would go back to being a virgin if you could?"

"You are a complete liar," Edel said lightly. "I never said anything like that."

"So what are you telling me now or do I have to read between the lines?"

"I have to admit that you are a gentleman, or that is what I thought until I say your little soldier standing to attention."

"That soldier has a mind of his own. He will lie down at any moment now."

"He will if he is let. I think it might be too late to put the genie back in its bottle."

"I think it is fading away like the morning dew," Óran replied. "Maybe we should take some time to think things through. What plans have you for tonight? We could meet up and talk things out."

"I have an appointment with Mary From The Mountain and her supporters," Edel answered. "The sooner that I tell them that I am going to accept the part of the Virgin Mary in the film the better for us all."

"Is she likely to go ballistic?" Óran asked.

"I don't know. I don't think so. I think she will see it like an opportunity to disturb the enemy camp."

"Good for you," Óran said. "What made up your mind to accept the part?"

"You did," Edel answered.

"There must be more to it than anything that I said."

"I was lying there in the quiet of the morning listening to you snoring peacefully as I tried to think things through. It occurred to me that I have gone too far to the right politically because of the editorial post I have and that there was more to life than that."

"So you just went over to the other side?" Óran asked.

"Not completely," Edel answered." I am still the woman I was yesterday. Some aspects of Irish life have swung too far too fast and they need to be questioned honestly. That should not stop me from being the woman I was, the actress I was and much as I despise Dowling I am grateful for his offer of the part of Mary in the film, whatever his motives. It will actually give me time out to consider the future."

"Nothing like a few drinks with a decent man to bring about a conversion."

"You have a lot to learn if you think I am a decent man. Are you actually thinking of packing in your job?"

"Not until I get something else, of course, but a part in a fairly big film might open a few doors for me."

"I would prefer to see you in a different job than in that magazine that seems to be to the right of Hitler from what I hear."

"It provides balance to all the liberal stuff. What is that phrase? Virtus in media stars? Virtue stands in the middle?"

"I think some of what your paper stands for is so far away from the middle that it has gone out of sight."

"Have you read any of it, or are you hearing what you want to hear?"

"I am hearing what I don't want to hear," Óran answered. "I am not hearing the Edel I used to know Though Maybe I am now.."

"I am that same person but certain things need to be said and read all of the same. There are such things as principles."

"On every side," was Óran's answer.

"I have been considering using more acceptable language and being more understanding," Edel said. "Now that my identity has been established I am in a position to be somewhat more open in what I write."

"You could nearly pack the job in altogether if you take the part in the film. To be fair to Dowling, he pays well. You would have enough to take you through the year and you would surely get other film and theatre stuff after that."

"I would be accused of taking the shilling, selling my soul for a mess of
Porridge or whatever it is they call it."

"Pottage," Óran said.

"I will pass on the pottage and have it both ways if you want to put it like that, I will take Dowling's money and I will keep my options open at the same time. I can't just ditch the views that I have held for a decade or more. I am not some kind of a snowflake that melts when the sun comes out."

"Snowflake is certainly not your middle name," Óran said, "but you can go too far to the right and be stereotyped, you are far too intelligent for that."

Edel did not seem to be listening to him as she thought out loud. "I will speak to my editor, and if he allows me to be a spy on the wall in the making of Dowling's film, I will take the part."

Óran smiled "I am tempted to get in beside you in the bed, now that you are softening up and getting back to your old self."

"I wouldn't advise it," Edel answered. "I smell like a dung heap after the drink and the sleep. We will have to put it on hold."

CHAPTER TWENTY

Tadhg Ó Maoldomhnaigh began to worry as soon as the young people who had tied him to his cross ran away in all directions. The blast from the shotgun had obviously scared them and he was sure in his own mind that they would not be coming back. He was aware of his own strength compared to the young people so he felt he would be able to free himself from the ropes tying him to the cross without too much effort. When he failed to free either hand from the wings of the cross he started to curse whatever scouting training had taught the young people to tie ropes. By dint of kicking he felt that his feet had come looser but what good was that when he could not loosen his hands? At the same time, he felt that constant shaking and pulling might loosen the ropes on his wrists. There was the opposite danger, of course, that the knots would get even tighter.

The one thing that gave Tadhg hope was that the young man with the stones in his mouth had said that they would spread the word online so that local people would come and see this overweight Christ on his cross. That statement had been made of course before the gun had gone off and the youngsters scattered. From what he had been reading in the gospels as he prepared for his part in the film, this reminded Tadhg of the way the disciples of Jesus had scattered in the Garden of Gethsemane when he had been taken prisoner. None of those had come back in a hurry. What was the point now, he asked himself, was there about thinking he was some sort of a character in a film? He had to find a way of getting off his cross and getting out of there. There was always the chance that some hill walkers might come by and save him. On the other hand, they might just walk by at the other side of the trees. But they would not walk by unknown to him, he promised himself so he started to roar and shout at the top of his voice.

It would be one thing, Tadhg thought, when his shouts did not bring any result, was to die from a heart attack, but it would be awful to lose his life in such a stupid way. He roundly cursed Nicólás Dowling who had forced him to give up alcoholic drink so that he could take part in the film. He would give anything at that moment to be suiting by a pub fire anywhere in Ireland with a pint of Guinness in his hand. It wouldn't matter how dirty or ugly the bar was so long as they served nice black pints with creamy white tops. Using all the strength he could muster Tadhg made another effort to free his hands but soon found that he was just helping the ropes to tighten on his wrists.

For one second he thought a voice was answering his shouts, but he soon recognised the cry of a curlew. He had heard that same sound as a boy on his way home from school and went home and told his mother that a bird had called his name "Thai-agh, Thai-agh." It had reminded her of the story of Saint Patrick hearing a call to "come back and walk among us." It was seen as a vocation to be a priest and bishop, and his mother was more than open to him getting such a call. "Little did she think," Tadhg said to himself, "that her son would play the part of Jesus Christ in a film. That is if he doesn't die stupidly on a cross he fashioned himself." The nerves really began to jangle at that stage.

Tadhg had never thought of himself as being in any way a religious person, but he began to seek God's help with every fibre of his being. What else would a person do when his back was to the wall? He asked himself. Or in his case his back was to the cross? His back was to the ground. He screeched out the words Jesus had roared on the cross "My God, my God, why have you forsaken me?"

"Do not forsake me, O my darling," Tadhg shouted sarcastically. Then he switched to seeking mercy. "If you don't forsake me I will see that the crowd making this film do not make a mockery of all that you stand for, God and faith and forgiveness and all of that stuff. We will turn it into the greatest bit of propaganda ever produced on behalf of God and Jesus and the Holy Ghost or whatever they call him now. Not to speak of the Blessed Lady herself who took he dead son into her embrace which was to create the best piece of sculpture evet shaped, as the Pieta. "I will get Dowling to make his film as if he was a believer and not a cynic" he promised the darkening sky. "Can anyone hear me?" he roared.

Tadhg felt that neither God or man or woman was listening. "Fuck ye," he shouted "Fuck every single one of you. Go to fucking hell the lot of you." He felt at this stage that he had been forgotten completely by the young people that had tied him to his cross, or that they had not the courage to come back to set him free. By now little midges were tickling the skin of his face and he was unable to scare them off. He spat in the air in the hope that the spittle would fall back on his face to drown them, but if anything, it seemed to be drawing more of them onto him. He wondered could he deafen them or scare them by shouting. He began to roar again at the top of his voice but the lack of any kind of a response deepened his misery and discourage him even more..

"I wonder is it true that your whole life runs before you when you are dying?" Tadhg asked himself in his anger and despair. "Isn't that often said, but is it true. I should soon find out. On the one hand he felt strong enough to get through the rest of the day or even the night, but he was haunted by the thought "death from exposure." He asked himself "What have I done with my life? I have walked on many stages, acted in many plays, featured in a couple of films, married, divorced, a son and daughter that I have not seen in years." He wondered would they come to his funeral. A lump came to his throat as he remembered them as babies and children. But then he had just drifted away. He was then consumed by a great anger with his wife even though he knew in his heart that they were both responsible for the break-up.. He mixed curses, prayers and tears together as he called on God and man or woman to come and help him.

Tadhg gradually got some respite from the midges but something worse began to eat into his bones, the cold. The way in which the cold entered his bones reminded him of the way in which hot water enters a heating system when it is switched on, but it seemed as if the cold was somehow taking its revenge on him for something or other he had done wrong in an earlier life. He did not feel ready to pray for death at this stage, but it might be better than waiting for it for half the day. It would be a relief at that stage to let life slip away if that was in store for him.

There was one other plan even if it was a strange one that Tadhg thought he would try before he passed away. It was something that he had heard about years earlier that an Indian Shaman has used to send a message through his mind or consciousness to people he needed to contact, and most of all the young people who had wrapped themselves in plastic and hidden their faces who had left him there tied up and ultimately in danger of death. He had been told to always have his mobile phone with him when he went for a walk in the wood. What good was that now that his hands were tied to the cross? He would have to try anything and everything, no matter how stupid it seemed, to alert someone to his plight. There were about eight billion people in the world, he thought to himself, and not one of them was any good to him at that moment..

Tadhg thought that the girls or young women who had tied him up would be more soft-hearted than the young men. They had seemed reluctant to follow the other's instructions, which made him wonder why they had tied him so tightly. They were probably in some scouting or sailing group and good with ropes. Was that not true too about the women he had been reading about in the New Testament in preparation for the film? They were tough. They were brave. They went where the men other than John had not the guts to go. They were soft-hearted. Wasn't a woman, Veronica who had wiped the dust and dirt and spittle and probably the midges from his face? When he spoke to the "daughters of Jerusalem" he knew they were softer in their hearts than the boy soldiers pushing and kicking him up the hill.

How was he going to get his mind and emotions to reach out to those teenage girls?

Although those girls had looked to him earlier like scarecrows, he tried to address them through the evening air as he roared out. "Set me free in the name of God. Set me free in the name of Jesus fucking Christ." He corrected himself immediately. There was no point in insulting the very person you were asking to help you. "Set me free in the name of Jesus. I don't want to fucking die." He imagined his plea going first to the girl who had tied his left hand and then to the one who had secured his right. "In the name of God and the Blessed Virgin Mary, get me out of here safe and well."

"It is probably all a waste of time," Tadhg told himself as his voice fell on deaf or too far away ears. He tried to send a mind message to the girls first and then to the boys. Who would want to have it on their conscience that they had left a man to die on a lonely hill?. When he was visited by a big black Labrador dog that licked his face as if he had a taste for nudges he wondered was this real or was he losing his mind. The dog was very real, he felt when it lifted a hind leg and pissed on his shoulder. It was beginning to get dark and Tadhg hoped for a moment that the dog's owner was not far away. He shouted long and hard and all he succeeded in doing was to scare off the dog.

CHAPTER TWENTY-ONE

"Penny Lane" was the name the Migos used for the shed in which they practiced their music. Their parents had been Beatles fans all of their lives and it had taken the young people a long time to write or sing a song that did not in some way reflect the "Fab Four." They loved the group and played their music at every practice session but they were trying hard to develop a sound of their own. Their minds were far from their musical heroes as they came together in dribs and drabs on the evening they had abandoned Tadhg Ó Maoldomhnaigh in the wood after the unexpected gunshot scared them off. They had scattered in different directions before heading shamefacedly towards their shed.

"I am completely shagged," Eoin said. "I never in all of my life ran so hard or so fast as when the gun went off,."

Alan sat on a wooden bench by the table, before saying "We were here practising our music all evening as far as anyone else is concerned. We were practising for the Christmas show in the college."

"But we were not," his sister Eithne said. "I know that and you know that." There was silence in the shed for some time. It was Alan who spoke first. "The four of us have had great fun together down through the years and we have been through amazing stuff together. It all worked out great until today." He held up his hand "It was me who made the mistake. I should have checked the shotgun beforehand. Dad never before left a live cartridge in it. Maybe he is getting old and forgetful. But nobody died. I am sorry, but so far as anyone else is concerned we were here all evening practising out music."

Aisling said bluntly "We should have let that man in the wood go."

"I am sure he has managed to free himself by now," Alan said, looking at his watch. "That was hours ago and there always people walking the wood on a Sunday afternoon. Anyway, it would have been dangerous to loosen the ropes."

"Why?" Eithne asked.

"He could have beaten the shit out of us," was Alan's reply. "He is a big brute of a man."

"We could have loosened one hand," Eithne said, "and we would have been miles away by the time he loosened his other hand and his feel."

"We will stick to our story," Eoin said." We were here for the evening."

"We will pay for it one way or another," Eithne said regretfully.

"Listen to the queen of regret," Alan said. "I agree with Eoin. Stick to our story. We are all planning to go to University in a couple of years. Are we going to blow our chances in life because of one small mistake?"

"What if he dies out there in the wood, tied to a stupid cross?" Eithne asked.

"He won't die," Alan insisted. "If we are cute and stick together we will come through this. Look at it like this, I am not saying we never did anything wrong, but it was for a bit of fun. We were never caught. None of us has a black mark on our copybook. Nobody except ourselves knows that we were there today. Our own families even do not know. OK, we went too far today with our messing up that actor I accept that but are we going to ruin our futures because we messed up for once in our lives?"

"We need to free that man," was Aisling's blunt statement. "I never felt so bad in my life."

"That is because you are a snowflake," her brother said. "You need to harden up and not melt at every little crisis."

Eithne agreed with Aisling. "That poor man," she began, "We should get torches and go to the wood to find out if that man managed to get free, and to cut the rope from one hand if he didn't. That will give us time to run if he is dangerous. I tied my rope like you would be tying a boat to the pier. At the time I thought it was just a bit of fun."

We don't have a sharp knife and we don't have a torch," Eithne said. "And that man might be dangerous when we let him loose. He could be very angry and who could blame him? What if he tried to rape us or something like that"

"You are going over the top now," Eithne replied. "It will take him a while to even stand up if he is still there, and his back will be as stiff as a poker and he will have to free his other hand. We only have to loosen one hand and he can do the rest. We will be gone like the wind as soon as we cut the rope on one hand."

"Could we not just ring the police and say where he is?" Aisling asked.

Eithne was not so sure "I have my doubts about bringing the law into it If they find out it was us that did it we might never hear the end of it. The lads could be right about that. It could affect college and travelling to places like America if we still have a band in years to come."

"Are we making too much out of a prank that went wrong?" Aisling wondered. "It looks bad now, but it is not as if we were setting out to do damage to that poor idiot of an actor."

"Tell that to him lying there on the cross. If he is still there. What if he is found dead in the morning? I am going back to the house for a torch and a knife. Are you with me or me?"

"What about the lads?" Aisling asked. "They might have come to their senses after playing their music."

"They have washed their hands of it." Eithne answered. "It is something we need to do ourselves or we won't sleep a wink until we find out is he dead or alive"

"He is probably having a pint in the hotel at this very moment," Aisling said.

Eithne jumped to her feet "Let's go. We are out of here. We will cut the ropes off that man if it is the last thing we do."

"What will the oldies say if we go looking for a torch in the house at this time of the evening?"

"We are going for a walk in the fresh air. That is the truth."

"And the knife?"

"There is an old penknife of Eoin's in the drawer of the old dresser over there."

Aisling and Eithne walked closely together when they had collected the torch. They used the mobile phones to light the way too when they reached the forested area and began tripping from time to time on brambles and fallen branches. They virtually hung onto one another's shoulders as they made their way up Poteen Hill. They surprised and were surprised by a young deer that leapt out of the undergrowth and stood dazzled by their lights. It trotted ahead of them as if looking for a way to escape but at the same time did not want to leave the light.

"Everything looks different in the dark." Eithne seemed to be thinking out loud as she murmured the words.

"I hope we are not going to get lost too." was Aisling's comment. "Where exactly was that poor man on the cross?"

"Listen for a minute. We might hear him."

"Shouting or snoring?" Aisling asked, and suddenly they were laughing out loud with a mixture of tension and fear.

"Hang onto me, no matter what else," Eithne instructed.

"What if the light goes out on the torch?"

"What can we do except hang onto each other until morning"

As they moved along slowly stepping on and through the undergrowth, Eithne asked "Why are we whispering?"

"We don't want to disturb the wildlife or to be attacked by some wild thing."

"We could just walk by the man on his back on the cross without hearing a thing." Eithne said.

Aisling replied with a mixture of fear and black humour "We won't hear anything if he is dead."

Her companion roared out at the top of her voice "Jesus the actor, are you out there? We are here to help you."

"You put the heart crosswise in me there," Aisling commented. "If you go on like that you will waken the dead."

Eithne roared again "Jesus fucking Christ, where are you?"

"Don't say that. He doesn't like cursing. Isn't he supposed to be the son of God? You will just upset him."

"My Dad says that every five minutes" She shouted again "Jesus fucking Christ... Answer us. We are looking for you. We are sorry we tied you up. We will get you home if you tell us where you are."

"I bet he has got loose and that he is back in the village for hours," Aisling said. "I think we are wasting our time."

"Shut up," Eithne said suddenly. "I think I heard something.

"We are probably beginning to hallucinate"

Eithne shouted again "Jesus man! Actor! We don't know your name. Just give one more shout as loud as you can."

"He's over there," Aisling shouted and immediately tumbled on the undergrowth. Eithne helped her to stand up "I hope that there is nothing broken. That is the last thing we need."

When they reached Tadhg Ó Maoldomhnaigh he was sobbing with relief. "I never understood the word Godsend until now," he said. I was sure I was a goner"

"Will you attack us if we cut the ropes?" Aisling asked.

"What kind of fool do you think I am and the two of you after saving my life.? If I was not so old I would want to kiss you."

"We are sorry we didn't come earlier," Aisling said as she cut the rope from one wrist. "The gunshot frightened the life out of us."

"What happened the brave boys who were with you?"

"What boys?" Eithne asked. "We didn't see any boys."

"In other words, ask me no questions and I will tell you no lies." Tadhg said.

"They thought that a big strong man like you would free himself in no time." Was Eithne's reply.

"Was it in the scouts you learned to tie knots like that?"

"We have been messing with boats all our lives."

"Are you good to go now?" Aisling asked, "or do you want us to go on ahead?"

"Quite honestly, I don't know. I am not sure if I can even stand up. I am bound to be disoriented for a while. Go on ahead if you like. I will find my way later on. I have been looking up at the stars all night until now. I recognise the plough or the big dipper as they call it in the States and the North Star and a few others. I have seen enough shooting stars to last me a lifetime."

"Aren't they say those are souls going to Heaven?" Eithne asked.

"I was sure that I was going to be one of them, though I am not sure about the Heaven bit." By now Tadhg was sitting up massaging his wrists. "I would say that I am destined for the other side."

"Aren't you supposed to be able to rise from the dead?" Aisling asked.

"I couldn't even rise from this fucking cross," he answers, "with or without the ropes on my wrists. My back is aching me."

"Could we ring an ambulance or something for you?" Eithne asked.

"How would you explain how I got here?"

"We could be gone long before they get here," was Aisling's answer.

"Why don't the three of us try and make our way back to the village together?" Tadhg said.

"You probably want to beat the shite out of us," Eithne asked, "and we would well deserve it."

"I never hit a woman in my life, not even my wife and I can tell you that I was tempted. I am not going to attack a couple of girleens who have saved my life now."

"I am so delighted that we came back," Aisling said. "My conscience was at me all evening, even though everyone was saying you would manage to free yourself."

"You came because I called you," Tadhg said bluntly.

"How do you mean, called you?" Aisling asked.

"Don't come the heavy Jesus stuff on us now," Eithne said.

"It has nothing to do with Jesus as such," Tadhg answered, as he told the story of the Shaman that led him to try and make mind to mind contact between him and the girls.

"You are freaking us out now," was Eithne's comment. The girls were sitting at the end of the two arms of the cross and were, despite everything, enjoying the conversation.

"Will there be repercussions?" Aisling asked after a little while.

"The only cushion I am interested right now," Tadhg said. "Is to get my head on the pillow of that comfortable bed I have in the hotel. Tomorrow I will drink myself silly and forget all about it."

It was a long slow journey for Tadhg and the two girls to make their way downhill to the edge of the forest and along the road to the village. The actor walked the last couple of hundred yards to the hotel so that his companions would not be seen on CCTV. A middle-aged man slows on his feet being led by two young women would have aroused suspicions. As they parted Tadhg had said. "Thanks be to God and to his Blessed Mother and to all the angels and saints, to Allah and Jehovah and all the rest of them. And thanks to you two angels for coming back to rescue me. I will be forever grateful."

"Good luck with the film," the girls said. "It was the least we could do after treating you so badly."

"I don't give a fuck about the film," Tadhg answered. "I am going to drink myself silly and Nicólás Dowling can stick his part where the monkey stuck the nut. I am done with crosses and Jesuses from now on. It is just great to be alive, and it will be even better to be alive and kicking and drunk all at the same time."

Drunk he was later in the day when Nicólás Dowling approached him after hearing that he was "on the tear" in the hotel bar. He told Tadhg that he was no longer in the film, that he would collect his wages and go, before or after he got sober.

"Would you believe where I spent last night, Nicólás?"

"I couldn't care less."

"I spent it on the cross. My cross. Your cross. The cross of Christ. He told him what had happened, without drawing the 'Migos' into it, just referring to his attackers as "a crowd of yahoos."

"And your answer is to drink yourself to oblivion rather than telling the police?"

"I am a stranger in a strange land. I did not want to draw attention to myself, or to your film for that matter."

"Is this the truth or are you making it up?" Nicólas Dowling asked.

"I am smart but not that smart," was Tadhg's reply. "Shit happens, they say, and it certainly happened to me. I am out of here as soon as I get sober." He put an arm around the Producer's shoulder. "I can tell you one thing, Nicólas Dowling. It is great to be alive. I know now how Jesus felt when he came out of the tomb. Elated, happy, without a thought of the bad things that happened the night before. Or was it the night before that again? The bottom line is He got the fuck out of the grave."

Dowling looked him straight in the eyes "You still have the part you fucking idiot, but you need to get sober in the next two days or the part will go to someone else."

Tadhg tried to kiss him and Dowling pushed him away "Get off me you dirty fucker. And get sober.!"

CHAPTER TWENTY-TWO

Fr. Éamonn Ó Sé took a book from his bookshelf that he had not read since he was a student for the priesthood in Maynooth College. It had been written by a Spanish priest called Juan Arias with the title. "The God I don't believe in." It was not that he had no religious faith but the opposite. He was of the opinion that many people rejected religion not because they hated God, but because they had been given a false picture of what they referred to as their Saviour. "And who has given them that picture?" Fr. Ó Sé asked rhetorically, "but us, our church, every church or faith group that went over the top in portraying God as an old man in the sky just waiting on an opportunity to rain on everyone's parade and make life as difficult as possible for people."

Fr. Ó Sé wanted to sharpen his thoughts on religious matters before he would meet Nicólás Dowling or Edel Nic an tSaoir or Mary from the Mountain again. As far as he was concerned it was Jesus, Son of God who best represented the religion he himself stood for. Juan Arias in his book had a similar message. He was somewhat surprised that the film that was being mooted by Nicólás Dowling had slipped somewhat from public discourse in the previous week. It reminded him of waiting for a storm that did not come. He had been expecting that it would divide his community but it looked now as if the sting had been taken out of it. It was not that everyone was of one mind. Far from it, but it seemed as if that particular storm had blown itself out.

It was at a time like that the priest felt that his prayers and the prayers of the public at home or at Mass had been answered. As the Lord had said, "Blessed are the peacemakers and there was hardly a weekend that he repeated such a blessing on those who had brought peace, fragile as it was, to Northern Ireland and other places that had worked hard for an end to violence. For many years people would have thought praying was a waste of time, and then "peace came dropping slow" as WB Yeats had put it, even if that was not exactly what the great poet had meant. Even though the priest had known what "peace" and "process" had meant, he had not understood deep in his heart what exactly those two words together conveyed, a step by step approach, one step forward and two steps back at times, but coming to a fairly satisfactory solution in the end.

Fr. Ó Sé had learned much from his experiences on islands and the mainland how fragile peace could be. The same was true of people's relationships not to speak of the many inter-faith and inter-church difficulties. He had often felt that not even the United Nations would be able to solve the problems that even a small community or a family might throw up. There were such things too as problems that could not be solved. That was why he feared that problems that emanated from Nicólas Dowling's film would not blow his community apart. He raised his eyes jokingly to the picture of the Sacred Heart at the other side of the room. "Thank you for getting us through this week. Good man yourself. Keep up the good work."

The priest liked to speak to God in an easy-going way as someone would speak to a friend. He had always liked Old Testament stories in which God and Abraham spoke to each other like two man making a bargain at a fair. Not exactly spitting on your hand and slapping another similarly spitted hand as he had seen at fairs in his youth as they came to a resolution of the difference between two cattle jobbers.

It was on an Atlantic island that the priest had heard what was one of the most heartfelt prayers of his life. An old man at the back of the local church talked to God straight from his heart. He did not realise that anyone other than God was listening as the church building was empty. The priest however was in the sacristy preparing a sermon for the weekend Mass "Do you recognise me?" the old man asked God out loud, as he began a conversation in which he would do all the talking and imagine the answers.

Another example of the down-to-earth faith of his community came to mind as the thought of an old woman praying the stations of the cross: She had her own comments as she walked from picture to picture. As she came to the station on which Jesus is seen to fall for the third time, she spoke straight from the heart "Oh Jesus, you are down again." That was faith that saw God as one of the family.

Fr. Ó Sé's thoughts left memory lane when someone knocked at his front door. It was unusual to be disturbed so late in the evening without having received a phone call in advance. Some of his colleagues had been beaten and robbed in their homes down through the years and people generally had come to the conclusion that is was preferable not to disturb someone such as a priest living alone in case they were seen as easy targets who had collection money in their houses.

Mary from the Mountain was at the door and she blurted out "Did you hear that they are after crucifying a man up at the top of Poteen Hill? What are you going to do about it?"

The priest invited her to come inside and he asked her would she like to have a drink as she was obviously in shock.

Mary looked at the bottle of brandy on the table in the office and asked "Do you think that the drink is the answer to everything?"

"Tell me who has been crucified? Who crucified him? Is he still on the cross?" He did not know what he should say.

"That big fat actor that was brought in to play the part of Our Lord, even though he doesn't look one bit like him. They tell me that the poor man has a bit of a problem with the deink."

"Where is that actor now?" the priest asked, "Were the police called? Is he still nailed to the cross?"

"I'm told he is in the hotel throwing back pints of Guinness like it was going out of fashion."

The priest was trying to understand what exactly Mary was telling him "When you tell me the man was crucified, do you mean he was nailed to the cross?"

"How do I know? I was not there, but I am told that there are bandages on his hands like poor Saint Padre Pio used to wear. I doubt he is doing miracles though, with the way they say that he is drinking."

The priest asked as if talking to himself: "How have things come to this?"

"It is people like me that are getting the blame," Mary from the Mountain said, "Because we took a stand against their rotten film."

The priest tried to ease her worries "Everyone knows you were not there with a hammer and nails crucifying him."

"I was against the film from the start," Mary said, "as you well know from the meeting of the pastoral Council. Maybe I went a bit too far and that I gave out too much anger, but you know yourself how people get worked up."

"It would be a funny old world if everyone was of the same opinion," was the priest's answer.

"Edel Nic an tSaoir is after telling me that she is turning her coat and taking part in the film," Mary said.

"You mean the girl from that right-wing paper in Dublin?"

"You met her here Father when she came down first to supposedly check out Dowling and his film, she has taken the shilling and gone over to the opposition"

"That is a turn up for the books. They must have made her an offer she couldn't refuse."

"I could tell you what the offer was, father, but it is not something I could say in polite society like yourself."

"I am a man of the world, Mary. Try me."

"She was seen coming out of a room in the hotel the other morning."

"I thought it was staying with you she was?" the priest answered.

"They used to talk in the old days of politicians turning their coats. It looks as if the bold Edel has turned more than that. As far as I know they offered he the part of Mary Magdalene and now herself and the fellow playing Judas have become what is called an item. They are well net, the pair of them."

"I don't believe every rumour that goes around," the priest said.

"Isn't' it you that is innocent, Father. There is no smoke without fire.

"It's a free country, even if some of us wish it was different."

"The priests that came before you had very different attitude than you have."

"That was then, and this is now."

Mary from the Mountain answered "Not many of them went astray the way lots of clergy have in recent years. Most of them were held in high regard in their communities because they preached the gospel straight out with none of the shilly shalleying we get nowadays."

"I don't understand what you are getting at there, Mary." the priest said.

"Saying the things that will make them popular instead of good old-time religion is what I mean. Trying to be great with everyone. Talking about "him and her, he and she" as if people were stupid. As they used to say in the old days "man embraces woman" in the Bible. You don't have to mention both of them all the time."

"It looks like men still embrace women," the priest joked.

"And there are lots of them embracing other men as well from what I hear.

And there is no need to make a laugh out of everything just to try and make yourselves popular. We need serious priests and not stand-up comedians in the clergy. Religion is a serious business."

"You can't please everyone all the time," said the priest. "By the way do you think that God has a sense of humour?"

"He would certainly need to have," Mary said, "with the way the world is going these times." She sat into an armchair as if she was there for the long haul. "Now Father, what are you going to do about this film Dowling is trying to make in spite of the rest of us?"

"As I said earlier, it is not really any of my business. It is a fee country whether we like it or not. I am happy to wait until it is finished and look at it then before giving my opinion."

"Yourself and your opinion," Mary answered as if she had completely lost all trust in her Parish Priest, but was hoping he might change his mind if she pressed him hard enough. "What about the scandals that film is about to cause in your parish?"

"Scandals? What scandals?"

"I have already mentioned Edel who has obviously thrown her principles out the window. And then there is Margie in the Post Office who is going at it hammer and tongs with Nicólás Dowling. And that is only the half of it. What else is going on unknown to us?" She stopped suddenly before asking the priest. "Have I said something funny? You seem to be having a laugh behind your hand?"

"Sorry Mary. My mind just wandered for a moment."

"It would help if you concentrated when someone is making a serious point, Father. I can't be repeating myself all night."

"I was just thinking of the strange rumours that go around about people, and how they start, or how do people find out about them. I hope that there are not others in the room when a couple is going hammer and tongs as you put it yourself"

Mary from the Mountain answered more in sorrow than in anger. "You are such an innocent, Father. This stuff is going on all around you night and day and you don't have a clue. It is happy for you, in a way."

The priest replied with a question "What will people think, Mary if they see you leaving this house in the darkness of night? Will people be saying the same about both of us as you are hearing about other people."

"They would know instinctively that was not the case and that neither of us would look at each other in that kind of a way."

The priest was tempted to say jokingly that he found her attractive but after the earlier lecture about trying to be funny, he held his tongue except to say "I know what you mean, Mary."

Mary tried to clarify what she had said earlier "I was not talking about you personally, Father, because I see you as a priest and not as a man. I have too much respect for God's representative on earth than to think of you other than as a priest, even if I do not always agree with you."

Fr. Ó Sé could not help laughing "I am safe so, Mary, thanks be to God."

Mary looked him severely in the eyes "Not everything in this life is a laughing matter."

"If we didn't have a laugh from time to time, we would be crying all of the time, Mary."

Mary made her own effort at a joke as she got up to go home "It is coming on to midnight. It is time for Cinderella to go to the party."

"I hope you meet your Prince Charming," the priest said, "or am I mixing up the fairy stories?"

CHAPTER TWENTY-THREE

Nicolás Dowling called together a meeting of his actors, camera crew and advisors in the local hotel. He announced that work on the film would commence the following week. This was of course in addition to the preliminary work that had been proceeding for weeks as actors had got into their characters and extras were interviewed and prepared for their parts. "As usual money has been slow in coming in despite being contracted for some time, but we are now in a position to let the cameras roll."

Edel Nic an tSaoir raised her hand and Dowling gave her a signal to make her point "A small question, not as a journalist so much as an actor. What, if any part is the Tourist Board, known as Bord Fáilte playing in this production?"

"They expect, and it would seem they are right in that regard, that this film will be shown all over the world and that it will have the kind of influence that films such as 'The Quiet Man' or 'Ryan's Daughter' which were filmed in the west of Ireland had in days gone by. That basically of course, is none of our business, but if it brings in millions of dollars and euros in revenue for this part of the country, none of us will complain." The Film Director noticed that Óran Breathnach had his hand in the air and he beckoned to him to speak.

"Now that you have mentioned money, those of us who are not millionaires would like to know when are we going to be paid?" A ripple of laughter went around the room that ended in a round of applause. Óran continued "We are here a couple of months now, and although food and other beverages as well as our room expenses have been covered, there are such things as mortgages, direct debits and other matters that need to be looked into as a matter of urgency."

"All of those matters will be brought up to date," Dowling said, "now that the monies from the Film Board have come into our coffers. Everyone will be paid to date by the time the cameras are rolling."

Tadhg Ó Maoldomhnaigh interjected jovially "We will all be rolling in it then, I hope." He went on "What about danger money? I have been crucified already and according to the script that we don't have, I am due to be hung out to dry again one of the days."

Nicólas Dowling answered in the same kind of joking mood "I presume that you will be able to rise from the dead the next time as well." He then went on to outline his plans for the film. "As those who have worked with or for me in the past we will not start at the beginning, but at the end. "The Last Supper" will for instance be the first supper as it leads to betrayal by Judas and denial by Peter. So-called friends of Jesus are falling like ninepins. Apostles and disciples are shitting themselves as the whole Jesus-myth breaks down and they find themselves being left to their own devices. Herod is mocking. Pontius Pilate is washing his hands. The young Roman soldiers are caught up in a drama not of their own making. By contrast the crucifixion and death are like a bit of a walk in the park. Everything is predictable except the so-called resurrection.

"What do you mean so-called?" Margie from the Post Office asked. "Even an atheist like me believes in that, or how else did the church find its way back?"

"All of that is up for grabs. As most of you know already we will be thinking it through as we go along."

"It sounds like not knowing your arse from your elbow," Tadhg Ó Maoldomhnaigh said, "not knowing the chicken from the egg, and we are supposed to work it all out for ourselves. I have heard of 'the never-ending story', but this looks like it is taking the biscuit altogether."

"We will work our way backwards from resurrection and crucifixion to the public life of Jesus"

"What about his private life?" Tadhg Ó Maoldomhnaigh asked. "We don't really know anything about that."

"And you won't learn it here either," was Nicólás Dowling's reply. "We will not speculate, just stick to the evidence."

"You mean guesswork from a couple of hundred years later?" Tadhg said. "All that is there before that is guesswork and gospels attributed to Matthew, Mark, Luke, and John. Why are they all so different from each other?"

"Because they were written for different audiences," Dowling replied, "Greek, Jew, Aramaic speakers, written by some scholarly men and others like Mark who never wasted a word or polished a sentence."

"Are we going to spend the day speculating?" Edel Nic an tSaoir asked, "or are we going to get on with the job in hand? I am all for telling it like it is, rather than trying to impress scholars, many of whom are only guessing anyway."

"Thank you, Edel," Nicólás Dowling said. "I am glad you decided to join us and put your own acting training and ability at our disposal by taking the part of Mary who is named at the very end of the Bible stories as being there on what became known as Ascension Thursday. It is a name I remember from my youth when I was, believe it or not, a Mass server.'

Edel raised her right hand and when she got Dowling's attention, and said. "They have dropped the words Ascension Thursday in recent times because the church felt there were too many holidays of obligation, so the feast is celebrated on the following Sunday."

"That crowd really know how to magic things," Tadhg interjected, "like putting a Thursday on a Sunday. Is it any wonder they have lost their way? Next thing we will have Easter Sunday on a Monday to suit the crowd that make Easter eggs."

"We need to stick to the point," Dowling said, "or we will be here all day. We need to get on with what we are here for. Let us get back to Ascension Day which is where the Jesus story about the man himself ends when he is, as Tadhg might say, magic up to heaven. In other words, Jesus has left the building."

"I thought we were supposed to stick to the Bible," Edel said.

"I did say that I would start at the end of the Jesus story, and I have just described how it ended according to my edition of the Bible, this is what happened forty days after the so-called resurrection."

"What do you mean, so-called?" Edel asked.

"Just let him continue," Óran said. "We will get into the niceties later. There will be time for questions I am sure when the plan for the film has been outlined."

"Look at it like this," Dowling said. "Supposed Jesus had enough of it after all that had happened to him and that he wanted out. He still wanted the good things he had started to continue, but someone who was an organiser was needed for that. Someone to organise the rabble of good-hearted but disorganised fishermen of great faith for the most part that had followed him and kept the show on the road for three years. Saul of Tarsus fitted that bill. They won him over, came up with the Damascus story. Paul became the new Jesus without the long hair and the beard but a tongue on him that could melt stones when he started to talk. They didn't need a stable in Bethlehem, an ox and an ass to launch Paul. He came along on his pony spouting gospel in all directions."

"I never heard such bullshit in my life" Edel Nic an tSaoir said. "How did they get rid of Jesus, the innocent fool from your point of view?"

"He returned to Nazareth," Tadhg Ó Maoldomhnaigh said and cynically, "and he spent his life making bread, as well as crosses for the Roman army in his carpentry worship. There is no better man than yourself Nicólas to invent a story, but I can tell you now that this Jesus will not be handing on the baton to any Saul or Paul of Tarsus."

"That is the great thing about imagination," Nicólas Dowling said. "We can go in any direction we want."

"What about going in the direction of truth?" Edel Nic an tSaoir asked.

"The very question Pontius Pilate asked Jesus," Dowling said. "What is the truth? What I have been doing up to now this morning is throwing around different scenarios. Of course, I am not going to follow any of those, but I would humbly suggest that I have got you thinking."

"Thinking you are crazy," commented Tadhg.

"OK," Dowling said, "so I was sending some things up, but there are those who would say the ascension of Jesus was the greatest send-up of all time. I am not saying that here, just appealing for open and imaginative minds. What is it the man himself, Jesus used to say at the end of many of his parables or stories. Let those who have ears hear." To my mind that is just saying "Make up your own mind. I am not asking any of you to stray from the gospel story as you enter your characters, but keep an open mind, see some things differently even if you do not agree them or go down that particular road."

Edel shrugged her shoulders "Say what you like but it will not be easy or not be possible maybe, to send Mary the Mother of God in a different role. I certainly have no intention of going down that road."

"This is cow creativity works," Dowling said, "probing and questioning, arguing and becoming angry and fighting sometimes, without violence, of course. There is no harm in it as such, at least unless we start knifing each other.." He continued. "That is why we don't do everything in this case one after another as they are in the Bible. Sometimes it comes down to who is available on the day or what great epiphany someone had overnight. The crucifixion may come before the trial, for instance, but that adds to the tension. It helps to make you the actors or me the Director think more deeply about what we are doing."

"And you will be able to put your own slant on it at the end of the day?" Edel commented.

"Why shouldn't I?" Dowling asked half joking and half seriously, "after the Apostles and the Evangelists putting their own shape on it for the past two thousand years or so."

Tadhg Ó Maoldomhnaigh stood up said he wanted to share what he had learned from his experiences the previous weekend when he had felt close to death on his own cross. "I have this much to say," he said, "after what I felt in the loneliness that is part of expecting to die for no apparent reason on a cross of my own making. It is no laughing matter. I am and I have always been agnostic with regard to religion. I have to some extent kept a foot in each camp as I am sure have thousands or maybe millions of others. In some ways we are neither for it or against it but are caught in that halfway house. On the one hand I have a great time for the Nazarene, whether he is man or God or both, but hate a lot of those who claim to speak on his behalf. I don't need to relive the scandals of child-abuse or the terrible treatment of so many women for any of you. I understand what Nicólás Dowling is trying to do here today as he raises questions right, left, and centre about Jesus and about religion. He is not trying to hurt or upset believers or look on them as stupid idiots as some in the so-called national media do a lot of the time. He wants to look at the other side of the story as well." This much I will say "I am not a betting man but I would wager that not one person in this room will have more or less faith when this film is made than they have today. It is not that easy to change minds to sell people dummies."

"I fully agree with the last speaker, Tadhg isn't it" Edel Nic an tSaoir said.

"As a journalist I am aware that many involved in the national media and the art world in this country have a hatred of religion. They don't have any interest in my opinion in dealing with it in any way except to mock or condemn it. I don't agree with Nicólás Dowling on many issues but at least he has the courage to deal with religion in an honest way even if that questions it or raises issues with regard to it. It is pathetic to see so many self-styled liberals fail to see any value in religion even for people other than themselves. Jesus spoke of 'whited sepulchres' back in his time, but that is really what some of our so-called liberals are."

"Everyone here is entitled to their opinion," Nicólás Dowling joked, "but of course I don't agree with any of them."

Tadhg took to the floor again "It seem to be hogging the conversation, but then again I am the only one here that has nearly died for the cause this week. We all know that Hollywood called the film we are planning here. 'The Greatest Story Ever Told.' He might be right and he might be wrong, but there is no doubt but it is one of the most often told story in this world, on screen, in church or in schools. We are offering to retell it in our own way. What a challenge. We have a job to do and let us do it to the best of our abilities."

"Let us all agree about that, if nothing else," Nicólás Dowling said as he announced a break for lunch.

CHAPTER TWENTY-FOUR

Margie from the Post Office was keeping a close eye on the "Migos" as they called themselves as they wandered slowly about in the grocery part of her building.

She had always thought of them as mannerly sensible children as they grew up down through the years. Now that they were teenagers she was wary of them as she was of everyone of that age. Sweets and fruit were within easy reach and were open to be stolen by anyone with a less than honest disposition. She could not keep an eye on everyone who came in or out, particularly when she was occupied with pensioners collecting their weekly income. The CCTV system was her biggest fall back but she could not be watching it all the time. There were nights when she would not even look at it after work because she was tired, or in some cases when she did nit was clear that nothing untoward had happened all day..

She was surprised when Alan asked her "Do you like to watch yourself on the screen?"

"Do you mean the CCTV screen?" Margie asked. "That is for everyone else but me. I look in and they look out so I am not captured on it myself except on rare occasions."

"It is not the only screen around," Alan answered. "There are much more interesting things happening on other screens."

"What are you talking about? Are you on drugs or something?"

"Only on the love drug. Like yourself."

"What are you talking about?"

"I have seen you in action. Having it off with that Dowling guy. I am not complaining. It certainly made my night. You don't just sell lollipops. You sure know how to suck them as well."

"You are gross," Margie said. "You were so nice when you were growing up, and now you are just nasty."

"Do you fancy me? I hear you used to have a big crush, if that is the word, on young fellows who used to work here. Now you have a crush on that old fellow in the film, I thought you were literally going to crush him with your fat arse when you got up on him."

"I am going to tell your mother and father what a nasty little bollocks you are." Margie said.

"And if you do I will show them the footage of yourself and that Dowling fellow going at it hammer and tongs."

"It is a free country," was Margie's reply, "and there are such things as rules of privacy."

"Are you going to call the police now? They will really enjoy that piece of footage. It might even put them off their doughnuts while they are drooling over it." Alan did not wait for a reply. He picked up a box of sweets as he headed towards the door.

"You haven't paid for that," Margie said half-heartedly after him.

"Charge it to Dowling for film expenses."

"What are you looking for?" Margie angrily asked another of the "Migos," Eithne, who was wandering around the shop.

"Nothing in particular. Just a few sweets and drinks for a party we are organising. You can put the sweets Alan took on the slate. He was in a hurry so he will see you again."

"Not if I see him first," Margie said. "You can tell him that he is barred.

"Okey dokey," Eithne answered casually.

Margie moved away. "I will be in the Post Office area for a while. If you need anything, call me." Before moving away, she asked Eithne. "Is it somebodies' birthday or something that you are having a party?"

"We are just having a bit of a blow-out in Penny Lane."

"Penny Lane?" Margie asked "Doesn't that have something to do with a Beatles song?"

"That is what we call the shed in which we practice our music. So that we do not disturb the oldies. Our parents, I mean."

"A good plan," Margie said. "Enjoy it."

Alan had not left the building but just waited behind the front door. When Margie went into the Post Office section he returned and started to put items, including alcoholic drinks into a shopping basket.

"What are you doing?" Eithne asked. "We don't have enough money to pay for all of that."

"The Red Bull drink will make us fly. Isn't that what the adverts say? We will just fly out the door."

"Margie will have it all on CCTV."

"So, what?" Alan said. "I have a way of paying for it."

"You have just won the lotto?" There was deep irony in Eithne's voice.

"In a sense I have," said Alan. "Did Margie stop me when I took the sweets? No way. We have the whip hand over her. She can't do anything to us without bringing the footage we took of herself and Dowling and herself having it off into the public arena as they say. We have both of them over a barrel."

"That is what they call blackmail," Eithne replied.

"But are they going to let the guards and the whole country see it? That is why we did not go viral with it at the beginning. We just showed a clip or two. That full frontal stuff can be rolled out at any time."

"Parents will be delighted," Eithne said sarcastically.

"Who is going to tell them it is us?"

"I might, or Aisling might," Eithne said.

"Both of you are as guilty as Eoin and myself."

"We are the ones that went to save that man's life that the two of you were prepared to leave to die on his stupid cross."

"What has that to do with anything?" Alan asked.

"We did the right thing," Eithne said. "That is what it is about."

"Look here Goody Two-shoes," Alan said. "Just walk out of here and You will be off the hook. I will sort out the rest with Margie.

"I am on CCTV," Eithne said.

"You think you are, but I disconnected it when I was down there behind the door. Just go. You do your thing and I will do mine."

Eithne shook her head in frustration and walked out.

Alan called out to Margie when he has hidden the alcoholic drinks inside his coat. "Could you come here for a minute, Margie?"

She felt that Alan was being deliberately bad mannered, but that was not unexpected in dealing with some teenagers, especially when they wanted to show off to others. She checked out the items in the basket. "I won't charge you for the plastic bag but you will need one to carry the stuff."

"Everything is free today," Alan said.

"How do you mean?" Margie asked.

"No film footage of yourself and Dowling on line. No charge at the counter. Those are the new rules" Alan said.

"You must be joking?"

"I won't be greedy. Just a few items like this from time to time. I will not be doing the week's shopping for my mother or anything like that because it costs well over a hundred euros. Just a few items here and there between ourselves."

"Just wait there," Margie said as she took her phone from her pocket. "I need to clear this with the police."

"I don't think so," Alan said, "unless you want to see your well-shaped backside all over the world this evening."

"I will tell your parents, you nasty little brat."

"Hold the wagon, Margie. Do you want my mother to see that lovely piece of white pudding you had in your pretty little mouth? And a fine piece of meat it was. Don't they say Dowling's prick is hung like a donkey?"

"This is blackmail," Margie said. "You won't get away with it."

"It is just an arrangement that nobody else needs to know about."

"What if I tell Nicólas Dowling?"

"I couldn't imagine him to be very pleased seeing that the work is about to start on his film from what I hear. By the way we did offer our services as musicians to him, but we have not heard anything back yet.

"Would you lay off me?" Margie asked, "if your band was allowed to do something in the film?"

"That is not the worst plan in the world at all, Margie," Alan said.

"You would have to destroy the footage you took."

"That could be arranged for a fee."

"This is the fee," Margie pushed his purchases across the table.
Don't lose the run of yourself. Be thankful for small mercies."

"You are beginning to sound like my mother now." Alan took his goods and went back to "Penny Lane."

When Margie locked up soon afterwards she sat for a long time thinking over what had just happened. Her mind was in a spin. How could she even share what had happened even with Nicólás Dowling when he returned after his meetings? She had never been too sure what the phrase "catch 22" meant, but she knew that she was caught in a bind from which she would be able to extract herself without losing whatever dignity she had left. She asked herself why should she be ashamed of what had happened in what was supposed to be her private life, but had been spied on by a group of kids. It was none of their business, none of anyone's business, but who wanted what they got up to in their bedroom splashed all over the media or shown in Tabloid newspapers.

What would the pensioners she dealt with in the Post Office every day think of it? Would they be able to look her in the face? Would they take the bus to collect their pensions somewhere else? It was not that anyone thought she was a saint. They were well aware of the young men who had stayed with her during summer holidays, but that was her private life. This was about to be public.

"Most of all the pensioners liked her and trusted her," Margie thought. Didn't Tom Dharach tell her he loved the look of her. Even Mary from the Mountain who was not easy to please trusted her with money and with sensitive transactions to do with property or matters to do with members of her family who had emigrated. Down through the years she was used to hearing people use the phrase. "Soon it will all blow over." Well this would not blow over easily. It had only just started.

Mary from the Mountain was Margie's next customer after lunch, the lunch she did not have because her stomach was in knots.. Mary was in high good humour because of the part her friend, Edel Nic an tSaoir had landed in "Nicólás's film" as she put it. There was talk that she herself might get a small part as one of the women at the foot of the cross as Jesus died, she had been talking with the priest and he had told her that the film would not be nearly as controversial as people had said that it would. "Isn't Fr. Éamonn Ó Sé a great man all the same," she said. "He knows how to take the sting out of a situation that is getting out of hand. There are times you would think that he does nothing from morning to night except to say the odd Mass here and there, but he has his finger on the pulse all of the time. He does more by being quiet and easy-going, putting in the odd good word here and there than many of the old pulpit thumpers ever did with all of their shouting and roaring. He may not have built any mansions or churches, nor for that matter an Airport like Monsignor Horan did long ago, but his heart is in the right place all the same. If he stays around long enough he could even become one of our own the way that you have yourself, Margie. Despite what anyone says."

Margie got on with her work without commenting as she had more than enough on her own mind. She had never heard Mary so fulsome in her praise of herself, the priest or anyone else. She allowed the talk in one ear and out in the other as she signed documents and paid out Mary's pension in the usual way even though her mind was elsewhere. "Have a good day, Mary. I am delighted to see you in such great form."

Mary was in such good form that she even included Nicólas Dowling in her praises before she left the Post Office. "It is great to see that the film is starting at last and that it brings loads of tourists to the area."

"That is great," Margie answered, "but you can see yourself that there is a queue at the counter waiting for their pensions."

Margie even hurried Tom Dharach who always dallied for a chat. He drew attention to his rheumatism and the pain he had in his side from time to time. "The best thing you can do," Margie said, "is to go to the Health Centre tell the nurse or the doctor all about your pain." She organised the money he was due from his pension, put it into his hand and said. "Have a good day now, Tom."

Tom was not ready to move from the counter yet. "I will go to the Health Centre, but I am afraid that the doctor will find there is something wrong with me."

"Isn't that what he is there for, Tom. You managed to come through Covid and many another scare before now, so there can't be too much wrong with you. It could be arthritis or something like that, but the doctor is the one to tell you that."

"I am afraid that I might be sent into that Nursing Home back the road," Tom said. "Sure there are people dying in there?"

"That is actually one of the cleanest and healthiest places in the country," Margie replied. "You could eat your dinner off the floor there."

"I would prefer to have my dinner at my own table any day of the week."

Margie was getting impatient "Do what you have to do, Tom, but there is a queue of people behind you there waiting for their pensions."

"I know that, Margie. Sure, you have your own troubles."

"What do you mean by that, Tom?" Margie asked. "What troubles are you talking about? Don't believe every bit of gossip you hear."

The question surprised Tom and it took him a while to answer "I'm not sure what you mean. I was just making talk to pass the time. To tell you the truth I have no idea what women's troubles are. I was never married or anything like that. I have heard that women can be a bit contrary from time to time."

Margie gave a little laugh despite the worries that were gnawing at her after her experiences with Alan. "You are right about the contrary bits, but if I was ever contrary with you, I apologise. You are a lovely man. Always were and always will be, but I need to get on with things now."

"You are lovely yourself, Margie, and you have a lovely face. It eases my heart every time I come in for pension or to do a bit of shopping for the dinner. I just love to look at your handsome face."

A thousand thanks to you, Tom. You have no idea how much I appreciate what you have said. Whatever age you live to, keep saying things like that to women. Because we all need a bit of a lift sometimes."

"I can't tell every woman I meet that she is lovely, because I was always taught never to tell a lie. God bless and save you, Margie."

"I need every blessing I can get," she replied as Tom moved away from the counter. Some in the queue that replaced him commented on what a lovely man he was, "lovely to the point of innocence," as one woman put it.

Margie got on with her work, dispensing pensions, selling stamps, taking payments for electricity and phone bills, lodging money for people now that the Mobile Bank did not visit the area anymore because of the cutbacks that had closed up to half the Banks in the country.

As the evening wore on and some children came in for sweets, ice cream, or drinks on their way home from school, Margie began to worry that Alan might turn up seeking more goods for free. He had given the impression that his mini-blackmail the previous evening was a once-off, but who knew how greedy he might get after getting away with it once.

"I wonder has Nicólas come out of his meeting yet," Margie asked herself as the pressure eased at the Post Office counter when most of the pensions were paid out. Most of the older people came early to collect what was due.. She wondered was it because what they had received the previous week was barely enough to meet their needs, or did the regular Post Office raids by criminal gangs in earlier years lead people to worry that there would be no money for them when they got to the counter. Life really meant living on their wits for many people.

"Margie," Nicólas said when he saw her name and picture on his phone. He sounded in high good humour so his meetings must have gone well, she thought. She asked him was he finished work for the day. He began to talk of what good meetings he had, what Tadhg or Edel or Óran had said, what a positive vibe was about the place compared with previous weeks.

"We are in trouble, Nicólas." Margie said.

"You mean you are pregnant?" was his reply.

"Don't be an idiot. I am not that stupid. It is bigger trouble than that, though."

"I did think abortion straight away. It is easy now, but can have long-term effects."

Margie answered coldly "At least I know how you stand on that issue."

"What can be as bad or worse than that?"

Margie told him about Alan, his blackmail and other threats. "We are going to be outed in front of the whole world. Not to speak of the effect it will have on your film and reputation in general."

"We had a roll in the hay. Some fool filmed it. Who cares? It is not as if I have a squeaky-clean image anyway. I thought everyone knew about that already. It is months since it happened."

"It seems they were holding the footage back in order to have an impact when the film was being made."

"The little prick," Dowling said "Is it just one of that group that is in on this or are all four involved?"

"It is hard to know," Margie answered. "I got the impression that he was peeved because they did not get an interview to be extras in the film."

"That would not be an issue if those kids surrendered the film footage. We will want soldiers and hangers on for the Calvary scenes."

"It does sound like giving in to blackmail."

Tadhg seemed to be impressed by the two girls that cut the ropes on the cross and probably saved his Tadhg's life that night. "There might be an opening there to split up that little group."

"Divide and conquer, the oldest trick in the book," Margie commented.

"We need all the tricks that are going right now. I will work on it. We can offer them something to soften their cough. I hear that they play some kind of crazy music. There may be an opening there."

Margie said "That Alan is some operator, He scared me a bit."

"That little prick needs a good kick in the arse. I will deal with that down the line, but for now we should aim at getting the film footage onto the fire."

"From what I have heard they have not shared much of it online so far. That is not to say that they have not passed it around among their peers at secondary school, Margie said.

"If they had, some parent or teacher would probably have copped it. Or some people would be staring at us a bit more than they are" was Nicólas Dowling's opinion.

Margie answered "The threat is the worst part of it. In some ways I wish they would just put it up online and be done with it. We would have to take a bit of flack for a while, but people would get over it."

"I am sure that it is no worse than some of the porn that half the country is watching in their homes without batting an eyelid," Nicólas suggested.

Margie was not too sure about that: "Oh yes," she said sarcastically. "That was what I have always wanted. To be a porn star."

"You would be good at it," Dowling laughed. "Even if you say so yourself."

"I can tell you right now that is not funny" Margie said. "Another thing I am worried about is that I could be charged with supplying alcoholic drink to kids."

Dowling asked "You mean you let him have booze?"

"There was none in the shopping bag but there is some of the Red Bull missing from the shelves."

"I am sure it can be proved that was stolen."

Margie said "It is alright for you, Nicólás, but I have to live here. You will be gone as soon as the film is completed."

"You could come with me."

"Where?" she asked.

"Everywhere. My work takes me all over the place."

"My life is here now, that is if the locals don't decide to give me the road."

"All of this will be over in no time at all," Dowling told her. "It is like any other emergency. Nine days wonder or maybe not even half that."

"I would miss some of the people. They are part of my life now." Margie told him some of the things that Tom Dharach had said about her. "I was embarrassed with all the other customers lined up for their pensions, but it was nice all the same."

"Who age is this admire?" Dowling asked jokingly "He has me worried. What age is he?"

"I actually checked that on his pension book. Seventy-nine next birthday."

"I should be able to fight that fellow to get you from him."

"It is not the fight that works for me," she said, "just the silver tongue."

"The tongue must have been the start of our troubles."

"I am referring to the spoken word, the sweet words that come from some tongues."

"That is all well and good," Nicólás Dowling said, "but we have a film to make. But I feel like of getting hold of that cameras those kids have and smashing it."

"Youngsters would not forget to make a copy, or twenty or thirty of them, one for everyone in the classroom maybe."

"What gives me some hope," Dowling replied, "is that those children, and they are still children in the eyes of the law, have fathers and mothers and teachers. I am pretty sure that they would not want their parents looking at that footage if they knew it was their kids that had filmed it."

"I would not like to see it either," Margie had a touch of despair in her voice. "Even though I would consider myself a woman of the world."

"Why didn't we just pull the bloody blinds or curtains or whatever they are? asked Dowling."

"You should put that question to your stiff prick. Isn't there some phrase that that part of the anatomy has no conscience? We have to deal with reality, not what might have been. Would there be any point in approaching their parents? Margie asked."

"The problem I see to that," Dowling answered, "is that we would be exposing ourselves in more ways at once to the parent's anger, and right now they don't need to know anything about it if we can come up with a better plan. Parents or police or teachers, no, I would say. A bit of quiet diplomacy, yes."

"It might be a good plan," Margie suggested, "to bring the priest into it. Are they not supposed to keep secrets?"

"With respect, I would see that would be the worst thing in the world to do. Do you want to have the poor man going around with a horn on him for the rest of the month after looking at the two of us in action?"

"He is not a bad person," Margie said. "He seems openminded and understanding. I have heard him from time to time giving sermons. Not that I am in the church apart from Christmas and the odd funeral. He seems to have his head screwed on and the people I meet in the Post Office think highly of him."

"Leave the clergy out of it. Leave the police out of it. Leave God out of it," was Nicólás Dowling's advice. "At least until we have time to think it through and get a better handle on things."

"Time is passing and Alan is getting itchy feet. You would never know what he might get up to next."

"You know him. I don't. He might think he is calling the shots, but if its money he is after or a place in the film he actually needs us. OK, he could ruin us by putting the footage that he has online, but if he does that he can say goodbye to money or booze or anything else as far as the shop is concerned. I think he needs us more than we need him and that is not a bad bargaining position."

"You are thinking of offering him money?" Margie asked.

"That, or maybe a bit part in the film."

"What kind of a part?"

"Nothing serious, so long as it makes him think he is a film star, a spear-carrier in the Roman army maybe."

"It will make the others jealous if he gets a part and they don't."

"Divide and conquer," was Dowling's answer to that. What matters most is that he hands over that footage or destroys it in front of me."

Margie questioned that "What about copies?"

"We will have to take a chance on that one. The main thing right now is to get over the immediate panic. He can be threatened with arrest for stealing alcohol from your shop if he pushes things too far."

"He will, of course deny it"

Dowling answered "As American President Lyndon Johnson said in a more serious context. Just watching him denying it, he will tie himself in knots doing so, and it is probably on CCTV anyway."

They left it like that as both had to return to work. Margie was still worried, but less so than earlier. The last thing she wanted was to have turned the community against her and she promised herself that it would not happen again.

CHAPTER TWENTY-FIVE

Tom Dharach had no idea what was wrong with him. He had pains where he never had pains previously. He could not understand why he felt so bad ever since he had come back from collecting his pension. He bent down to give a drop of milk to his cat, Síbín. As he straightened up he felt a lot of pain in his chest area. He then felt as if there was something heavy inside one part of his head. For some reason the sight of his cat reminded him of what customers used to say in the pub when he announced that it was time for him to go home. "I will be killed when I go home," he used to joke even though everyone there knew that only Síbín the cat awaited him there. His smart remark still drew a laugh every time.

"Why did I not go to the doctor when I was out?" Tom asked himself. He could call him on the phone, of course, but he did not want to bother the doctor with a little pain in his head. The pain was not so little at that stage. It felt as if some kind of a lump of iron like they used to have in the shop years earlier to weigh the flour and sugar was sitting on one side of his brain weighing it down. He felt he would recover if he stretched himself in his bed. If he was not, he would call the doctor then.

Tom found it hard to settle in his bed. He could not get any comfort as the heavy part of his head felt sore on the pillow and was top heavy when he rolled over on his other side. It seemed strange now to think that he had never previously had a serious pain in his head. The word migraine came to his mind. He had often heard women especially complain about that, but he had never experienced it. He took the little bottle of baby Power whiskey he had bought from Margie from his trouser pocket and allowed the liquid to slowly flow on his tongue into his throat If it did not take away the pain, he felt, it might at least help him to sleep and he would wake up without pain.

Tom felt that he had never seen Margie as agitated as she had been that morning in the Post Office. It occurred to him that the new man she had, Nicólas Dowling and herself might not be getting on with each other as well as they expected when they had first met. It was none of his business, of course, but he felt that he himself had loved Margie since the very first day she had come to work in the Post Office. What he had told her that morning was no lie. He had often gone to the shop to get something he didn't need just to see her lovely face. He did not love her the way a married couple were supposed to love each other. His was a different kind of love. He knew of course that Margie had no interest in an old codger like him, but he would not like to think that any man was cruel or hurtful to her in any way. That was the way that he loved her.

That was the way too in which Tom had loved his mother, and he could see her now in the eye of his mind, as she was when she was young. She was not very young at the time as she had been nearly forty years old when she married. His father had been nearly twenty years older again, and Tom did not remember much about him as he had not even started National School when his father had died of Tuberculosis.

That was the disease that had prevented his mother from marrying younger than she did. She had spent many years in a Sanatorium but some new drug had helped to give her back her life. "His mother's pet" were words often applied to Tom when he was at school but it was a comment that never hurt him, even if was intended to. He loved his mother, and what else could a widow's only son be other than a pet?

"Tom will die of loneliness," people had said when his mother had passed away in her eightieth year, but for whatever the reason, he had never been lonely.

He had missed his Mum, of course, but it felt as if she was still with him even though he could not see her. He was still her pet, Tom thought as his mind strayed back to the years that followed her passing. He could hardly boil an egg, or ready a meal, because everything like that had been done for him, but he learned how to do those chores. He would boil bacon, potatoes and cabbage together to avoid having to do a big clean-up afterwards. The days had come that oven-ready meals were available in the local shop but Tom had not bothered with them as he tried out new methods and new tastes, to pass the time as much as anything. He learned too how

to keep the house as clean as his mother had done. She had always been house proud and he was not going to let her down. "How could I leave the place in a mess?" he used to ask neighbours who offered to help with housework. "Isn't she sitting on my shoulder watching me herself?"

"I wonder have I put them in the fridge?" Tom asked himself as he lay on the bed. He had taken frozen herrings from the freezer one day and left then to defrost on the table where Síbín had eaten them to the bone by the time he was ready to cook them. It had taken a long time for the cat to cough up a small piece of bone that stuck in its throat: "Good enough for you" Tom has told the cat, not that he wished her any harm but so that she would learn a lesson. Tom tried to rise from his bed to check was there something he could have for his lunch in the fridge. But he felt that his head was too heavy. The pain was not just in one part of his head mow, but all over. An image came to his mind of himself as a boy running through the meadow towards his mother so that she could lift him high in the air before hugging him. He did not remember anything else.

CHAPTER TWENTY-SIX

"You would be sorry for those youngsters," Mary from the Mountain said to Margie as she paid her for some items she had just bought. She was the first customer that morning as Margie opened her Post Office and shop. There had always been some tension between the two women. Mary was well aware that Margie would have heard some of the things she had said about her at the meeting of the church's Pastors Council. Such meetings were supposed to be confidential, but whatever remains under wraps in any local community.

Mary would prefer to shop somewhere else, but what choice had she? Travelling to the local town was expensive and prohibitive when all someone wanted was a few groceries. Anyway, money was money and Margie were hardly in a position to refuse payment. Mary was just trying to be civil when she asked about the shed in which the youngsters known as the "Migos" practised their music which had burned to the ground overnight. "They were lucky that none of them was there at the time," Mary said.

Margie had not heard the news "What fire?" she asked.

Mary told her the fire brigade had been called earlier that morning but had been too late to save the shed and its contents. "I am surprised that you did not hear it on the news?"

"I don't have time to listen to anything in the morning."

Mary could not help herself from commenting "You wouldn't, would you? You have to give Nicólas Dowling his breakfast."

"What do you mean by that?" Margie asked, "although she felt sorry immediately that she had opened her mouth at all."

"I am just trying to be civil," was Mary's answer." I was just bringing you up to date on the news."

"You are my first customer today, so I had heard no gossip of any kind until you arrived in."

"It is not gossip," Mary snapped. "I just thought you might be interested in what is going on around you."

"Thanks Mary. I am just a bit under the weather at the moment."

"If you ever want to talk about things, I could be a listening ear."

Margie thought to herself those words would be the last ones she would ever listen to, but she tried to be graceful and thanked Maty for her offer. Her own mind was actually elsewhere as she wondered if Nicólás Dowling could have had anything to do with the fire in what the "Migos" called "Penny Lane.

"I wouldn't mind," Mary from the Mountain said, "but there were musical instruments thrown around outside the shed that was burnt. Could those kids have saved their guitars and stuff before they torched the shed?"

"I presume that if they were trying to save their instruments they would just have taken them with them," Margie answered. She longed for Mary to just go away so that she could phone Nicólás Dowling.

Mary was putting her shopping in a carrier bag as she said. "It will give people something to talk about other than the film. There has been too much talk about that already."

"Everything is a wonder for a while." Margie answered. "The backbiters and the gossip makers move on to a different target after that."

Mary from the Mountain turned to scripture for her answer. "Nobody sees the plank of wood in their own eye, but it is the first thing they see in someone else's. Did I say that right, or was it meant to be the other way around?"

"You know that stuff better than I do," was Margie's answer.

She rang Nicólas Dowling as soon as Mary had left. "Had you anything to do with the fire that burnt down the shed in which those four young ones practice their music?"

"What in the name of God are you talking about?" he asked.

"You did say yesterday that there are ways and means of sorting out that crowd?" She told him then what Mary from the Mountain had told her about the fire.

"I had no intention of setting fire to anything or anybody."

"Who was it so?"

"I haven't a clue. Those kids have rubbed up a lot of people the wrong way."

"I hope that any footage they had about the two of us has gone up in flames too," Margie told him.

"They were probably just messing about after drinking the Red Null they stole from you," was Nicólas Dowling's opinion. "There was nobody killed or hurt. That is the main thing."

"Do you think it might have been an insurance scam" Margie asked. "Mary from the Mountain told me that anything of any value was scared outside."

"How would I know? There is always speculation when something like that happens. As for the instruments and stuff, they probably just dropped them and ran. That is certainly what I would do if there was a fire at my behind."

"Are you busy again today?" Margie asked Nicólas, as much to get their minds off the Migos as anything else.

The usual. At this very moment I am getting ready to rehearse the part of Caiaphas the High Priest in Jerusalem, before I move on to Pontius Pilate for a bit of a chinwag.

"He seems like an interesting character. Wasn't it he that washed his hands of Jesus, or something?"

"I think he would have let Jesus go if he could, but politics got in the way. He managed to have a little revenge on some of the Jewish leaders when he put the statement 'Jesus of Nazareth, Jung if the Jews,' at the top of the cross. He was either being brave or just showing them the two fingers, but those seven words have lived two thousand years."

"If you had as much interest in the realities of life as you have in the tales of the past," Margie told him, "there would be a bit of a shape to you."

"The past is the present," was Dowling's repl. "What shaped us shaped us."

"I won't even try and answer that. You have lost me completely."

"It is what you called the realities of life a few minutes ago, this is the reality of my life, just as your little shop is the reality of yours."

"My little shop, you say? Dismiss my life that brings more joy and satisfaction to me and my customers than anything you have ever done."

Dowling dug an even deter hole for himself. "It is hardly what you or anyone else would call a supermarket?"

"Insult me and my shop all you like, but I still have to make a living here. We can't all be bigshot film makers."

"Sorry," Nicólas said. "That came out wrong. I didn't mean to insult you."

"We are both under pressure," Margie answered, "and arguing among ourselves will not get us anywhere. I am sorry too. I know that you have your own job to do and that puts you under pressure. But I am worried that Red Bull cans will be found in the ashes of that shed that burnt down, and I will be in the spotlight for selling them to youngsters."

"But you didn't sell them," Dowling argued. "They stole them."

"It would be my word against theirs, and the police would sympathise with them because of what happened to their shed."

"I'm sure the paper receipts on your checkout will show no record of sale of alcohol to children. You are making a mountain out of a molehill" Dowling said

"It is easy for you to say that but it is my livelihood and reputation that is on the line."

"It will all blow over in a few days, like everything else."

"That is your answer to everything," was Margie's reply.

Nicólás tried a bit of humour to ease the situation. "That is because I am always right."

"I give up, but you are probably right. I worry too much."

"So do we all, but it doesn't get us anywhere."

The ordinary work of the day proceeded in the Post Office and shop. There was plenty of gossip about what happened to the "Migos" shed, but little clarity about anything. The overwhelming mood was of satisfaction that nobody had been killed or injured.

When one of the Migos, Eithne entered the shop fairly late in the day Margie sympathised about the fire before saying "I don't want any trouble from you or anyone else. Two of you were out of order here the other night."

"I don't want trouble either the young woman answered as she left a packet on the counter. I want you to get rid of that and we are sorry for what happened."

"Is this some kind of a scam?" Margie asked.

"It's that dirty film. I am sure you know what is in it."

"What about copies? So you can blackmail me again?"

"Alan thinks it was burnt in the fire, so let that be the end of that," Eithne said.

"What do you want me to do with it?" Margie asked.

"Do what you like with it. Send it in for the Oscars if you liked," was Eithne's sarcastic answer. "The porn Oscars."

"I am sorry you had to see it," Margie said, "but it was something private between mature adults."

"Is that what you call it? Mature? Still it was better than any sex education we ever got at home or at school."

"It was stupid of us. I'm sorry." Margie did not know what to say.

"I hope that you wash your hands before you pay out people's pensions," Eithne said. She turned on her heel and walked out of the shop.

Margie felt deeply embarrassed but happy that that particular episode was over. She rang Nicólas Dowling, hoping his day's work was nearly over and that she would see him soon. She told him about her visit from Eithne.

"Are you sure that is the end of it and that there is not a copy somewhere?" He asked.

"I am fairly sure. She was a bit nasty about the contents but I think the fire wakened them up to the reality that you can't mess with people's lives."

"I hope we are not being naive," Dowling said, "but is should take off some of the pressure and worry for both of us."

"What do you want me to do with the footage?" Margie asked.

"We could include it in the film to show off who are the real film stars."

"Be careful," Margie told him. "Mocking is catching."

"I never really understood what that old cliché means." Dowling answered.

"Maybe I am a bit superstitious, but I don't want anything else to go wrong."

"You said that young girl was a bit nasty. What did she say?"

"It was obvious she had looked at the footage. I never felt so ashamed. She said it was the best sex education she had ever got."

"It just shows how good we are in the blankets."

"That was the problem. There were no blankets, no curtains, no clothes. I was so embarrassed."

"What age is she?"

"About seventeen or eighteen. She is in this year's Leaving Cert class"

"A lot of kids of that age have seen it all. They are big into porn."

"The boys maybe, not the girls," Margie answered.

"Don't be naive. They could teach lessons to the rest of us."

"Not to you, I would say, Nicólas."

"Thanks for the compliment."

"I knew very little at that age," Margie said.

"But you soon caught up?"

"It was you that taught me most of it in recent weeks. Did I tell you what the little bitch said? She told me to close the curtains the next time."

"A message that she and the rest of them had seen it all," Dowling said. "By the way where is the footage now?"

"It is right here in front of me."

"Gey a hammer and make smithereens out of it before someone else comes across it."

"I will leave it to you to do that. I think it was you that invented the phrase, hammer and tongs."

"It is great to hear you in such good humour compared with this morning."

"Is that another way of asking me to close the curtains in case we are filmed again?"

"Just destroy that tape or whatever it is. It is time to close that chapter."

CHAPTER TWENTY-SEVEN

Alan was angry when he could not find the footage he and the other "Migos" had filmed of Margie and Dowling.

"What is the problem?" Eoin asked him. "Aren't we lucky to be alive. We could have been toasted in that she'd be thankful for small mercies."

"That footage was our meal ticket," Alan answered. "It could have made us money in the long run. That is why we didn't put it on line straight away. It was our bargaining chip to get food and drink for free. Now Margie probably won't even serve us."

We are lucky the police are not on to us," Eoin said. "On to you for stealing alcohol and other stuff. We have to be more careful. At least the guitars and the other stuff were not ruined. Someone must have thrown them outside when the fire started."

Alan did not admit that it was him or that he had lit the fire that burnt down the shed they referred to as "Penny Lane". It was because he had found Eoin and Eithne having sex on the couch beside the table in the middle of the floor. He wondered now why he had destroyed the place. He had drunk a few cans and was angry to find his sister being fucked by his friend. It was one thing to see Dowling and Margie having it off, another to see his sister and her and his best friend shagging away. They must have been trying to recreate what they had seen in the footage, he thought.

His memories of the previous evening and night slowly came back to Alan. "What the fuck is going on here?" he had shouted when he found the two of them having sex. He tried to beat them with a guitar as they ran half naked from the shed.

When they had gone a memory came to his mind of something from a religion class. It was about Jesus chasing out those that were abusing the temple. Alan told himself that was what he was trying to do with the guitar He wanted to clear the place that he had loved and was now defiled. He had cleared out the instruments and other items that seemed important before using candles to set fire to "Penny Lane." When he met Eoin the following day it was as if nothing had happened. He had acted as if it was just another schooldays. He had seemed upset when he heard about the fire as he acted as if having sex with your best friend's sister was of no consequence.

Alan's father and mother had seemed more upset by the fire than the young people were. What would they think or what would they do if they knew that their daughter had been defiled by the son of their next-door neighbour? It was one thing to fuck someone else, Alan felt, but to do it with someone who had been like a sister to you smacked of incest.

His father had asked him "Why did you do it? Start the fire, I mean?"

"Ask your daughter?" he had replied.

"What has Eithne to do with it?" was his mother's question.

"I am not a snitch," he had answered.

"You told me to ask her," was his father's comment.

"We will find out one way or another. Was there anyone else involved?

"No Dad. There wasn't."

"We will try and keep the police out of it so," was a statement agreed by both parents, "but we will have to cancel our annual holiday to replace it. And it will be a bog standard wooden shed the next time."

"We won't need it anymore," Alan said bluntly.

"You are not giving up music," his mother said.

"I intend to go solo."

"What do the rest of the group say to that?" his father asked.

"We are all agreed," Alan said. "We are getting too old for the childish stuff, and anyway the Leaving Cert is coming up and we won't have as much time to practise."

"When did you decide on that?" his mother asked.

"We have been considering it for a while," was Alan's answer. "We are not kids anymore."

CHAPTER TWENTY-EIGHT

It was Ann Joyce from the Home Help organisation who found Tom Dharach dead in his bed when she came to deliver his "meal on wheels" in the afternoon. It was part of her remit to spend two hours on house work once a week as well, a service she provided for him and six others a couple of times a week. At first she thought that Tom was having a late lie-in and did not disturb him as she felt he may not have slept well the previous night. She prepared porridge for him while cleaning around the place as well, and it was when she arrived in with the food she realised he had passed away.

It only took the local doctor a few moments to confirm Tom was dead when he was called. Fr. Ó Sé gave him the last rites of the church and continued to pray for some time with traditional prayers in times of death, ending up with the words. "May you see your Saviour face to face, and may you delight in the vision of God for ever and ever."

The doctor called the police to confirm that there had been no foul play in question as was the norm in such circumstances. Despite the fact that Tom had been under the doctor's care for heart problems, his body was brought to the nearest hospital for a post mortem and in until after the funeral. A wake in his house was seen as an integral part of the fumetto have the body embalmed nearby so that there would be no question of the body decaying as neighbours and friends began to prepare for the wake, as was the local custom.

Neighbours as well as the doctor and priest and a few relatives sat around Tom's bed in what was a kind if mini-wake before a hearse came to remove the body to the hospital. A piece of cloth was tied around Tom's head from crown to throat to keep his mouth closed while a book was placed against his chin for the same reason. This time around the need was known in Gaelic as the "Marbh Faisc" or the tie of death and down through the centuries it had developed into one of the meanest curses you could call anyone because it basically wished someone dead. The doctor spoke of his own father, a doctor too who arrived at the house of a person thought to have died, but there were little bubbles of air being formed between his lips. "He was a blunter man than I am," the doctor said. He immediately ordered. "Take that thing off the woman's head and let her breathe."

"She wasn't dead at all?" one of the neighbours said. "Wouldn't it be nice to be able to say that about Tom Dharach, but unfortunately it is not true in this case."

When the stories of deaths and funerals had dried up, talk of the film that was about to be made in the area replaced it had become a normal subject of conversation as actors and actresses were to be seen coming and going in their working clothes such as garments depicting apostles and disciples, Roman soldiers, Jewish dignitaries and hangers on of various kinds could be seen coming out of taxis and buses on their way to and from their work.

Much of the work had already been done without too many problems according to the feedback that local people were getting. There was no talk in the house of the dead of course about which actor was sleeping with which, as would have been some of the conversation in the shop or hotel. "We will miss the actors when they are gone," some people were saying. "At least they brought a bit of life to the place." For a few moments it even seemed as if Tom Dharach who was laid out on his bed had been forgotten, but when there was a break in the conversation, someone would say something like. "Lord have mercy on the dead. Poor Tom will be missed around here: He was one of the greats." Then someone would quote Tom's farewell line before leaving the pub. "I will be killed when I go home. At least it was not the cat that killed him," his Home Help, Ann Joyce said. "Which reminds me, who is going to take the cat now?" After some discussion it was decided that Ann herself would, unless some relative of Tom of whom there were few at this stage, offered to foster it.

That raised the question of who and where Tom's nearest relatives were as well as who was going to contact them. When that much was sorted talk turned to who would dig the grave, who would carry the coffin, who would read scripture at his funeral Mass, and what symbols would be brought to the altar to represent his life.

It was agreed that his flat cap would be the number one symbol as he was never without it. "A pack of cards" was another suggestion, as well as his penknife, even though it was years since he had cut tobacco for his pipe. The blackthorn stick he had used as a walking aid in recent times was seen as an important symbol too. "He never raised it in anger in this life," a neighbour said, "and he won't need it in the next."

Everything comes to an end and the little circle of conversation that had surrounded Tom Dharach's bed came to an end when the hearse came to take the body to the morgue. Those present helped as much as they could when it came to lifting and carrying the body. The priest blesses him with holy water. Within ten minutes the body of Tom Dharach had left his home for the last time, the house in which he and his ancestors before him for more than a hundred years had lived their lives. The final wake was scheduled to take place in the Funeral Home at the top of the village as Tom's little cottage was deemed too small to accommodate the number of people who would want to attend the wake.

The little church was full to overflowing, with many people standing outside for Tom Dharach's funeral Mass. It was not just people form the parish and surrounding areas who were gathered to say their goodbyes, but people who had known himself and his family and extended family in the tradition of Irish country funerals. Many of those who had come to the locality for the making of the film about the passion and death of Jesus Christ were present too, out of respect or possibly in some cases to just experience a west of Ireland funeral. Some of them had met Tom in the hotel bar or in the Post Office and had been draws to him because he was such an outgoing man.

    Mary from the Mountain had heard that Ann Joyce the Home Help had taken Tom's cat temporarily and she offered to take it home and mind it, which suited Ann as she spent so much time going from house to house caring for the aged and infirm. "I hope that I will not be the next one to follow Tom to the cemetery," Mary had said "but I want to mind Síbín in his memory for whatever time the Lord leaves me. I loved him once. I loved him all of his life, but he was so attached to his mother I could not break that bond. He was a Mama's boy from start to finish. I thought he might have gone in for the priests. I even thought he might marry me when I came home from America after his mother died, but he was too set in his ways at that stage. And now I have only a little bit of him left "Poor Síbín."

    It was the men's Choir that officially sang Tom Dharach's requiem Mass even though many women's voices joined in too. Such choirs had become fashionalle in the Gaelic speaking areas about fifty years earlier due to the work of Peadar Ó Riada in Cúl Aodne in West Cork and other musicians and singers like him. For once it was not a matter of male dominance in the Roman Catholic church as much as a reaction to having much church singing "left to the women." In previous times. It was not every Sunday that the male voice choir sang, but when it was one of their own and particularly someone with a rich voice and a commitment to be available when required, they tend to come out of their shells and wow the community. Tom Dharach had been one of their stalwarts, and they did him proud.

    As he sat at the altar while the music and singing filled the church, the priest, Fr. Éamonn Ó Sé felt a great sense of loneliness. "Was it for Tom Dharach or because of his death?" he wondered. To the listener or viewer Tom had never done anything out of the ordinary in his life. He had no wife or child and very few relatives left alive, but he was his own man, traditional, sensible, easy-going, a good and honest man, one of the old stocks who had never wilfully harmed anyone. Just a nice decent man. That sounded like an understatement but it was at the same time a compliment of the highest order. He noted in his sermon that Tom had never craved money, fame or success in the eyes of the world. For him enough was enough and that was one of the greatest compliments of all. He finished with Tom's own catchphrase "I will be killed when I go home." You are at home now, Tom, not dead, but alive in the eyes of the Lord for ever and ever.

Young men from the village carried Tom's coffin on their shoulders for the half a mile or so to the cemetery where he was buried in the deep sand that had been blown in from the shore for centuries to form the sand dunes as well as shape the burial place of its citizens. As is common in the highlands and islands of the country, the grave was not covered with imitation green grass but filled in shovel by shovel to reflect the reality of death rather than trying to cover it over. The final prayers were said and the crowd gradually scattered, some to their cars or other transport, those who had walked, returning on foot to the church carpark. Some laughed and talked, others took time to ponder the events of the day.

Tadhg Ó Maoldomhnaigh and Óran Breathnach walked with Nicólas Dowling Nicolás Dowling. Filming had been cancelled for the day as a mark of respect.

"I must say," Tadhg said, "That was the nicest Mass I attended in years. The music was spectacular for a country choir."

Óran gave a little laugh. "I would go so far as to say that it was the only Mass you attended for years."

"That is true," Tadhg answered, "but it stirred feelings that have been locked away inside me for years. I went there expecting long boring ceremonies, boring me to the hilt, but I have to say that I actually enjoyed it against my will."

Nicólas Dowling asked "Did those ceremonies bring to mind the words of the great dramatist and poet, Oliver Goldsmith. Those who came to mock remained to pray."

"I wouldn't go that far," Tadhg said, "but it was a lot different from what I had expected."

Óran said "It probably gives a lot of satisfaction to a community to have a send-off like that for one of their own."

"In some ways it is related to the kind of drama that we do." Dowling said, "and when it is dome well it can be impressive."

"As funerals go," Tadhg said, "I suppose we can declare it a success. It is not that long since I lay like a fool on my back on a cross. It could have been me there today lads. Make the best of what you have."

"You would have got the best send-off of all time, Tadhg," Óran joked.

"It was closer to being a send-up than a send-off," came Tadhg's quick reply.

"You could say that funerals are one thing that Christians generally do well," Óran suggested.

"What about Hindus and Muslims, not to speak of Humanists?" Dowling asked. "I was at one of them recently where there was music and poetry as good as anything that we heard today?"

Tadhg suggested that it was a mistake to leave God and religion out of public discourse. "What have you left without it but societies that have been castrated, a society without balls, a society without any kind of direction."

"I thought you said a society without erection," Óran said. "It reminded be about Brendan Behan's quip when suggestions were being made for a new slogan for what I think was the Labour Party. "From the cradle to the grave" was one idea that was mooted. Brendan capped it all with "From erection to resurrection."

Nicólás Dowling said "The biggest mistake ever made, and it has been made a million times, is to force religion down people's throats."

"It can't have been that effective," Dowling said, "when all three of us were able to reject it and leave it behind us."

Óran laughed "So say three men on their way home from Mass who are preparing to make a film about Jesus Christ. We are never able to escape it no matter what we do."

"The hound of Heaven hunts us down, day and night," Tadhg commented.

"I was glad to be able to turn to him when I was on the broad of my back on that cross."

Nicólas Dowling suggested "It was the best thing that ever happened to you from the dramatic point of view. You did some fine acting in that scene in which you were being crucified in the film. You looked and sounded as if you understood what exactly Jesus went through on Calvary."

"Feel free to compare me with himself any time you like," Tadhg joked.

"What amused me," Óran said was when you said. "I thirst" I expected a burst of laughter from the film crew, and that they would be joking. "It is not the first time that you thirsted, but you carried it off so well that there was not one laugh. They felt your pain."

"People still remember John Wayne in his yankeee accent saying 'This truly is the Son of God,'" Nicólas Dowling said "I was tempted to change it to 'This truly is the son of man,' but I would have all the naysayers on my back because I had messed up the crucifixion scene. "

"You would be hung, drawn and quartered," Óran said.

"The death of Jesus was more human than divine as I see it" Nicólas suggested. "Even he had a wobble as he hung between life and death. I have no doubt that it was Paul or Luke or John that added in the line attributed to a Roman

Officer. 'This man was truly the Son of God.' That is not in character, that is what I call rewriting history."

Tadhg did not agree. "In this business we have character on the brain, but not everything that happens in life is in character as if everything that happens in life is part of one big drama. The rules of life are broken day after day and if anything, it is the people of faith that break them. They go against the stream, against the waterfall,

Against everything that the so-called wise and wonderful seem to have agreed among themselves in their little hearts and minds."

"Why do they tie their wagons to the Kingdoms and the Empires of this world so every chance they get?" Dowling asked "from the Empires Greece and Rome to the Spanish and British and Portuguese down to our own day?"

Tadhg answered "They do so because it suits them, to spread their faith, for instance, or to earn a wage. Not every country is like this upstart of a country in which the name of God cannot be mentioned without an outcry from the media. The name of God is on the tongue of every American President, for the wrong reason, maybe. But it is used without shame unlike in our spineless Parliament. If our Taoiseach or our President was to speak like that, they would be eaten without salt.. Despite that narrow-mindedness, people say publicly that there is freedom of religion in Ireland. As a healthy agnostic I now proclaim that to be a lie."

"You have changed your tune in the last while," Dowling teased. "It is not long since you hated God and religion according to yourself."

"I hate many of the things done by some priests and nuns and so-called Christian Brothers," Tadhg answered, "but that is not to say that I am against God. I am not a believer or a follower as such, but the world would be worse off without at least the idea of religion."

"In other words, you are going soft in the heart at last," Óran commented.

"I am sure you learned as much about Judas as I did about Jesus from your experiences in the making of the film," Tadhg answered.

Óran joked "It didn't put me on the road to Damascus like it put you, but I suppose I did get some insights to the man."

"Do you love him or hate him now?" Dowling asked casually.

"Does it matter? That film is made. I do not need to answer any questions."

"You sound like a man being questioned by the police," Tadhg quipped.

"Not guilty," Óran answered. "Neither Judas or myself."

"If you have any new insights," Dowling said, "we could shoot that scene again."

"You will have to shoot me first," was Óran's answer. "My work here is done," After a little while he mentioned. "But he will live with me for a long time."

"Tell us more," Tadhg said.

"To my surprise, it took a lot out of me."

"No wonder," Dowling told him. "You lived the character for weeks."

"A complex character he was, too," Óran replied. "There must be many like him in religious life just now. People who signed up to follow Jesus as best they could, only to end up full of regret, mourning their lost youth, the lost families that they never had. Basically, betrayed by life. Their own fault in many ways, but thankfully there are not as many going down that road to oblivion anymore."

"A lot of people thrived in that calling, as they used to call it," Dowling said. They spread their faith halfway around the world and many of them helped people out of poverty by starting and sustaining projects with the help of people at home. Even I try to see the other side of the story."

"It was celibacy that screwed up lives more than anything," Óran said. "That and the failure of the churches to deal with homosexuality. I have played the part of Judas but I have no idea was he gay or straight, or did he have a wife and children. I am actually thinking of writing a play along those lines."

"Good man yourself," Dowling said. "There could be a film in that"

"There could be a minefield in that," Óran replied. "There would be one crowd saying that Judas was gay, another would blame his suicide on that, or the fact that he was accused of robbing from Jesus and his followers. It looks like that particular play will be a nonstarter"

Dowling suggested "The best thing to do with an idea like that is to sit on it. Let it come to the boil in its own time. Scribble a few lines every now and again and go back to it in a year or so. If it ever comes to anything, I would like to be the first to see it."

"There could be spin-offs for everyone that is in this film," Tadhg said. "Mary from the Mountain might come down the hill with a story in her hand. Your friend Margie might publish the inside story of her dalliance with Nicólás Dowling."

"The film director countered and Big Tadhg might regale all of us about the day he died and went to heaven. Or was its hell?"

"That was no joke, I can tell you. I still get nightmares about lying on my back on the cross, my hands tied to both wings, my feet to the bottom, midgets eating into my face..."

"I thought midgets were little people," Óran said.

"Don't split hairs," Tadhg said. "I don't know what water boarding is except that it is some kind of a torture, but however bad it is, it wouldn't hold a candle to the midges eating into your face; I had no trouble turning to God at that minute, even though I tried the devil before and after."

"Was it him that saved you?" Dowling joked.

"It was not funny, Nicólas," Tadhg answered. "You were lucky you did not have a dead man on your hands the next morning. It was some of the people that tied me to the crodd that saved me.. Maybe it was God or their faith or their consciences that brought them back. But I am thanking God one way or another."

"Have you ever reported them to the police?" Tadhg asked.

"I was so happy that they came and set me free that I didn't have the heart to drop them in it."

"You are a big softie," Dowling said. "Myself and Margie have had problems with some of the same crowd in so far as I understand, and if there was proof I would not be as soft as you are."

"Live and let live," was Tadhg's response. "I was so happy to be alive that I hardly gave revenge a second thought."

Nicólas Dowling said. "There are a few little shits of teenagers around here that need to learn a few lessons. There have been a few dirty incidents around the place in recent times and nobody is prepared to open their mouths about them."

"What kind of stuff are you talking about?" Óran asked.

"Invasion of people's privacy is one thing." Dowling did not want to mention what exactly he had in mind."

"Are you talking about on-line stuff here? Tadhg asked: "I don't understand any of it, and I don't want to."

"There was a time when priests used to sort out that kind of thing," Tadhg said, "but there are not many of them left and they don't want to get on the wrong side of the youth. It looks like they have lost their courage completely because of all that has happened down through the years."

"As they walked along on their way back from the cemetery they were approaching the priest as he walked slowly towards the church, still in his vestments after the Mass and funeral 'Why don't we ask his opinion?'" Dowling asked.

"He looks to have the weight of the world on his shoulders," Tadhg suggested.

"I imagine that dealing with a funeral service is not unlike having a serious part in a drama," Nicólás mentioned. "Especially when the person who has passed was an icon in the community even if he was a bachelor who never did anything great with his life."

"Why don't we just let him be?" Tadhg said. "he has the head down like someone that is praying or meditating. I don't think we should bother him."

"Come on," Dowling said. "Why don't we catch up with him? A compliment or two about the funeral might raise his spirits. Anyway, I have a few questions to ask him yet about the apostles and disciples of Jesus before we finish the film. Strike while the iron is hot as they used to say."

"What is to stop you going to the house to talk to him?" Tadhg asked

"The rest of you might think I was going to confession," Nicólás joked.

"A week wouldn't be long enough or a penance strong enough for your confession, I would say," Óran quipped.

"You did a great job there with the ceremonies in the church today," Dowling said when they caught up with Fr. Ó Sé. "You sent the poor man to his reward with a lot of dignity."

The priest thanked him for the compliment and told a sorry about a time he was at his uncle's funeral in West Dublin. When the Parish Priest who was presiding came back to the sacristy he made a gesture with his arms as if sinking a putt on the golf course. "That one went down very nicely," he said "I thought it was referring to my uncle he was. No. It was to a putt sunk by Seve Ballesteros the previous day that he had watched on television. I was thinking in my own mind of how far the man's thoughts were from my uncle who was being buried. I promised myself that day that I would give every funeral I attended or was involved in my full attention and interest. To tell you the truth I have hated golf ever since."

"I was impressed by the choir," Óran said. "It is mostly in a pub you would hear men singing, or at a match, but those male voices were lovely today."

"Leave it to the Welsh," Dowling said, "when it comes to men's choirs. If they were as good at the rugby as they are at the singing, they would wipe the floor with every other team."

Dowling asked the priest as they walked along "Would you have any interest in coming to the hotel with us for a while, Father? To wet your whistle."

The priest pointed to his vestments "I would look a bit out of place at the bar in my fancy skirts. I will drop in as soon as I have changed. They say Tom had left an envelope of money to get drinks for the house after the funeral?"

"I am ravenous for a lemonade myself," Tadhg said as he pointed at Nicólas Dowling. "This old fucker won't let me drink any alcohol."

"You are off the hook now. You have played tour part and played it well in the film."

"Do you mean to tell me I could have been drinking for the past few days?"

"I was waiting to see the footage in case you would have to called back," Nicólas answered."

Tadhg laughed "Do you know what. I might pass on the alcohol. Just to spite you. To be honest I could do with a break from it."

"What will you drink, Father?" Dowling asked. "It will be on the counter waiting for you when you take off those clothes."

"I have heard of the Naked Civil Servant," the priest answered, "but not the naked clergyman. I will have a pint of Guinness so, please."

The priest went to the bar when he had changed his vestments. He took a bowl of soup and a sandwich from the table laden with food before sitting down in the seat that Nicólas Dowling had kept free for him. He sipped his pint with relish before asking Nicólas "Have you the film nearly finished?"

"Don't worry. We will be out of all of your hair soon", the Director said "The filming is nearly finished, but not the film of course. There could be close to a year to get it from here to the screen, with editing and correcting and that involves in the meantime."

The priest smiled as he said "I have only one question about your film?"

"What is that?" Dowling queried.

"Did Jesus rise from the dead at the end of it all?"

"I can give you a typical Irish answer to that," Dowling replied. "He did and he didn't. We have prepared two different endings, the traditional rising from the tomb and the 'what if he didn't rise' one, but the apostles and disciples went on as if he did."

The priest answered that there were some theologians in the Roman Catholic church that would have no difficulty accepting that Jesus had not risen physically from thee dead, but that he had lived on as the "Spirit of God" or "Holy Spirit"

"I am not trying to be smart when I ask this," Dowling said, "but is there any proof of resurrection?"

"In typical Irish fashion again, there is and there isn't," the priest said. "But we are not without proof of a kind that might even stand up in a court of law."

"Wasn't the tomb empty?" Tadhg interjected.

"It was, but one of the stories at the time had it that the disciples had stolen the body and hid it," the priest answered. "But that is not the most important evidence."

"Pray tell," Tadhg said bluntly.

"The word of the apostles,." Óran interrupted the priest. "That was pretty questionable at the time. They didn't have a leg to stand on."

"Not after Gethsemane and Calvary, they didn't," Fr. Ó Sé said, "but what about the change that came over them between Calvary and Pentecost?"

"Remind us again about Pentecost?" Tadhg said. "It sounds a bit like pantyhose. The church has a lot of strange words. You would wonder if they understand them all themselves?"

"They are strange to this age because they are almost as old as the hills," the priest replied. "Pentecost, Whit, whatever you want to call it is about the Holy Spirit. Sometimes call the Holy Ghost, but that was changed so as not to scare people," Tadhg said. "Continue please, Padre."

In our tradition," the priest said, "the Holy Spirit is basically the spirit of Jesus risen from the dead doing the work Jesus did while he was a man on earth. As a man, of course, he was confined by space and time so he could be in only one place at any time. As Spirit he can be everywhere all of the time."

"So very handy," Tadhg commented. "So that was the big trick really. Turn Jesus into a ghost and let him loose on the world. Note that I say 'Let him' because there is no talk of a her. Or are there female Holy Spirits fluffing around in the sky above us as well?"

"Sorry Father," Dowling said. "Tadhg needs his flights of fancy especially when he is not drinking."

"I am as entitled to my opinion as much as anyone else," Tadhg answered.

Fr. Ó Sé took another tack "There are some wonderful resurrection stories in the forty days after Jesus rose from the dead until he ascended into Heaven according to the Bible. Stories of the risen Christ flitting about like a butterfly from flower to flower, appearing among his disciples in the Upper Room even though the doors are locked, walking the road to Emmaus with two disciples who do not recognise him until he breaks bread like he had done at the Last Supper. He even had a barbeque ready on the beach for some of the apostles when they came back from fishing one morning. Not to speak of Doubting Thomas probing the wounds made by the nails in his hands and feet and the hole the spear left in his side."

"And then he took off like a rocket into the sky," Tadhg said. "He passed by the Moon and the stars like a shot and was parachuted in at the right hand of God."

"You know it better than I do," the priest said, "and you tell it in much more spectacular language."

"But do I believe it? Tadhg asked. "That is the real question."

"To be quite honest," Fr. Ó Sé said," I don't care if you do or if you don't. It is not my place to push religion down anyone's throat."

Óran Breathnach suggested "I always thought there was a touch of composition about that story of the resurrection, imaginative thinking I must admit, but just too imaginative."

"I always liked Doubting Thomas," Tadhg said. "One of our own, a man not afraid to ask a question. I could believe the likes of him."

The priest told that he had always liked the story of Jesus walking the road to Emmaus with two disciples who didn't realise it was him until they saw him breaking bread. "It carries that image of God being with you no matter what, even if you do not feel or realise his presence."

"He must have looked over my shoulder many a time unknown to me when I was drinking a pint," Tadhg mentioned cynically.

Nicólas Dowling had sat back enjoying the conversation without taking part other than at the beginning. "It looks I will have to remake the film from what I have learned in the last while," he joked. "The proofs you have mentioned are interesting but they don't see very watertight."

"It is not really about the kind of proof needed in a court of law, but from a couple of thousand years of faith," the priest said. "As far as I am concerned the nearest thing we have to proof is the change that came over the followers of Jesus after his death. What changed the craven cowards of Gethsemane and Calvary into those brave preachers who went out at Pentecost to proclaim the resurrection of Jesus? Not only were they willing to die for that faith but most of them actually did, all of them except John the Evangelist."

"It is really all about men," Óran said. "Like the church until this very day?"

"There were women there too," the priest answered, "and they had a lot more courage than the men. They were there on Calvary when most of the men were hiding. They were there at the Ascension. They were there at Pentecost. It could be said that women were the church for the best part of ten thousand years. OK, they were not on the altar, nor are they now, but without them there would not be a church. I admit that it is a church on one leg until women are admitted to the altar, but they are gradually getting nearer to that goal.."

"I think you are pulling the one leg you say the church is standing on," Dowling said. "It might be on your Wishlist, but not on many such lists in Rome."

"A famous American bishop used the phrase 'No broads on the alter' many years ago when Pope John Paul was coming to Dublin," the priest said. "I hope I live to see the "broads" taking over in my lifetime.

"Keep wishing," Óran said, "but it sounds like pissing against the wind. The only result is getting your own back."

"Why did Jesus leave the building?" Was there a coup d'Etat in Heaven or something?" Dowling asked. "Or was its Red Bull that made him fly? Red Papal Bull, if you really want to pun."

"He left this earth as a man because he had done all that he was able to do," the priest answered. "He had lived his life. A short life I must admit, but it was probably as long as anyone was getting at the time."

Tadhg interjected "Didn't John the Evangelist live to be a hundred or something. The virgin Mary had to be at least fourteen or fifteen years older than Jesus. Wasn't it the same Herod that was around at the time Jesus was crucified that was trying to trying to kill him when he was a baby? So, some people were obviously getting fairly long lives?"

Fr. Ó Sé ignored that question as he wanted to continue what he had started to say earlier. "Jesus basically had done the job he had come on earth to do: He had taught and preached and had given good example by helping the poor, the sick and lonely He had died and risen from the dead. What more could a man do because a person is constrained by his or her body? So, he left in order to send his spirit, what we now call the Holy Spirit to carry on his work on earth."

"Very neat," Óran said. "Some would say too neat."

"Nice and cozy," was Tadhg's version, and the priest began to wonder had he been drinking too fast and talking too much.

"An interesting take on the story," Dowling said. "Whatever about the resurrection part of it being able to stand up in a court of law, the Holy Spirit bit is pure fantasy. It does not have to be that complicated. A good and decent man was put to death in the wrong. He left a legacy..."

Tadhg interrupted "Judas left a bit of a legacy too."

"Don't be facetious," Dowling snapped. "Why do we have to treat it as other than a human story? A good story that exploded and boomeranged throughout the world for a couple of thousand years. A story that has inspired millions but has hit the rocks in this part of the world, but is blooming in many countries and cultures."

"Faith can not thrive or flourish without imagination," the priest suggested. "Imagination is not the same now as it was then or many times in between."

Nicólas Dowling said gently "I have no faith of the kind you have, Father, but are you suggesting I lack imagination because I reject some fairy tales? I have made films, written books. That was hardly without imagination."

"I am sure that you could buy and sell me in that department," Fr. Ó Sé answered, "but the way I see it is that all imagination is limited by upbringing, background, memory, tradition. My imagination would include concepts that yours would reject such as angels and spirits, what happens after death and that kind of thing. My faith imagination includes those concepts though I do not have nearly enough imagination to understand them fully."

"I am not sure what you are trying to get at, Father," Tadhg said.

The priest gave a little laugh "Maybe I am not so sure myself, but take that funeral we have all attended today, Tom Dharach, the Lord have mercy on him as we say around here. We have no idea of how many of those who attended believed in the resurrection of the body or life everlasting. There was a priest in charge of Galway University many years ago, An tAthair Pádraig De Bruin. He is often quoted as saying that Irish people have three different understandings of death, all of which are held at the same time. First you have the traditional Irish Roman Catholic hope in life eternal. Then there are the beliefs you would get in India and other places that people are reborn in different ways. The third is that there is nothing after death. All as I said are believed by the same person at different times, or sometimes at the same time.."

"That man hit the nail on the head," Tadhg said. "That sums me up to a tee."

"You yourself seemed very sure about it all when you spoke at Mass this morning?" Dowling said. "No doubts at all?"

"I suppose that was because I couldn't imagine Tom Dharach going anywhere except to join his mother in Heaven."

"Between ourselves" Dowling said. "How could there be such a thing as another life? It is beyond reason. There is no head or tail to it."

"We are back at the imagination question again," the priest answered. "The way I see it for instance when I am speaking about the dead during November is that those who have left this life are still with us in spirit..."

"The bloody spirits again," Tadhg said. "maybe those midges that were eating me on the cross are the spirits. I was in spirit hell. If I hear one more word about spirits here today I am going to vomit up my lemonade."

Fr. Ó Sé ignored his comment and went on "Getting back to imagination again, take any of the developments of the past century for instance. A hundred and twenty years ago that church that we were in today which would have been new at the time would have been surrounded by horse and traps that had brought people to Mass. Could anyone who was there then have imagined it being surrounded by horseless carriages, the fancy cars that were there today?" He answered his own question. "No, they didn't have the imagination. So how can be begin to imagine a life after death? We just do not have the imagination to do so."

"You could be on to something there," Óran commented.

The priest was in full flow now as he started on his third pint of Guinness "If you were to suggest to people back then that most people would have a yoke in their pocket on which they could speak to and see their relatives in the United States or

Australia, they would say you were crazy. They would not believe you either if you told them that you could watch sports of every kind on a box or a flat screen in the corner, hey would be equally disbelieving. When such wonderful inventions have been developed in our own lifetime, how can we write off a next life or anything of that nature?"

"Call me when you raise the next Lazarus from the dead," Dowling answered

with a cynical smile. "All of the things you mention came about because of advances in science and the work of very talented people. You are still talking about a magic world of the imagination side by side with this one."

"I have enjoyed our chat," the priest said, "but we will have to agree to differ. We don't need to fight about it but of course you are right and I am wrong. When we get to the next life the opposite will be proven. He told of two bishops who both felt that they were the real bishop of Cork. When one of them died suddenly, the other remarked: "He knows now which of us is the real bishop of this diocese.."

"Have you any designs on being a bishop yourself?" Óran asked.

"I may think of myself as the salt of the earth," Fr. Ó Sé answered, "but as far as bishops are concerned I am at the bottom of the barrel."

"Are you being humble?" Dowling asked, "or are you persona non grata?

"Let's say my thoughts on celibacy and the place off women in the church are

considered too daring. But I am alright for weddings and funerals and harmless stuff like that. And I wouldn't want it any other way.."

The men talked about everything except religion for a while, about Gaelic football and hurling, soccer and rugby and many other non-controversial matters even though each of them had loyalties to their own county or country district. It was Fr. Éamonn Ó Sé who put religion back on the table when he was on his fourth pint." He winked at Óran and Tadhg before asking Nicólás Dowling "Have you and your film succeeded in putting Jesus not just to bed, but to a tomb he can not escape from this time?"

"He didn't escape the last time either" Dowling said. "He was spirited away by his apostles and disciples so that they could start on the big lie that has haunted the world ever since. DNA was invented or discovered far too late. Otherwise we would have the answers to those questions for a couple of thousand years."

"So we will all wallow in our own opinions and just get on with life," the priest said.

"The biggest mistake your crowd ever made was to get rid of the devil. At least that used to put the fear of God into people," Dowling suggested.

"A fearful faith is no faith at all," was the priest's answer to that.

"It was the devil that put people on the seats of the churches," Dowling said. "It was the devil who put money in the baskets. When ye killed the devil ye killed religion as we used to know it."

"That is not the faith of Christ," the priest answered, "but the opposite."

"Bring Nicólás here to Mass with you at the weekend," Tadhg joked, "and he will scare the shit out of people and you will return three baskets full."

"If I was in it for the money," the priest answered, "I would have left long ago. He recalled a priest who had been in his home parish at some stage "He put up his foot over the edge of the pulpit one Sunday and announced to his congregation. You are the most useless people I have ever seen. You can't even keep half-soles on my shoes." When the priest realised that the drink had gone to his head and that he was rambling on too much, he used Tom Dharach's mantra in memory of the man that had brought them together: "I will be killed when I go home."

CHAPTER TWENTY-NINE

The "Migos" had not been together since the burning of "Penny Lane," the shed in which they used to practice their music was burnt to the ground. Apart from Aisling and Eithne chatting from time to time at the Secondary School there had been very little contact between them. They were lying low because their parents were angry and the feeling that the quieter they kept the less chance there was that the police might become involved in checking what had caused the blaze.. Alan had given no explanation on why he had set fire to the small building. Aisling got a shock when he came up behind her on the road and put his arms around her. She struggled to free herself as she asked "What the hell is wrong with you?"

"I want to make love to you," he blurted out.

"Are you gone completely out of your mind?" she asked. "I don't fancy you. I never have and I never will. You are OK as a friend but that is it."

"When the other two are having it off," he said. "Why shouldn't we? I would prefer to be with you than any other girl at school."

"What makes you think that Eoin and Eithne are at it?"

"I caught them at it hammer and tongs on the bench. That is why I set fire to 'Penny Lane' To get rid of the dirt and to sanitise the place."

Aisling seem dumbfounded "You are talking about Eithne and Eoin?"

"Did she not tell you? I thought you two talked about everything."

"We used to. The stupid bitch. I hope she is up the pole. That will teach them a lesson."

"There are ways to get out of that," was Alan's answer. "They have no shame, My sister and my so-called friend. Going at it like rabbits."

"But you were planning to use me in the same way?"

"I was planning to make love. Not just to fuck you. We could have done it in a bed or even a car, not on a wooden bench like they did, the dirty shameless whores."

Aisling sounded as if she was talking to herself. "Out of all the students at the college, Eoin and Eithne had to pick each other."

"To pick and to fuck each other," Alan reminded her. "If everyone is at it, why shouldn't we?"

"Because that is not who I am, whatever about you."

I thought you were my best friend. Among the girls, I mean."

"Are you telling me that your real best friend is a boy?"

"I thought Eoin was my best friend. Until he fucked my sister."

"So I am your revenge?" Aisling asked.

"If you put it like that. To show that we can do what they can. Sauce for the goose and sauce for the gander."

"I can tell you now," Aisling told Alan. "I am no goose and I would say you should think twice before picking on some other girl."

"I just want to get my hole like every other young fellow."

"If you want to get your hole put back your hand, but stay well away from me." Aisling told him.

"I'm sorry," Alan said.

"Sorry for what? For coming on to me or for being a stupid idiot?"

"I don't know what got into me."

"I do. Jealousy that your friend was getting his oats and that you were not."

"I was a fool to burn down 'Penny Lane'" Alan said.

You were angry, and not without cause considering what you saw that night, But the fire was away over the top as was what happened a while ago when you came on to me.. I am not a toy or a rag doll and no other girl or woman is either. You need to get over yourself and start concentrating on your Leaving Cert."

CHAPTER THIRTY

"Show a bit of breast" Nicólas Dowling told Edel Nic an tSaoir. "You are a fine looking woman, young, beautiful, a virgin." The Annunciation scene where Mary the mother of Jesus was told she was about to become a mother was one of the last scenes to be filmed as part of the story of the Passion and death of Jesus Christ. True to his word the first had become last in Dowling's scheme of things, as that was how he went about his business whether his actors liked it or not. Edel had downloaded many of the pictures painted by artists down through the centuries which featured that seminal moment in the conception and life of Jesus.

"Have you studied all of the pictures now, Edel," he asked, as he took her phone from her hand and asked one of his assistants to switch it off. "Forget everything you have just seen," he told her. "You are as beautiful as ant of them."

"I am no fifteen-year-old," she answered. "I am more like a scary old witch,""You are in your character now," Dowling said. "You are a young girl on her way home from the well with a pail of water when you need the most handsome man you have ever seen. A vision in every sense of the word. You hold on to your bucket because your parents, Ann and Joachim need water for the cooking and cleaning, you are a tough little girl even if this vision of a man has your heart fluttering. Take it from here as if there is not a person or a camera in sight."

"Where is Joseph?" Edel asked.

"You are supposed to do this on your own, Edel," Dowling said. "God is supposed to be the father."

"You know and I know that is a myth," she answered. "Joseph must have had a part to play, even if it was unknown to himself, or unknown to both of them maybe."

"How are we supposed to film that?" the Director asked.

"What if Joseph happened to be a sleepwalker?."

Nicólás Dowling mused for a moment "Interesting," he said. "I thought you of all people wanted to act the story in the traditional way, with the angel Gabriel being the Daddy."

"It could be done in a way that would not question Mary's integrity as someone venerated all over the world. I am not talking about having a naked scene or anything, just two people on the same floor and let imagination do the rest."

"Keep talking," Dowling said. "You could be on to something here."

"I am one of Mary's greatest admirers, so I am not talking something sordid. I have not thought it true fully, the Angel Gabriel as a spirit alighting on Joseph and the rest of it left to the imagination."

"A Jesiutil solution to an Irish problem," Dowling said. "But wouldn't that be making Joseph the real father."

"What did we say about imagination?" Edel asked. "I don't expect anyone to do a DNA test. It is only a film all the same. Even if was true that Joseph was the actual physical father, he proved his fatherhood in a more important way by caring for Mary and her child, and teaching him his idea as a carpenter."

"While the angel Gabriel flapped his wings all the way back to Heaven," Nicólás Dowling said with some satisfaction.

"I don't see the need to overthink it over complicate stuff," Edel replied.

"You could have a long future in the film industry," Dowling said admiringly. "And you were the one trying to put the kibosh on the whole project a couple of months ago."

"All I wanted was for it to be done with dignity," Edel answered.

"I read some of the stuff you had written on that right-wing Catholic newspaper, and I certainly was not expecting the kind of broadmindedness from you that we have seen today." Nicólás said.

"Don't lose the run of yourself," Edel answered with a wry smile. "I could be putting the boot in yet before the end of the week."

"Are you happy enough with the film footage you have seen so far?" Nicólás Dowling asked Edel.

"What I have seen is OK. I don't want to see too much or I might lose the rag altogether. It is your film all the same and good look with it as long as you don't have a complete dog's dinner out of it."

"I will take that as a compliment," Dowling answered. "And I got an equally good compliment the other day from Fr. Éamonn Ó Sé. He called me another Christ."

Don't lose the run of yourself," Edel told him. "That is straight from the Paul of Tarsus hymnbook. That is how we are supposed to treat everyone."

"How do you work that out?" Dowling asked.

"That is what was said to Paul in his vision at Damascus, when Paul asked Jesus who he was, and the answer comeback. I am Jesus and you are persecuting me. In other words, he put Jesus in the shoes of every other woman and man."

"I think he might be too big for my shoes," Dowling quipped before saying. "Some of that stiff seems childish to me."

"Childish in what way?" Edel asked him.

"You mean to say that if I walk past an old woman or man begging by the side of the street it is Jesus Christ himself that I am refusing to help?"

"Maybe not Jesus himself as such," Edel replied, "but someone equally important, that is part of the faith."

"A pure Catholic guilt trip is what it is," Dowling said. "a way to make people feel guilty so that they will part with their hard-earned earnings to help what is in many cases people who never did a day's work in their lives."

"That is an arrogant rich man's answer," was Edel's reply. "I know now why I had doubts about you before I came down here to check out your film. That was part of the faith for centuries, long before there was talk of Orthodox, Protestant or Catholic and it has remained part of those religions ever since. That are the reason people turn out to help the Saint Vincent De Paul society as well as the myriad of groups set up to help the poor and deprived all over the world. There are many areas in which Christianity can be criticised, especially after all of the scandals, but not for helping the poor and deprived of the planet."

"You really are a born preacher," Dowling said. "I can see now why you didn't keep up the acting after college."

"There are more important things in life even than acting," Edel answered,

"Not for me," Nicólas answered, "but we can agree to differ once again, I have a film to be getting on with."

CHAPTER THIRTY-ONE

There was a "monster party" announced for the "wrap" at the end of the filming. Jokes were made about what kind of a "monster" would be coming to the party while the word "wrap" drew its own puns from people asking what rapper was coming to supply the music. Everyone was invited. Mary from the Mountain met Fr.

Ó Sé after the First Friday Mass and she asked him would he be going to the wrap party.

"I will probably step in for a few minutes," he answered, "but I am not a fan of that rap music. I presume we are talking about the 'Migos.'"

"They seem to be back on their feet again after that fire," Mary said. "Nobody knows what caused it, but I hear that Dowling fellow is being blamed for it like he is for everything bad that happens around here. Of course, I don't take heed of any gossip. They say it is him that is paying for that new wooden prefab shed that they have moved into, so it must have been bought with guilt money."

"The main thing is that nobody was injured in the fire, Mary." Was the priest's diplomatic answer.

"People like you and me have been left behind by the world," Mary said "Everything is moving so far."

"God be with the days of dancing the Stack of Barley" and the "Siege of Ennis" the priest replied. "Are you going to the monster party yourself."

"How could I?" Mary answered, and poor Tom Dharach not cold in his grave yet. There are still things like decency and decorum in this world even though the youth don't understand that.

"Tom himself was fond of the old step on the dancefloor," Fr. Ó Sé said to Mary from the Mountain "I don't think it would be a bit of harm to turn up at thee dance and do a bit of a twirl in his memory."

"You could be right there, Father. He will hardly be turning in his grave at this stage."

"It might do us all good to step out in Tom's honour."

"So much has changed," Mary said, "since the churches were full and the faith strong."

"The psychiatric hospitals were full too, Mary," the priest said, "in many cases by people who were not sick, but had babies out of what we used to call wedlock."

"Drugs are the worst scourge of all, Father."

"The raw whiskey we call poteen killed as many or more than drugs ever did," was the priest's answer."

"Did you ever drink it yourself, Father? I heard you had a few scoops of Guinness after poor Toms funeral. You needed that."

"Nothing ever goes un-noticed in this parish. I drank poteen at Station Masses when I was young. I didn't want to insult people by refusing. People were so proud of what they had distilled themselves. It did me no harm, but that was the best of stuff. Bad stuff was the killer."

"I often said to Tom Dharach, the Lord have mercy on him, that it was a pity the way the world fell apart compared with long ago."

"Not everything was great then Mary. Do you remember TB, like I do and the whispers that 'so and so' had been taken to the Sanatorium and that they would not be coming back? It was as bad or worse than cancer is now. We all know the problems the church and state have had, but we are still here, thanks be to God."

Mary did not reply and then the priest noticed tears running down her face.

"What is it, Mary?"

"You know yourself, Father."

"I know what?" he asked.

"I am sure that you have seen it in the book?"

"What book?"

"The book where you write in the Baptisms."

"What about it?"

"That was why I went to America. I am sure you have seen the Baptism certificate in that big book with the black cover."

"All I ever look at is what people ask me to look at when certificates have to be produced before Holy Communion, Confirmations or weddings."

"My child was christened here before I left, Martha Mary. I suppose it is away back at the start of that book and that you didn't notice it."

"And where is Martha Mary now?" the priest asked.

"She was adopted to a couple in Canada,"

"Have you looked for her or has she looked for you?"

"She didn't contact me, and when she didn't, I presume I was not wanted in her life."

"She is probably thinking the very same thing from the other way around, if you understand what I am saying."

"Would you look for her, Father?"

"Of course I will, but there are no guarantees. I will do my best."

There was silence for a moment, which Fr. Ó Sé broke when Mary had not said anything. "So you have carried that pain all of your life since"

"It was complicated, and that was the way people dealt with things at the time. Now that Tom Dharach is gone, I suppose it is alright to mention it."

"You mean Tom was the father and he didn't stand by you?"

"He never knew because I never told him."

"Why not, Mary? You two could have a lovely life together."

"His mother was alive at the time and it would have broken her heart."

"It is a pity people didn't take a chance on breaking hearts other than their own." The priest shook his head "So many have suffered for so long, and we in the church were the cause of most of it."

"Don't blame it all on the church. We were the ones sinning at the back of the dancehall."

"If that was sin you have paid for it many times over. There is hardly a day that I am not ashamed of belonging to this organisation."

"As they say nowadays, Father, don't beat yourself up about it." Mary reached for her purse "Say a Mass for Tom when you get time." She paused for a moment. "And for his little girl who is obviously a big girl now. She is probably about the same age as yourself. Say one for me too, please."

CHAPTER THIRTY-TWO

The film was completed, the so-called wrap was ongoing. Traditional Irish music and dance mixed with musical influences from all over the world. The "Migos" played a couple of their own compositions.. People of all ages danced and sang as they shared the floor. Locals and film people mixed together as if they had known each other all of their lives.

"Isn't it a pity that we don't have more nights like this," Mabel Uí Chionnaith, the chairperson of the Pastoral Council to the priest, Eamon Ó Sé.

I see that all of your own family have returned for the occasion," the priest said.. "I seem to see one of them everywhere I look."

"That is because there are so many of them in it and they are all here for the weekend for the first time in a long time. As soon as they heard about this hooley they were all planning to come home. Little did we think when we had that emergency meeting earlier in the year that it would all end like this."

"You did a great job of it, Father," Mabel said.

"I did nothing at all. It is the only thing that I am good at," the priest answered.

"That is the most important thing to do, sometimes. Keep your cool. Don't rush in where angels fear to tread, as the old cliché has it. The biggest mistake many of us who are involved in communities is to try and settle situations in which people are not sure what they want or unwilling to give an inch on anything. I suppose that I always admired the approach people in Trade Unions have most of the time, that is to allow for what they call a 'cooling off period,'" Mabel said.

"The young people have certainly put life into the situation tonight," the priest remarked. Those "Migos" as they call themselves are not half bad.

"It will be interesting to see how the film turns out," Mabel said. "I suppose it all comes down to editing at this stage. There are still some people that think Dowling will have his own agenda and that he might mess up the story."

"At this stage I don't give a damn one way or another," Fr. Ó Sé answered. "The pressure is off from our point of view. Peace has broken out between our warring tribes. As for the film it will be good or bad. Good I hope, but it will be forgotten in no time apart those who are into that kind of a thing. If it creates a job or two, or brings in a tourist or two, it will be a bonus."

"The best of luck to all of them." Mabel pointed to a table at which members of her family were gathering for something to eat. "My chickens are waiting for this old hen to join them," she said "We don't see each other often enough."

At the counter Tadhg Ó Maoldomhnaigh was drinking slowly and steadily as he knew that he had a long night in front of him in which he looked forward to a long session. As far as he was concerned his work there was done. His Lenten Fast as he referred to his period without alcohol was over. When there was a lull in the music he sent drinks to the "Migos" with the message. "No hard feelings." They waved their thanks and got on with their music.

Margie from the Post Office crossed the floor to speak to him. "Are you happy that the film is finished?" she asked.

"Happy is not the word for it. Delirious, because there were times when I thought I would chicken out. Literally playing God was the biggest challenge I have ever had. What about yourself? I hear that you were splashing your bucket around Jacob's well?

"It was my first and last effort at being a film star, and I just about got through it without falling into the bloody well. I have faced many a challenge at the counter of the Post Office, but having the camera aimed at you is a bit like having a gun pointed at you. And trying to think of your lines at the same time. It's not for me but I got through it."

"Who knows but yourself and Dowling might set off on a world tour to sell the film to the world? You could bring your bucket so that he could take a piss without having to go to the jacks."

"Don't worry. I will be here and he will be gone. He can take the piss somewhere else."

"So it is a temporary little arrangement, as a certain politician once said?"

Margie laughed: I haven't seen any sign of him taking a ring out of his pocket yet, so I am not sweating with anticipation."

"Here today and gone tomorrow," Tadhg said. "I heard of a priest once whose bishop used to change him from place to place year after year. He bought two greyhounds and named one of them. 'Here today' and the other 'Gone tomorrow.' The penny dropped for the bishop and he never changed him again. I will have to tell that one to Fr. Ó Sé before I leave this place."

"I suppose you could say the same thing about the part you were playing yourself, Jesus. He didn't last very long, but his fame has lasted a long time."

"For a lot of people, I know," Tadhg answered, "he was here yesterday and gone today."

"Is that your way of telling me that you haven't found Jesus?" Margie asked, half serious and half joking.

He is a slippery customer," Tadhg said "Love him. Hate him. Can't forget him no matter what you try. But tonight, I am putting him on hold. He was part of my work for the past couple of months, and I am letting him go tonight so that I will be drunk enough to sleep."

When Margie had crossed the hall to sit beside Nicólás Dowling, Óran Breathnach sat down beside Tadhg "Isn't it a great night? Everyone seems to be enjoying themselves."

"All good things come to an end," Tadhg said, "and I hope that all bad things will come to an end soon, but there is always some trouble somewhere around the world. But tonight's the night as the fellow said when his wife offered him his yearly shag. We are trying to make the best of it."

"Are you telling me someone has made you an offer? I saw Margie and yourself putting your heads together a while ago."

"Purely platonic," Tadhg answered.

"You might be the one to put tonic into platonic," Óran joked.

"Dowling would have my guts for garters. What about yourself and the lovely Edel? Has she won you over to that Catholic Action group?"

"It is hard to say. We are not living in the same country so that always creates difficulties," Óran replied.

"It can also make for great fun when a couple gets together."

"Speaking from experience, I am sure?"

"Not as much experience as I would have liked" Tadhg said with a sigh. "Anyway I am gone past it now."

"When shall we two meets again" Óran asked in a mock dramatic voice.

"As you know about this job the one thing you can be sure of is that you can't be sure. Still if this film goes alright we could be in demand for a part or two in times to come.."

"Still, what part is bigger than that of Jesus" Óran teased.

"I would not be averse to playing a Pope or an Emperor," Tadhg joked. "The next one is always going to be the big one."

"A person doesn't get much time to settle down. We have to always follow the work, even though I must say there is more of it available in this country now than there was for years, between soaps and adventures and murder stories."

"Edel will pin you down yet," Tadhg promised him. "I can see the magnetism between you. You would be good together in a soap opera and there is plenty of that stuff in this country now, between English and the Irish language."

"The trouble is that we don't believe in much of the same stuff."

"Edel does not seem as much hung-up on that right-wing stuff as people were saying at the beginning," Tadhg told Óran.

"In some ways I suppose that she is playing a part when she is at work, writing or whatever," Óran answered. "If you take a stand on something you have to be able to back it up with arguments."

"Look at all the politicians that have softened, or should I say grown up, down through the years. Coalitions were formed by people with some very different views, and they were successful enough in their own ways."

"You could be right, Tadhg," Óran said, "but for tonight let us just let down our hair and have a blast."

"Keep your eye on this, Óran," Tadhg said as Edel Nic an tSaoir literally dragged the priest, Éamonn Ó Sé out on to the dancefloor. While he insisted "I can't dance." As she led him around he told her. "It is a big mistake to try and dance with me unless you are wearing army boots. Otherwise you will have no toes when you look down tomorrow morning," It surprised him that she drew him so close to her. He could feel the warmth from her body. For some reason it made him lonesome as he thought of all the years he had spent without a woman's love.

"Will you be going back to the journalism?" he asked Edel, to make conversation more than anything. "Or will you go acting fulltime?"

Edel smiled and said "At least you did not ask me the traditional dancehall question. Do you come here often?"

"Is that what I am supposed to say?" he asked nervously as he tried to follow her light-footed steps.

"It was the awkward question people asked each other in the old days when they did not know what to say," Edel answered as she swept him around in circles as he wondered to himself why was this coming so easy to him.

"You ae a brilliant dancer," Fr. Ó Sé said. "I have not managed to stamp on either of your feet yet. He got even more embarrassed when some people stopped dancing to look at Edel and himself in full flow. They were even applauded when the dance came to an end."

"That was brilliant," Edel said as she sat down beside him on the bench that was built around the floor of the hall.

"I have not danced since I went to college to train for the priesthood forty years ago. They were playing 'Those wedding bells will never ring for me,' and I wondered how did they know that I was in the crowd."

"You asked me about the Catholic newspaper," Edel told him. "I will be going back to journalism in a couple of weeks. That is not to say that I did not enjoy my time in front of the camera. I think the actors looked on me as a spy in their midst but they were all very nice to me, as were the local people. There is a built-in Christianity you would not feel everywhere, but that might have to do with the fact that I do not know country areas very well. It is true of some parts of the cities and big towns too. People look out for each other."

"It was good to talk to you," the priest said, "without having to deal with other agendas like the first time we met. I will let you back to Óran now, as he might want to have the next dance."

"He is an even worse dancer than you," she replied, before correcting herself. "Let's say he is not an expert, but I will talk with you again before I go back to Dublin. You might give me some impressions of how the film impacted on the area for my column next week."

"Work, work, work," Fr. Ó Sé said. "Just take it easy, and if I was you I would hold on to that Óran."

"I hadn't realised you were a matchmaker as well," Edel quipped as she left him. Nicólás Dowling sat beside the priest and asked "Will ye miss us when we are packed up and gone?"

"All good things come to an end, but you have helped to put some life into the place."

"It is a very special place, and from what I have heard from tour congregation you have a lot to do with that."

"It costs me a fortune for me to get them to say that." the priest said. "Don't believe a word of it."

When he went back to his house Fr. Ó Sé had a shower and lay on his bed looking at the ceiling as he tried to process the evenings happenings. His hands still smelt of Edel's perfume despite the shower and he held them close to his face. He tried to pray and he realised that he was fairly drunk as sentences ran into each other. "O Jesus, what a God. You are the best. You love us despite everything. Love your neighbour. Love your enemies. Love every single fucker... Sorry about that, Lord.

Be good to those who hate you. Bless those that hurt you. Pray for those who persecute or calumniate you. Or is it culminate you or contaminate you? Whatever. You are a great fucking God, one of the best. I mean the very best. A constant in our lives even if we give you the two fingers half the time. Jesus forever near, forever now.. FN for short. Jesus Forever Now Christ. Jesus FN Christ, I love you." He laughed himself to sleep.

www.ingramcontent.com/pod-product-compliance
Lightning Source LLC
LaVergne TN
LVHW021801060526
838201LV00058B/3197